A PLUME BOOK

THE SPARE WIFE

ALEX WITCHEL is a staff writer for *The New York Times Magazine* and also writes "Feed Me," a monthly column for the *Times's* Dining section. She is the author of *Girls Only: Sleepovers, Squabbles, Tuna Fish and Other Facts of Family Life* and the novel *Me Times Three*. She lives in New York City with her husband, Frank Rich.

"Alex Witchel is already treading on Henry James territory as a chronicler of wealthy Manhattan. . . . *The Spare Wife* serves up a skirmish in the firmament of the Upper East Side with all the careful maneuverings of a Jamesian fortune hunter . . . a tight comedy of bad manners."
— Ellen Wernecke, *The Onion*

"A blast to read. In Witchel's scintillating second novel . . . [she] writes with an informed, natural voice."
— *Los Angeles Confidential*

ALSO BY ALEX WITCHEL

Me Times Three

Girls Only:
Sleepovers, Squabbles, Tuna Fish and
Other Facts of Family Life

THE SPARE WIFE

THE SPARE WIFE

Alex Witchel

A PLUME BOOK

PLUME
Published by the Penguin Group
Penguin Group (USA) Inc., 375 Hudson Street, New York, New York 10014, U.S.A. • Penguin
Group (Canada), 90 Eglinton Avenue East, Suite 700, Toronto, Ontario, Canada M4P 2Y3 (a
division of Pearson Penguin Canada Inc.) • Penguin Books Ltd., 80 Strand, London WC2R
0RL, England • Penguin Ireland, 25 St. Stephen's Green, Dublin 2, Ireland (a division of Penguin Books Ltd.) • Penguin Group (Australia), 250 Camberwell Road, Camberwell, Victoria
3124, Australia (a division of Pearson Australia Group Pty. Ltd.) • Penguin Books India Pvt. Ltd.,
11 Community Centre, Panchsheel Park, New Delhi - 110 017, India • Penguin Group (NZ), 67
Apollo Drive, Rosedale, North Shore 0632, New Zealand (a division of Pearson New Zealand
Ltd.) • Penguin Books (South Africa) (Pty.) Ltd., 24 Sturdee Avenue, Rosebank, Johannesburg
2196, South Africa

Penguin Books Ltd., Registered Offices: 80 Strand, London WC2R 0RL, England

Published by Plume, a member of Penguin Group (USA) Inc. This is an authorized reprint of a
hardcover edition published by Alfred A. Knopf. For information address Alfred A. Knopf, 1745
Broadway, New York, NY 10019.

First Plume Printing, February 2009
10 9 8 7 6 5 4 3 2 1

 REGISTERED TRADEMARK—MARCA REGISTRADA

The Library of Congress has catalogued the Knopf edition as follows:

Witchel, Alex.
The spare wife / by Alex Witchel.— 1st ed.
p. cm.
"This is a Borzoi book."
ISBN 978-1-4000-4149-7 (hc.)
ISBN 978-0-452-29530-8 (pbk.)
1. Divorced women—Fiction. 2. Socialites—Fiction. 3. Upper-class families—Fiction.
4. Rich people—Fiction. 5. Manhattan (New York, N.Y.)—Fiction. 6. Domestic fiction.
I. Title.
PS3623.185s63 2008
813'.6—dc22   2007040320

Printed in the United States of America

PUBLISHER'S NOTE
This is a work of fiction. Names, characters, places, and incidents are either the product of the
author's imagination or are used fictitiously, and any resemblance to actual persons, living or
dead, business establishments, events, or locales is entirely coincidental.

For Frank Rich,
the indispensable husband

THE SPARE WIFE

Chapter One

Jacqueline Posner stood at the edge of her dining room and aimed a blow-dryer at the center of a pale peach rose. It just refused to open the way it should, and she was running so late she hadn't even checked the place cards Ponce had set out that afternoon.

"Are you still fooling with those flowers?" Ponce asked impatiently as she made her way from round table to round table, seating charts in hand, checking the last-minute changes. "Honestly, Jacqueline, I've told you a hundred times, you don't need them. You've got poinsettias everywhere and mistletoe and that enormous tree in the living room. No one is going to focus on the centerpieces. I hope you've paid as much attention to stocking the bar."

Well, that comment made Jacqueline even more flustered, if such a thing was possible, and she thought for maybe the thousandth time that she should never have asked Ponce Morris to throw this party with her. Jacqueline opened her mouth to speak, but before she could say a word Ponce headed into the library to check on the bar. Jacqueline watched her go, relieved. She had known from the beginning that Ponce was no coddler. She had never been the sort to coo over shoes or diamonds or even men, and she had little tolerance for the dithering that so often passed for girl talk. She was a straight shooter, an option that had simply never occurred to most women in Manhattan—at least not the women Jacqueline knew.

She unplugged the dryer and sighed. Then again, there was absolutely no one better at throwing a party than Ponce, everyone knew that—like they knew the best plastic surgeon for the upper eyelids, as opposed to the best plastic surgeon for the lower eyelids—so Jacqueline really hadn't had a choice. After a twelve-year marriage to one of the richest men in the country, as the tabloids all noted when trumpeting news of their impending divorce, Jacqueline was giving this dinner in her last weeks at her Park Avenue duplex to show a brave face to the world, the world she had worked so hard to make for herself. And had.

There. The last stubborn petal fell into just the right pose of ripeness—maybe it was too much, would they even last the night, these silly roses?—when Jacqueline glanced at her watch and saw that she had only twenty minutes before the guests would arrive at eight. She stowed the dryer hurriedly in a drawer full of antique Wedgwood—which would have been *the* perfect breakfast china for the Cotswolds cottage, but never mind—and started toward the first table.

She nervously studied the cheat sheet Ponce had made for her so she could remember who some of these guests were. Why couldn't she just have the people she knew, she'd implored Ponce at the very beginning, but Ponce wouldn't hear of it.

"The entire point of this exercise is to make a statement

that you're strong, your design business is strong, you're still social, and you're not disappearing," Ponce had instructed. "Moving to a maisonette on Gracie Square is not exactly going into exile." She spoke in her courtroom voice, strong and centered and sweetened not at all by her Southern accent. "When this is done, your good friends can eat off trays with you in front of the television and watch you cry your eyes out, but this event is official. It's meant to be written about in the gossip columns and talked about the next day and the day after that, and when you go to Sir's to have lunch, everyone will look at you and say, 'Honestly, that Jacqueline was a damn good wife to Mike Posner. Whatever was he thinking?'"

Well, Jacqueline had liked the sound of that, so she went along with Ponce's list, even though a good third of them were people she had never had in her home before. Wishing now that she had not let herself be bullied, she looked pleadingly at Ponce as she swept back in.

"That is an exceptionally well stocked bar, though there's no ice in sight," Ponce said, stopping her flight to the kitchen only when she caught sight of the paper fluttering in Jacqueline's unsteady hand.

"Need some help?" Ponce strained to keep her tone light and forced herself to ease up on the triage and remember how difficult this was for Jacqueline. For a dozen years Jacqueline had been at the top of social New York—a fluid mishmash of the rich, famous, and notorious—and had been envied her sumptuous lifestyle. The Posners owned twelve homes around the world—one for each year of their marriage. Every February, on their wedding anniversary, Mike would give his wife an envelope with a key inside and, once aboard their private jet, hand her a "destination folder," and off they would fly to see their latest plot of paradise—the mansion in Lyford Cay, the flat in Paris, the killer condo in Aspen. The problem with each of the properties, Jacqueline had told Ponce, was that Mike only liked buying them. Living in them didn't seem to interest him. Or at least living in them with her.

"No, I'm just fine," Jacqueline said bravely. She knew that no matter what happened—fainting dead away in the front hallway as she greeted her guests, or succumbing to a paralyzing sick headache midappetizer—with Ponce in charge the party would still go off without a hitch. She just didn't want her friend to know what distinct possibilities those scenarios were.

Ponce smiled encouragingly and pushed through the doors into the kitchen, leaving Jacqueline to squint at her list in the dim overhead light. The candles would not be lit until right before the guests were seated.

She read the name Mary Elizabeth Shaw and sighed. Shawsie, as she was known, was Ponce's best friend, had been for twenty years. To Jacqueline's way of thinking, Shawsie was a dreary-looking girl with her rust-colored hair and wardrobe of khakis and kilts. That Shawsie managed to still look like a member of the field hockey team from Greenwich High, despite years of exposure to Ponce's style and flair, was a mystery to her. But that sexless quality seemed to make people trust Shawsie and like her. In her capacity as the celebrity wrangler for *Boothby's Review*, that appeal worked magic, because who could be threatened by Shawsie? If she promised a movie star or a rock star that she would stay in the room every minute once a photographer showed up, Shawsie was right on time, stalwart and true, like the house mother in a girls' dormitory. No matter what tantrums or crises arose—hair extensions the wrong shade of red!—she could always fix them.

Jacqueline scanned the list for Robin's name. Yes, of course he was there. Shawsie had married Robin Brody a few years ago. They had eloped to the Bahamas, to Shawsie's grandmother's home, where the rich old woman pulled some strings and the happy couple stood barefoot on the beach whispering their vows. Shawsie's mother stayed holed up in Greenwich and, in a moment as rare for its insight as it was for her sobriety, assured her friends at the club that the entire endeavor could end only in heartbreak. Robin had written a novel in the late eighties about greed and power on Wall Street that had become a huge bestseller. He hadn't written a word since, though he continued to frequent the hot spots of the greedy and powerful and, his marriage aside, maintained a reputation as quite the ladies' man.

Gus Fisher. Jacqueline was glad to see that Ponce had seated herself next to him and far away from her. It wasn't that Jacqueline had anything against Gus Fisher, really. It's just that he was such a wunderkind news producer, creating that television magazine show *Real Time* that everyone thought was the greatest thing since, what, *Current Events*. Well, that was the problem, wasn't it? *Current Events*, a television classic since the late 1960s, had been created by Walter Gluckman, and Walter's wife, Annabelle, was an old friend of Jacqueline's. Walter was eighty; he had been a pioneer in broadcast news, and the show, incredibly, was still a hit now, in 2003. He ran it with the same iron hand he'd always wielded, in blatant disregard of whichever "kid" at the network challenged him, and it was an open secret that the top brass were collectively sick of him. Although they had been slow to push him out—the publicity would be atrocious—they would one day, soon, probably, and everyone wrote that it was Gus Fisher who would no doubt succeed him.

Jacqueline sighed. She knew that Annabelle would not be

happy at this turn of events, but Jacqueline had been power-less to stop it. She also was none too cheered by the prospect of seeing Rachel Lerner, Gus's new second wife, a contributor to *Boothby's Review* who had written a first novel about the magazine world that had become a marginal bestseller. (The boys at the Literati bookstore assured Jacqueline that the phrase "national bestseller," which ran in the ads for Rachel's book, resembled "*New York Times* bestseller" not at all.) Rachel was one tough customer, with her black clothes and flip remarks and trained eye for even the tiniest mis-step—whether someone didn't remember a fact or tried fak-ing that she actually knew where something like the weapons of mass destruction were hidden. You could practically see Rachel's pupils dilate as she filed that mistaken moment away in the cold metal cabinet of her heart. Or at least that's how Jacqueline felt the one time she had, oh so foolishly, gotten involved with Gus in a silly discussion about politics. Well, she would not make that same blunder tonight.

She peered again at her list. Red Evans's name was crossed out. That was a shame. She'd always liked Red, named for the same rusty head of hair that his niece Shawsie had. He had run Jimmy Carter's presidential campaign and for years had written a popular political column at *The Washington Post*. After Shawsie's father was killed in a boating accident when she was only thirteen, Red managed to be there in times of crisis for her and her brother, a long-distance daddy who always made time to fly up to New York on a weekend and sit for hours at the Yale Club listening to tearful—or angry—renditions of "Mother doesn't understand" as he drank an afternoon's worth of gin martinis, straight up, three olives. As "Mother" was his older sister, he knew exactly what his niece and nephew meant.

"Jacqueline, I think you need to put that away now."

Ponce stood before her in the candlelight, and as Jacqueline crumpled the paper in her hand she couldn't help but be stunned at how magnificent Ponce looked. Her friend's blond hair fell lush around her shoulders, her wide blue eyes dominated her perfectly heart-shaped face, and her skin was the poreless movie-star variety that doesn't exist in nature except when it does, marking its owner for eternal damnation by the bitter acne-scarred multitudes. Ponce wore a silver charmeuse top with skinny rhinestone pants, and the effect was simple and formal and absolutely devastating. How old was Ponce, forty-two? Certainly, as fabulous as she was now, it was nothing compared to how she'd looked twenty-four years earlier when she was new to New York, one of the last Aryans signed up by Eileen Ford before popular taste went ethnic. No wonder Lee Morris had lost his mind over her. In those days you could see Ponce's face on billboards all across the city.

"Oh," Jacqueline began worshipfully, but Ponce waved her off. "Never mind that. Let me take a look at you."

Jacqueline stepped away from the table and stood uneasily at attention, hands by her sides—a familiar posture from childhood, when her mother would measure her against the kitchen door. Ponce nodded slowly, examining Jacqueline from head to toe. Truth be told, she couldn't find a thing wrong. Jacqueline's puffy black hair framed her long pale face and made it seem less like a schoolteacher's. Her peach-colored dress was divine—Oscar, probably—and her long, thin arms were as perfectly toned as anyone's over thirty, not to mention forty, could be. She looked like a preacher's wife on a hot date, her prim face and tense manner softened by swirls of chiffon and years of assiduous applications of body cream. Ponce considered her own somewhat crusty elbows and nodded approvingly.

"You are *fabulous*," she proclaimed, and Jacqueline nearly melted with gratitude. But Ponce had already moved on.

"Okay," she said, leaning over one table to adjust a place setting. "This all looks wonderful. I'll go into the bar and double-check the ice. And you might stop into the kitchen and tell the very cute waiter who is on his cell phone with his girlfriend that he needs to put on his jacket, comb his hair, and pick up a tray."

As Jacqueline turned dutifully toward the kitchen, Ponce leaned over the nearest table and slipped a rose petal into her bag. Jacqueline had overdone it, as Ponce knew she would, and already they were falling.

The bar had been set up on the far side of the library between a Picasso and a Rothko, and as Jacqueline dallied in the kitchen Ponce sent the bartender back for still more ice. She put coasters on some of the tables—she didn't know much about antiques, that had been Lee's expertise—but a water ring on any of them could be a disaster worth thousands. And who knew if Jacqueline was even keeping these things? Granted, with twelve homes, there was an awful lot of plunder to plunder, but in Ponce's years as a lawyer she had handled her share of divorces and understood that a couple was never uglier than when they fought to the death over a lamp they each detested, just so the other couldn't have it.

"The kitchen is under control," Jacqueline announced as she came back in, stopping at a mirror to wipe a dot only she could see from her face.

"Well, I think we're ready." Ponce smiled and wished she still smoked.

The waiters went into the hallway, armed with their silver trays, and Jacqueline joined them, flushing self-consciously, before giving them their instructions. The bartender returned and Ponce said, "I'll have a white wine, please."

As he opened a bottle of Puligny-Montrachet she said, "Oh, for heaven's sakes, that is just wasted on me. Don't you have anything else?"

He shook his head, gesturing to a case of it stowed in a small glass-fronted refrigerator behind him, and Ponce realized that Jacqueline was doing a little housecleaning of the wine cellar for good measure on her way out the door.

Ponce instructed the bartender to fill her glass with ice first to dilute the strong taste—her usual was a bargain-bin Pinot Grigio she liked just fine—and started to sip. Then she went to the mirror and wiped an invisible dot of her own from her face. She glanced toward the living room, anchored by its spectacular ceiling-high tree, then down the length of the grand hallway, which glowed pink and gold in its candlelight, and felt pleased. No, Jacqueline Posner was not a close friend, but she and Ponce had come up together in the early, heady days of their marriages to rich older men, and Jacqueline had proved herself a pal. Ponce would never forget the charity ball at the Waldorf on the eve of her divorce from Lee when he'd skipped town at the last minute, forcing her to host their table alone. No matter where she turned she found herself face-to-face with that smarmy tabloid reporter hounding her with innuendo about her missing husband. Jacqueline saw what was happening, left her own guests to their cocktails, and swept her friend into a nearby elevator.

"I have the most fabulous client in the Waldorf Towers," she told Ponce, as lightheartedly as if she had just run into her at lunch. "He lives most of the year in Saudi Arabia and is just thrilled whenever I stop in to make sure everything is just so."

Within minutes the two women were on a top floor, shoeless, ensconced in a cream-and-gold boudoir, refreshing their makeup. As they made short work of a bottle of Dom Pérignon, Jacqueline called the front desk on the house phone and had someone instruct security to get rid of that reporter, pronto. By the time they glided back downstairs just in time for dinner, order was restored.

Now it was Ponce's turn to help Jacqueline. And Ponce knew all too well the precipice of doubt and dread on which Jacqueline balanced now.

Would the friends who came here tonight still be her friends by next Christmas? A few, probably. The rest would call once or twice, ask her out for a casual dinner or to come with them on a night when they had theater tickets. But that would stop soon enough. No one wanted an extra woman at a dinner party. Like apartments on Park Avenue and houses in the Hamptons, husbands and children were valuable real estate in New York. You would no sooner seat your husband next to a single woman with big eyes who laughed at all of his jokes than you would a diamond thief next to a duchess. It could only end badly.

If Jacqueline had had children instead of homes, she could have hung on more tightly. A man is unlikely to take away the twelve roofs over his heirs' heads, and being a mother would have meant that Jacqueline's rights to those roofs were safe. But that line of work held no interest for her.

Ponce didn't know many details about Jacqueline's childhood, but she knew she was one of six children who had grown up poor in a small town in Rhode Island, where her father was a lobsterman who also did maintenance work for the Newport Mansions. It was clear that Jacqueline had never located the romance in being the last one to bathe when the hot water was gone, and that sharing a bedroom with two sisters was a deafening hell of its own. So when she earned a full scholarship to the Rhode Island School of Design, she had walked out the front door and kept on going. Her greatest childhood joy, she told Ponce, had been visiting the Mansions with her father, who would turn her loose while the crew worked. Yes, the sconces and chandeliers had stunned and delighted her. But it was the silence, the vast roomfuls of polished, carpeted silence that promised new worlds ahead.

After she graduated Jacqueline went to New York and was snapped up as an assistant by Millicent Wilson, the society interior designer. Within two years, so many clients had found Jacqueline so charming—a beguilingly modest young woman who combined a sophisticated take on the traditional with a keen eye for the quirky and new—that she became an associate. When she married Mike she could afford to establish her own business and Madame Wilson was dismayed to discover more than a few defections. And as Jacqueline finished each of the houses Mike bought annually, it was photographed and featured in the top magazines. She was in demand both here and abroad.

Ponce slipped more ice into her drink and watched Jacqueline out in the hallway, flirting tentatively with the cute waiter. She would do just fine, Ponce thought. At least four of the homes were in Jacqueline's name already, or so Ponce had heard. She sipped her wine and absently rubbed away the lipstick print on the thin rim of the crystal with her thumb. Jacqueline had loved Mike, really and truly. She'd tried everything, poor girl. The sex wasn't the problem, Jacqueline had confided that afternoon—he'd never cheated, she was sure of it. Or at least that's what she'd told Ponce. The problem was the conversation—or, more specifically, its absence. It had gotten so bad that Jacqueline had hired a financial adviser to explain the market just so she'd have something to say at dinner. Ponce peered at her wineglass and rubbed it again. It was too awful to think about. But Jacqueline was a good egg, always had been, and if she made it through this ordeal and decided she wanted another man instead of another armoire, Ponce was sure she would find one.

The bell rang, the waiters stood at attention, and Jacqueline turned, searching for Ponce, who walked over and slipped her arm around Jacqueline's waist for a final, heartening squeeze. "Here we go," she said as the door opened, giving Jacqueline a gentle nudge forward then retreating into the library, where she could offer a second round of greetings as the guests drifted toward the bar.

The party was on.

"Robin, how *are* you?" Ponce asked the first guest to come her way. The dapperly dressed man kissed both her cheeks as deftly as if he had been born in Milan rather than Staten Island.

"Great, Ponce. You look great, too."

"Thank you. Where's your lovely wife?"

Robin raked his hand through his hair, which set the moussed mound slightly askew. Through the years, Ponce had noticed that this was a gesture women found endearing, designed as it was to make the listener feel he was considering a question's many ramifications, though it never did a thing for Ponce. As a lawyer, she appreciated a straight answer.

"Shawsie? Stuck at the office, I guess," he said vaguely, as Ponce watched him make not-so-subtle eye contact with a tall young woman, talking to Jacqueline out in the hallway, whom Ponce had never seen before.

"And who is that?" she asked, trying to keep her tone breezy. Honestly, she didn't know how Shawsie put up with it. Robin was genuinely smart and genuinely talented, so in her own exasperated moments she could still justify her best friend's attraction to him. That he was genuinely lazy queered the package for Ponce. Well, maybe not lazy, if she was going to be fair. It was a lifetime of cheap charm that had gotten him this far; his mother had died of cancer when he was only eight, and because his father drank, Robin moved in with two doting maiden aunts, whom he had quickly learned to play like craps.

Ponce didn't know many of the specifics when it came to Robin's night crawling. Shawsie did, certainly, but Ponce figured that wanting a child was important enough to Shawsie to help her look the other way. But there were times when she couldn't; a few months back she'd let drop to Ponce that she'd found a purple bra in the backseat of her car. After that it was a crystal chandelier earring, snugly deposited in a suit jacket pocket that Robin had left for the cleaner.

The young woman in the hallway saw that Robin was talking to Ponce Morris, and her smile brightened instantly.

"That's Babette Steele," he told Ponce casually, turning toward the bar. "Scotch, rocks," he ordered, knocking it back.

"And she is?"

"Right here, actually." He reached behind Ponce and took Babette's hand, pulling her forward. "Ponce Morris, Babette Steele. Babette works at *Boothby's*, with Shawsie. Jeez, Ponce, I'd think you'd know your own guest list."

Ponce greeted the younger woman warmly. "Hello, Babette, it's so nice to meet you. And do forgive me. Between Jacqueline's list and mine, we're both meeting new people tonight. Of course I know you work at *Boothby's*. And that you're a great friend of Annabelle Gluckman's."

Actually, when she and Jacqueline had been making the guest list, Jacqueline called Annabelle in desperation, searching for attractive women under thirty to amuse Montrose Merriweather, the Southern billionaire who had bought her apartment. Jacqueline said that as a top marketing executive at Solange Cosmetics, Annabelle knew them all. "She's a registry, like at Bloomingdale's," she told Ponce. "She meets these girls on shoots for the ad campaigns, then uses them as window dressing for her glitzy PR events. But she's careful to shut them out of the hard-core social ones like this so they don't ruin anyone's marriage. Especially hers. I mean, only in this crowd could twenty-five be considered jailbait." At that point, she and Ponce mustered weak smiles. They remembered when they were the young ones.

"Yeah, Annabelle, what a trip! I mean she's great," Babette answered. "I'm just really excited to meet *you*, is all." The girl flushed, tossing her glossy blond hair over her shoulders.

"Me?" Ponce's engagingly self-deprecating laugh was tinged with a shade of skepticism.

"When I was growing up," Babette said, "I saw you all the time, like in *Women's Wear Daily,* and *Harper's Bazaar* and *Town & Country*. There were your fashion spreads, and then when you married Lee Morris you went to all those parties and openings. But what I thought was so great was that you never hogged the shot like those other women who couldn't wait to show off. You were always so cool about it, like you didn't care if they took your picture or not." She flushed again. "At least that's what I thought."

"Oh, trust me, you were right," Ponce said, laughing. "Once I wasn't making a living at it anymore, it would have suited me fine to never have my picture taken again." She held out her wineglass in the general direction of the bartender, who automatically leaned over to refill it. "But never

mind that. A child reading *Women's Wear*! Do you cover fashion at *Boothby's*?"

Babette laughed, tugging self-consciously at the clinging
skirt of her red jersey dress. Ponce saw that a few of the red
beads that paved its plunging neckline had pulled free, leaving little shoots of naked thread in their wake. That was too
bad, she thought. The girl's bosom was simply not large
enough to prevent one from noticing.

"Me?" Babette said. "No, definitely not. My mom's a
librarian and I read all that stuff there, waiting for her after
school. Actually, I'm a writer. Or at least I'm going to be. I've
been an editorial assistant at *Boothby's* for the last five
months."

"Hiya, Ponce." Two arms grabbed her around the waist
from behind.

Ponce turned. "Oh, hello, Walter," she said, skillfully
shifting her cheek just out of his slobbering reach. Honestly,
he was simply too old to be this vile still, she thought. In his
younger years, Walter Gluckman was such a lech he made
Robin Brody look like a eunuch.

"Ponce, you look marvelous!"

Of course, where there was Walter, the clinging Annabelle was never far behind, her grating voice gilded not at
all by its stagy British accent. When she had first met Ponce,
Annabelle called her "Ponth," much to the Southern woman's
amusement. "Oh, I'm not Spanish," she'd said, laughing. "It's
just like it's spelled. Plain old Ponce." Now the two women
moved their faces toward each other dutifully as if to kiss.
Ponce glanced at Annabelle's deep V neckline and was horrified to see that the pancake makeup she had applied to her
décolletage had, in the overheated New York apartment,
melted into the furrows of her ample cleavage. Ponce forced
herself not to stare at the sticky mess, trying in vain to spot

Shawsie, who would have a delectable appreciation of a sight as heinous as this.

But Annabelle had already pressed past her. "Hello, dear," she said to Babette, who leaned over and kissed her cheek. Annabelle then went for the second cheek, the Continental double kiss which Babette hadn't expected. She stranded the older woman, who extended her neck back and forth in midair like a pigeon.

"Oh, sorry, right," Babette said, stepping forward too late.

"Hiya, kid." Walter slid his arm around her waist and turned her toward the bar. "Whattaya drinking?"

Ponce moved away to avoid being overheard by Babette and said to Annabelle, "I understand that girl is a friend of yours."

Annabelle sighed and, looking for escape, scanned the sparse crowd. The last thing she wanted was to get stuck having girl talk with Ponce Morris. Ponce had once given the most glamorous parties in New York, but then she'd just quit after her divorce, refusing to entertain again, so why should Annabelle bother? Now all Ponce did was that dismal legal work, for the city or some downtrodden agency—Home Again, wasn't it—placing poor children in foster homes. She had stepped up tonight to help Jacqueline, but that didn't really count, did it?

"Not exactly a friend," Annabelle said crisply, silently berating herself for arriving too early, even though she had been dressed and ready at six-thirty. Everyone knew this was *the* invitation of the holiday season, a front-row seat to watch Jacqueline Posner try to keep a stiff upper lip amid her nearest and dearest. Annabelle also knew that practically every guest tonight had been savvy enough to call Mike Posner's cigar broker personally to send along the financier's favorite vintage Cubans as a holiday token. And many of them had devised dinner parties of their own just to be able to invite him. Those were scheduled for mid-January, after the skiing and after Jacqueline had safely relocated to the estate in Bedford while her new place in the city was being renovated. His was by far the more important list to stay on.

Ponce was waiting for an answer, Annabelle realized. "Babette was an assistant in the beauty department at *Self* about a year ago," she said, "so I met her through shoots with Solange. She went around for a while with that handsome chef, the one downtown with the motorcycle who got all those raves for inventing that dish—what was it—the braised fetal arugula, I think. I can't quite remember, but it was very hot." She fanned herself with an antique linen cocktail napkin. "As it is in here. Can't you do something about that?" Her tone had slid up the scale from bored to imperious.

"Right away," Ponce said, grateful for the getaway. She knew just where Annabelle's napkin was headed, and she couldn't bear to watch that painstakingly preserved piece of fabric from a bride's trousseau in late nineteenth-century London meet its end with Solange's Tawny Continuous Coverage, SPF 15.

She turned back toward the bar and saw Sari Grossman, waiting patiently for a mineral water. Ponce practically hugged her.

"Sari, how are you, I haven't seen you forever," she said, pulling Sari away from Annabelle, who had already injected herself between her husband and the tall young girl in the red dress. Annabelle's tight smile was a sure sign that the evening was rapidly falling short of her expectations.

"Ponce, I know you got us invited here, thank you," Sari said kindly. As she always did, Sari Grossman made Ponce feel like a bum. Her husband was a doctor, she had three small children, and she ran one of the most successful pediatric public health clinics in the city, in Brooklyn. In her own pro bono legal work for foster children, Ponce had dealt with her and always found her so, well, earnest.

"Hello, Ponce."

She turned toward the familiar voice and smiled. It was Sari's husband, Neil, a fixture of late on all the television talk shows, having had terrific success as a fertility doctor impregnating "lost cause" women in their late thirties and early forties. He leaned toward her cheek, a move she neatly dodged by turning him toward the bar.

"Still Dewar's and soda?" she asked as Neil Grossman spoke over her to the bartender: "Vodka neat."

Ponce raised her eyebrows. "My mistake," she murmured, turning to engage Sari in what she knew would be a tedious conversation about flu shots and the city's budget woes. Neil, meanwhile, was shaking hands with Gus Fisher, who, not a moment too soon, had come up behind Ponce, laying his hand in the small of her back.

"Hello, darling," he said, kissing the immediate airspace above his old friend's cheek. He knew full well how she had been drilled as a model to consider her makeup as much a part of her outfit as her clothes.

"Dewar's and soda," Gus said to the bartender, and Ponce laughed. "Oh, that's your drink," she said. "I should have remembered. I am sorry, Dr. Grossman. As you can see, my hostessing skills are simply pitiful since Mr. Morris's demise." She sipped her wine. "And thank God he isn't here to catch me. Divorce or not, if I didn't remember something like a man's drink, he would be furious."

"What's this? Another allusion to your former life as a Sutton Place stewardess?" Rachel Lerner leaned toward Ponce and skipped the air kiss, squeezing her arm instead. "How great do you look?" she said, her tone a democratic mix of admiration and envy.

Sari Grossman looked confused. "I didn't know you were a stewardess, Ponce. I thought you were a model."

Ponce laughed as Rachel said, "She wasn't a stewardess. She only played one in her marriage. Hi, Sari, how've you been?" Rachel shook Sari Grossman's hand and thanked God that at least one woman here looked drabber than she did. Rachel always meant to go shopping, really she did. She must have worn this black dress with the matching jacket fifty times since she bought it on sale at Bergdorf's, the day she interviewed the fancy hairdresser who once worked there. She looked at Ponce. Not even in my next lifetime, she thought, and that meant the outfit, the face, and those hips in those pants.

Sari still looked confused.

"Oh hell, Sari, you didn't start coming around until it was almost over," Ponce said, again holding out her glass to the bartender. She raised an eyebrow, and this time he did not forget the ice.

Rachel opened her mouth to comment further, and Ponce saw Gus dig a cautionary finger into his wife's hip. "Oh, Gus, you are unfailingly polite and Lee always loved you," Ponce said, smiling conspiratorially, "but the truth was that when we gave those famous dinner parties, he made me go to the public library before each one and look up every guest in Who's Who—and I want to tell you, almost all the men at least were in there—and I had to memorize their biographies and ask them questions that were attuned to their interests."

Sari gasped as Rachel shook her head. "That you did it is the incredible part," Rachel said as the bell rang for dinner.

Ponce took Gus by one arm and Rachel by the other. "My

dears, I had no choice. Or at least I thought I didn't," she said mildly as they headed toward the dining room. A red-faced man in his early eighties staggered down a side hallway, zipping his fly.

"Fred Engel is here?" Gus asked, amused. "I didn't know he could stand up anymore."

"Jacqueline insisted on inviting him," Ponce said, disgusted. "He's the only famous writer she knows. Which reminds me." She stopped walking, and Gus and Rachel stopped on either side. "Do you know someone named Babette Steele from *Boothby's*?"

Rachel rolled her eyes. "Yes. Why?"

"She's here because she's friends with Annabelle Gluckman. And she seems perfectly pleasant, so why are you making that face?"

"Well, she hasn't been at the magazine terribly long, but she's very *helpful*, if you know what I mean," Rachel said. "She's always offering to sort the mail or answer the phone or run something down to the messenger room."

"Sounds downright sinister," Ponce said, shaking her head.

"I guess the point is, she says she wants to be a writer, but she's never writing," Rachel went on. "She's too busy hosting the office. And when she does write, I've seen a few small things she's done, it's completely generic. No voice at all. She's like the Stepford assistant."

Gus moved over to Rachel and put his arm around her. "That's my wife," he said affectionately. "Always a kind word."

"She's probably just hungry," Ponce said teasingly, and Gus laughed. Although reasonably slim, Rachel usually ate for six. "Take her in to dinner, Gus, so she'll behave herself."

Ponce turned and walked down the grand hallway, where a number of guests lingered with their drinks, murmuring over the string of Tissots that reached from the dining room entrance to the duplex's main stairway. It looked like an opening night at the Met. She moved from group to group, mentioning that dinner was served. Most people nodded and smiled and didn't budge, though a former senator, a man Ponce found unbearably pompous, caught her eye eagerly.

No wonder, Ponce thought. Beside him was the wife of a high-powered lawyer Ponce had known forever. It was this woman's habit, on the day of a dinner party, to sit down with *The New York Times*, *The Wall Street Journal*, and the *Financial Times*, read them front to back, and then spend the evening unloading her worldly knowledge onto the distinguished men in her midst—who had not only read the same papers but had created some of the news themselves. She was a terrible seat, Ponce often complained to Shawsie, because, her statistics on world hunger aside, she had never learned the most important thing about men: They didn't want to be told. They wanted to tell.

As the dinner bells sounded again, the crowd finally started to move. Ponce went to the entrance of the dining room and watched the waiters guide guests to their seats.

"*Where* is Jacqueline?"

It was Annabelle, in an advancing stage of outrage.

Ponce tried to hold her temper. "I don't know, Annabelle. What's the problem?"

"I want to know why Gus Fisher was invited to this dinner and why I, of all people, am seated next to him. I mean, really!"

Ponce's gaze was even. "Gus Fisher was invited because he is one of my oldest and dearest friends." She smiled sweetly. "And I think this is a marvelous chance for you to get to know him better. Think about it. You just might do your husband some good." A warning note sounded in that last sentence, and Annabelle heard it. She turned and left without a word.

"Ponce, there's trouble." Shawsie appeared, her eyebrows drawn together in a deep quotation mark of anxiety. Her gray satin pants, so early in the evening, were creased across the crotch in a sideways echo.

Ponce nodded, her eye on one of Jacqueline's friends, a slightly older woman whose strapless evening dress exposed spindly arms hung with loose, crepey flesh. "I see it," she said. "Why spend all that money doing her face if she insists on showing those arms?"

"No, Poncie, not that!" Shawsie steered her toward the stairs. "Our hostess is sobbing in the master bathroom because she found Fred Engel peeing into her bidet."

"Sounds to me like she's selling the place in the nick of time." Ponce grabbed a fresh glass of white wine from a waiter's tray and sent Shawsie in to dinner before climbing the stairs and pushing open the bathroom door. Jacqueline was sniffling on her makeup stool.

"Short of a death in your family, there is no reason for you to be in here," Ponce scolded. "Fix your face, Jacqueline, and let's go." As she started to protest, Ponce held up her hand. "Your left eye is fine, just redraw the liner on the right bottom and do a light powder over your nose." Jacqueline, seemingly dazed, turned toward the mirror and followed instructions. When she was finished, Ponce took her by the wrists and stood her up. Her tone was unexpectedly tender. "I know that this is your home, that you love it and you're losing it," she said, her voice low. "I know that to find someone doing something so awful is more than you can bear." Jacqueline's eyes filled again. Ponce tightened her grip. "But that is for later," she said firmly. "Right now, there are sixty people in your dining room waiting to start their dinners. So before Fred Engel pees into those roses, we had better head back there."

That got a wavy smile from Jacqueline, who started down

the stairs as Ponce stayed close and murmured encouragement. In the hallway, through the entrance to the dining room, Ponce could see Babette Steele throw back her head and laugh at something a gray-haired man seated next to her had said.

"That must be the great Montrose Merriweather," Ponce said.

Jacqueline reached for her friend's hand. "Two weeks from Monday," she said weepily, "he'll own this apartment."

"Let's get through tonight first," Ponce said, holding on tight. "I'm praying this Babette is up to keeping him entertained."

Jacqueline nodded. "So is Annabelle. As a matter of fact, I'm sure she's counting on it."

Ponce looked at Jacqueline sideways, surprised to hear a hardness in her voice. Jacqueline was never tough or bitchy: In the viperous crew that composed social New York on any given week—a tit-for-tat bunch whose acceptance had meant everything to Lee—Jacqueline's decency was one of the things Ponce liked best about her. It was why she was here tonight; realistically, the chances that the two of them would see each other—in the short term, at least—were slim. A few shrewdly timed guest appearances aside, Jacqueline would essentially leave New York for a year or two, making sure to find work as far away as possible. After that, anything could happen.

But for the last, what, decade or more, the two women had been each other's dependable allies, both subject to the whims of older, powerful husbands who had come from nothing and designated their young, beautiful wives their personal emissaries to the big time. And make no mistake, those endless parties had constituted work as crucial as any corporate board meeting. The dresses and the jewelry and the flowers aside, you could stand in a Park Avenue apartment and see the values of social power rise and fall above each coiffed head as clearly as if you were looking at the board at the Stock Exchange. The rich always mattered most, and the well known—an ever-changing group of the hot then the not, who were the evening's equivalent of the entertainment—always mattered less.

Which is why you would rarely find one of the rich women behaving like Annabelle—for the most part, they wouldn't need to. But Annabelle's desperation was justified. Some of the well known were still invited if their fortunes changed because, well, people actually liked them. Annabelle, who had never been above phoning a hostess to cry and cajole her way into a dinner from which she and Walter had been excluded, didn't have much in the bank when it came to goodwill. And she was canny enough to know that the minute he was deposed at the network, the two of them would find themselves convening nightly at the menu drawer, debating the relative merits of orange beef and moo shu pork.

So Ponce and Jacqueline, having learned together to navigate a world as treacherous—and absurd—as this one, had come to appreciate the simple reward of a kind word from a kind person, even if the two were never meant to be bosom buddies.

In the familiar grand hallway Ponce felt an unexpected pang, and Jacqueline caught her eye. They squeezed each other's hands, united in a wistful nod to their passing youth, its shining triumphs and terrible errors. Ponce wanted to pull her aside then, to say what—something like thank you, something like goodbye—but before she could say a word they had arrived at the entrance to the dining room and Robin Brody stood, holding his drink aloft.

"Ladies and gentlemen, your attention, please! A toast to our glamorous hostess and her spectacular home!"

Glasses were raised and cries of "Hear, hear!" rang out. Jacqueline blushed, and Ponce smiled appreciatively at Robin. Never had one of his showboating gestures translated into actually meaning something as much as that particular moment. It was a much smarter alternative to her and Jacqueline getting soggy in full view.

Flashing an all-clear expression to Shawsie, Ponce set down her wineglass at her seat next to Gus Fisher, who was manfully handling what Ponce could hear was a screed against the network delivered by Annabelle in defense of her husband's countless achievements, and made her way straight to Montrose Merriweather.

"I just wanted to introduce myself and welcome you to your new home," Ponce drawled in pure cornpone, which, she knew from long experience, worked potent magic against the forbidding elegance of her appearance.

"Mrs. Morris." Merriweather rose to a very full height. "I understand that you have been of incomparable help to our poor Jacqueline." In his pronunciation that last syllable rhymed with "clean," and Ponce was surprised to hear some cornpone of his own.

"Our?" she asked airily. Her smile dazzled.

"Well, after she spent so much time helping us with our home outside Atlanta, we started to feel she was one of the family."

This rang a faint bell with Ponce, who remembered something about the restoration of a former plantation so elaborate that even her relatives in South Carolina had heard about it. Jacqueline, of course, had never said much. When it came to her clients, she was always discreet.

"Is your wife here?" Ponce asked, looking around the table.

"No, Mrs. Merriweather and I have had a parting of

the ways," he said smoothly. "But allow me to introduce my delightful dinner partner this evening, Miss Babette Steele."

Babette leapt from her chair as she and Ponce said together, "We've met." Babette, on her way to standing, banged the table hard enough so that the water sloshed in the glasses. She grabbed at her own to prevent it from spilling.

"Babette and I have just realized something of a connection," Merriweather said to Ponce, looking amused. "Before she ran off and married a Yankee from New York City, Babette's mother was the prettiest girl one town over from where I grew up in Georgia, and I had the honor of dancing with her once."

"What a small world."

Ponce was surprised to see how awkward Babette was — like a kid, really. She was pretty enough, but she was so much of a type — blond hair, blue eyes, long legs. Ponce stopped when she realized she was describing herself.

"I meant to tell you before, I just love Shawsie," Babette blurted, trying to seize the moment. "I know you guys are friends and she's just the nicest person at *Boothby's*. You should come visit us there sometime."

Ponce smiled. "Of course I will," she said, placing a hand on the backs of both their chairs. "But I'm afraid I've interrupted your dinner, so please sit down. Mr. Merriweather, it was lovely to meet you."

"Likewise, but do call me 'M,'" he said, taking his seat. "Everyone does."

Babette remained standing. "Uh, do you know where the ladies' room is?" she asked Ponce, who led her to the guest bathroom, right off the dining room in the front hallway, which anyone but Fred Engel would realize was the right place to go.

On the other side of Babette's empty chair, Walter Gluck-man leaned over to M. "She's something, isn't she?" he said as Babette and Ponce exited the room.

"Which one?" M asked dryly, lighting a mentholated Ben-son & Hedges 100 and sliding a small silver footed ashtray nearer to his wineglass.

"Ponce, for chrissakes," Walter answered. "The other one's a kid."

M looked amused. "Perhaps," he said. "Though I suspect she's a tad older than the last Mrs. Merriweather."

Walter laughed knowingly. "Well, if I could do it again, I would have gone after Ponce." He glanced awkwardly over his shoulder, trying to remember where his wife was seated. "She's a knockout now, but then? You wouldn't have believed it." He spotted Annabelle, safely out of earshot, lecturing Gus Fisher two tables away.

"Yes?" M inhaled, pushing his caviar pie off to the side. Yankee pretense, nothing more. "So where is Mr. Morris?"

"Dead," Walter said importantly. The newsman in him rose to the occasion of delivering a scoop. In this tired group he and Annabelle traveled in—a world that meant more to her than anything except maybe his life-insurance policy— they all might as well have been fucking each other forever. You didn't just go home bored with your wife after one of these shindigs, you went home bored with every broad in the room. As the years went by, the collective tits drooped ever lower (except for the spooky rejiggered racks that now bounced), and the conversations remained the same, with their forced frissons of excitement ("I *loved* this week's show! How did you *ever* find that story?"). The result was that these dinners were depressingly like fucking your own wife—only they happened more frequently, and everyone's makeup was still on. And there was no chance of television for hours.

"Actually, Lee died a few years after the divorce," Walter told M. "He'd started to turn on Ponce when she became a lawyer and he treated her like crap, so she left. But I'll say this for her. When he got sick, she came back and took care of him. Stayed in the apartment, dealt with the nurses and all his kids, not to mention the first three Mrs. Morrises. And I guess he appreciated it, since he apparently left her a fortune. Though the women all say she earned every dime."

"That's what the women always say," M said pleasantly, and Walter laughed.

Ponce had reentered the room, and M watched as she made her way to her table. Rail-thin, with a big-city aura of money and confidence. An exquisitely balanced face that was pointed and kittenish at once. She stopped and whispered something to Robin, who threw back his head and laughed. M was surprised to see that ease between them. After Robin's third scotch, he had said a few things about Ponce that M had found somewhat curious.

"Yeah, she is a great help to Jacqueline," Robin had said. "She's a great help to everybody, really. That's her specialty."

"Sounds like you don't mean that too kindly."

Robin shrugged. "Look, she's my wife's best friend. Everyone loves Ponce." His tone was sour. "She's the only woman in New York who has threesies in the living room."

M raised his eyebrows but said nothing, hoping not to interrupt the stream of bile—and information—bubbling so close to the surface.

"Not real ones, my friend. That lady is no tramp. Unfortunately." Robin laughed.

M smiled. And waited.

"Ponce *hates* sex," Robin said in an exaggeratedly dramatic tone. "That's her whole gig, since Lee. I mean, she had some major affair after she left him, but since then she claims she's finished with it. So her big thing now is being best buddies with all these couples. Like me and Shawsie. Though I can tell you, she's always liked Shawsie a hell of a lot better than she's liked me." He laughed a little too loudly.

"She's a professional friend, is what I'm saying," he went on. "Shawsie needs some girl-talk manicure session? Ponce is there. I get some dumb-ass magazine assignment on something like premium vodkas—I'm between books at the moment—and even though Shawsie's dead asleep, we've been trying to have a baby, let's not even go there, Ponce is sitting with me in some Russian dive in the West Fifties, pounding pomegranate vodkas at two a.m."

"Sounds like a good sport," M crooned.

"Maybe," Robin countered. "She's also an old friend of Gus Fisher's, and she can listen to him spout Nielsen numbers and political polls forever. Lives for it. While Rachel, Gus's new wife, couldn't give a shit about all that. She's a cook. Spends hours on a meal. And you can see that Ponce is no eater. But she eats that food like she hasn't eaten in days. Which, by the way, she hasn't."

M smiled. "She sounds like a very good person to have on your side," he said.

Robin shrugged. "I guess so," he said, accepting a fresh scotch from a waiter who took his empty glass. "But all that bullshit with the wives aside, I think Ponce is really an imaginary friend for the middle-aged man. I mean, yes, with the women she goes shopping and gives parties and all that. But she watches football with Stan Crandall, while Bitsy reads magazines in bed and thanks God she doesn't have to; she plays golf with George Stein, because Carol only likes tennis; and not only does she go to Knicks games with Larry DeLynn but she lets him eat as many hot dogs as he wants and never tells Lila, who forbids him to have nitrates. But what's *in* it for her, exactly? Doesn't it make sense—for someone who invests that much time and effort—to actually get laid?"

M laughed as Robin went on, raking his hand through his already tilted hair. "I'll give her this, though," he mused. "The one thing she never does is get close enough to fight. She gets all the perks of being married before she disappears in the nick of time, leaving the rest of us to slug it out on our own."

Babette returned from the ladies' room, and M rose, pulling out her chair. She sat down and pulled it forward, banging the table again.

"Whoa, sugar, you're hard on the china," he said.

The appetizers had been cleared and replaced with dinner plates; a waiter quickly approached Babette, offering a tray of fried chicken. Another waiter followed, bearing a bowl of mashed potatoes. Once she had helped herself—she was the last guest served—someone hit the side of a water goblet with a spoon and Jacqueline stood, looking much more relaxed than she had a half hour ago. Ponce had apparently seen to it that Jacqueline's wineglass stayed full.

"I want to welcome you all to my home," Jacqueline said when the room quieted down. "And I want to give you all a chance to meet the man who will be the next resident of this apartment where I have spent so many happy years. He is Montrose Merriweather, the financier from Atlanta"—a rumbling went around the room; among rich people Montrose Merriweather was richer—"whose beautiful home, Twin Springs, I had the great privilege of helping to restore. And now that M wants to spend more time in New York, well, I can't think of anyone who would take better care of the place that has meant so much to me. So please make sure you all introduce yourselves tonight, he's right over there"—heads swiveled as M smiled genially and Babette turned the color of her dress—"and just by the way, in case you were wondering what in the world is going on in my kitchen, this dinner tonight is part New York, the caviar pie, giving way to Georgia, the main course you have now. So eat, drink, and be merry!"

The din in the room rose immediately, and there was much fevered speculation about Mr. Merriweather and the very young woman by his side, both new faces for this crowd, an unusual occurrence indeed. Needless to say, the young woman was the topic of much derision among her elders: What a cheap dye job! She looks just like the Wolfes' newest au pair, that girl whose every outfit shows her navel—how *has* Patricia stood it all these months? Jacqueline has apparently lost her mind seating such a nobody—what, a secretary— next to a man like Montrose Merriweather! He'll think all of New York to be simpleminded fools. Perhaps Jacqueline Posner isn't leaving town a moment too soon.

As the waiters went round to say that coffee would be served in the living room, people rose eagerly, though most made a beeline out the door. The time was exactly 10:50 p.m., and as the eleven o'clock news loomed, it was the undisputed witching hour for a New York dinner party. The shelf life for good sportsmanship never exceeded two hours, fifty minutes. A dismissal bell might just as well have rung, as it once had in grade school.

In the hallway, Ponce noticed Shawsie talking to Neil Grossman. She could see from the look on her friend's face that the news was not good. In the last year Shawsie had attempted three in vitro fertilizations, and it was now clear that the latest hadn't worked, either. Normally, of course, she would have gone to the office to speak to Grossman, but she was a tortured woman and he wouldn't be mean enough to know and not tell.

Seeing Sari give her husband the high sign that it was time to leave, Ponce walked over to say goodbye. "School night," Sari said apologetically, and Ponce kissed her on the cheek as Shawsie offered the couple a ride in the *Boothby's* car she had waiting downstairs.

"I'm going back to the office, actually," Neil said. "I promised to speak on a conference call to Sydney at eleven-thirty, and I was nervous about making it to Brooklyn in time." He turned to Shawsie and gave her a quick hug. "If you have more questions tomorrow, give me a buzz in the afternoon and I'll be glad to go through it with you."

She thanked him and collected Robin and they all got into the elevator together. Within minutes, the party was down to a handful. Ponce bid Gus and Rachel goodbye.

"Feeling better now?" Ponce asked Rachel, who had her arms wrapped around her new husband.

"Caviar, mashed potatoes, and Gus," Rachel sighed. "Remember never to speak to me on an empty stomach. I think Babette Steele is the loveliest editorial assistant I've ever known." She leaned over to kiss Ponce's cheek and was amused to see that even at this late hour she was still pulling away.

Ponce climbed the stairs and heard Jacqueline back in the master bathroom. When she pushed the door open this time, though, it hit the cute waiter full in the back. He didn't seem to notice, as he was busily bent over the hostess in a passionate embrace.

"Excuse me," Ponce said, but neither of them straightened up. "I guess we'll talk tomorrow," she called, shutting the door behind her.

Down in the lobby, the doorman signaled for a cab and once inside, Ponce gave the driver the address. Ten blocks away, he pulled up to an elegant brownstone and waited until she turned her key in the lock. She felt quite pleased, actually, about how the evening had turned out, its bumpy start aside. Even the dread Annabelle had made it a point to bid her a fond farewell, although Ponce knew that Annabelle was just hedging her bets in case she decided to throw a white-tie ball anytime soon.

She closed the front door firmly and double-locked it, then started down the darkened hallway. She had gone only a few steps when she was grabbed from behind.

She gasped as he pulled at her shirt and clutched her breasts—she wore no bra—pushing her against the wall. He yanked at her rhinestone pants, and a few small stones made a tinkling sound as they hit the tiled floor.

She turned, but before she could open her mouth he covered it with his, and when he entered her she groaned. She grabbed at his hair and pulled at his shirt collar and still he kept on, oblivious as one of her shoes flew off and she wrapped her legs around him hard and held on. She barely felt the smack of the wall against her back as she finally broke her mouth free of his and cried out as she came, just before he did.

They stood a moment in place, his arms making one circle around her, her legs making another around him. Slowly he eased her down, and once she was standing he bent over and kissed her gently on her forehead.

"Jesus, did you have to ruin my pants?" Ponce said, pulling them back on.

"What took you so long?" Dr. Neil Grossman panted. "You know I have to get home."

"Part of the thrill," she said wryly. She walked over to a wooden cabinet on the far side of his office and opened it. She poured him a vodka—the only liquor in the cabinet— neat. He took a sip, then held out the glass, offering it to her. She shook her head and pulled on her blouse. As he continued to drink, still standing in the hallway, she blew him a kiss and left.

Chapter Two

It was another short cab ride from Neil's office back to her apartment building on Fifth Avenue at Seventy-second Street. As she got out of the taxi, Ponce drew her sable coat tight around her.

"Good evening, Raoul," she said to the doorman.

"Mrs. Morris, good evening," he replied, rushing to close the taxi door behind her.

"Chilly night," she said, taking long strides through the lobby.

The elevator man waited for her, tipping his cap. "Oh, ma'am!" He started toward her, but she held up a hand.

"Mike, you'll get a broom and sweep it up later," she said as the rhinestones left a pinging trail on the marble floors.

"Yes, Mrs. Morris."

"It's my own fault for wearing something so silly, then going ahead and ripping it." She followed him into the elevator and he closed the door. Three flights up, he waited as she stepped into the tiny foyer and unlocked the door that led straight into her apartment. "Thanks, Mike." She turned and put two separately folded fifty-dollar bills in his hand. "Tell Raoul, too, sorry for the mess," she said. "Good night."

With the door closed, Ponce released her coat and the pants fell in a heap. She stepped out of them and her shoes, dropped her ripped blouse, and walked over to her answering machine. One message.

"Poncie, it's Red. I'm all ears on the postmortem. Talk later."

The clock read 12:35 a.m. Best to leave that for tomorrow.

She got into the shower, letting the water stream through her hair, feeling what little body was left at the end of the night flatten in her hands. Her damn hair was the bane of her existence. Thin and fine as spiderwebs—well, practically—it just hung without the help of a curling iron.

As she sat down at her mirror to swab away the remains of her mascara, Ponce scrutinized her jawline from both sides. Softening. Damn.

Yes, at forty-two, she knew she still looked good, but compared to Ponce Porter, fresh off the bus from Harding, South Carolina, she was just a whisper, really. She remembered how the booker at the Ford agency had come personally to fetch her from the Port Authority, taking her straight to the Fords' house, where she spent a summer grueling enough to give her pause about her new life. Mrs. Ford ran that house like a general, and Ponce and the two other girls who lived there had loathed the punishing curfews.

But Ponce never let her unhappiness show. Sure, this woman was tough, but Ponce's secret was that she was tougher. She had spent her life with a far worthier opponent—her very own mother. Oh, Mother had pretended to be lovely—and loving, for that matter—but her youngest child knew better. Dolores Porter had had three girls already when the fourth arrived to herald her forty-first birthday, so she named the child after Ponce de Leon and his fountain of youth. This was her baby, Dolores decided, the one who would stay home with her and keep her young forever. She took to reciting this unlikely notion to anyone—the postman, the group down at the beauty salon—and always in front of her youngest daughter as she reached greedily for the girl's hand, hair, or, hell, even a toenail would do. Ponce thought peevishly that she had spent her whole childhood trying to twist out of her mother's reach. The woman could never leave her be. So when Ponce got off that bus in New York City, she knew she was here to stay.

She worked hard, starting small, with catalog shoots and store ads. She auditioned for television commercials and actually got a few—where she didn't need to speak. Her accent was a killer, they all told her that. By the time she was twenty-one she was picked for Black Magic perfume's "Come Closer" campaign, and a shot of Ponce—her hair dyed ebony—stretched clear across one wall of Grand Central Terminal. That particular assignment had kept Mother busy for months, Ponce knew, boring the neighbors deaf, dumb, and blind with the rolls of film she had shot during her interminable trip to the city.

Ponce climbed into bed and snuggled against a mass of pillows. She had loved this apartment from the moment she saw it and was grateful it was hers. Her marriage to Lee Morris changed her life in every way she had hoped. During her five years of modeling, Ponce had lived on the Upper East Side in a series of dreary walk-ups all along First Avenue, with pitted linoleum floors and rust-stained sinks. At the sound of the buzzer you dropped the key from the window down to the sidewalk, where the beau of the moment waited. They all blurred together, those beaux, most of them long-haired photographers who liked to shoot her as she slept (God, she hated that), but she had especially liked that sweet-natured drummer, the one who wrote poems comparing her to the wind, who shared countless drinks with her at the Lion's Head, down in the Village. Then they would walk the streets until the sun came up.

But although the work she got was steady, and something like the Black Magic gig was a big success, her achievements were mostly local, and she never broke through to be a national star. Her look was too similar to Cheryl Tiegs's and Christie Brinkley's, Mrs. Ford told her. She didn't stand out. And people were ready for something new. Ponce reverted to her Black Magic hair for a while, but without the right lights and the right makeup her deathly white skin made her look like a corpse.

By her fifth year in town, Ponce found herself in the unwelcome position of scheming to make ends meet. She temped as a receptionist in some of the big advertising agencies, flashing her smile often enough to fill her appointment book with lunch and dinner invitations Monday through Friday. Weeks would pass when she didn't need to buy groceries at all. Although she had not grown up poor, she had grown up thrifty, and she knew how to stuff an overused pair of shoes with newspaper when she needed to—yes, even that pair of Chanel flats she had worn home from a shoot and never returned.

In between bookings—and those periods got longer and longer once she saw the back end of twenty-three, there was no denying it—Ponce would sit at the reception desk at some agency or other and study the help-wanted ads. She had barely made it through high school, and in her haste to escape South Carolina and see the world, she had never even considered college. That, she came to realize, was a mistake.

So when her Ford booker called one day, not with a job but to say that Lee Morris was throwing a party at his Sutton Place duplex and that Ponce should do herself some good and go, she didn't need to be told twice. She could either face the fact that her modeling career was ending and that her best shot at supporting herself was to become a saleswoman at Bergdorf's or Tiffany, where the commissions were high, or she could do exactly what she had been raised to do, and marry up—a time-honored tradition, not only in the South.

Lee Morris, half of the legendary team of Morton/Morris Productions, was notoriously brilliant, difficult, and drop-dead rich. It was he, in the early days of television, who figured out that the best way to sell suds to housewives was to give them suds to watch. His iconic soap operas—*Along Main Street*, *One Hope, One Heart*, and *The Sands of Time*—on all three networks were the first examples of what would later become known as daytime drama. He was written up everywhere— the women's magazines followed his every move—and four more of his soaps became hits as well.

But though he was beloved by the detergent companies and the networks alike, Lee could never bring himself to appreciate his own success. He simply could not shake the feeling that his contribution was cheap somehow, nowhere near as prestigious as that of, say, Walter Gluckman, who was, after all, a pillar of television news. When Kennedy was shot, Walter was right there, running his network's coverage. And what had Lee Morris begat by comparison? Serial weepers about women so dim they couldn't figure out that their own husbands were cheating on them in towns that measured six square blocks.

Like other hard-driving men of his generation, Lee over-did everything to get ahead. Raised on the Lower East Side of Manhattan, he'd dropped out of ninth grade to become a messenger boy for a local radio station, but he read all of Shakespeare's plays and every book in the public library. Twice. He was fluent in French and German (as were his immigrant parents), and once he started making money he traveled extensively, hiring Ph.D.s as his tour guides. He taught himself enough about modern art to become a major collector. And after two decades of daytime triumph, he finally consoled himself for missing out on a career in news by buying thirty television stations and a syndicated newspaper chain instead.

Through the years, Ponce had read some of these things about him. And she knew from the modeling grapevine (he often called the bookers to send over girls as last-minute win-dow dressing for his parties) that his diminutive height (5'5", people guessed) added to his insecurities. But that only sounded like a challenge to Ponce.

When she arrived at the party—in flats—she found her-self to be at least a head taller than Lee. Later, she liked to say she had already outgrown him, but that night she laughed at his jokes, told him all about her mama, and watched him fall in love. They were married within the year.

What she felt most was relief. She was twenty-four and he was sixty, and at that point she was grateful to be granted a supporting role in someone else's oversize life. She wasn't sure what to make of most of it, but Lee had opinions about everything and Ponce took them all as gospel. That he was so much like her mother didn't dawn on her until later. With all the traveling and the new friends and redecorating the duplex on Sutton Place, Ponce didn't realize that Lee wanted noth-ing more than to program her every move, to show the world that this stunner he had snared would do his bidding. And only his.

The other similarity between Lee and her mother concerned show business. As a girl, Dolores Porter had imagined a life on the stage. Or screen. Just how she thought that might happen hanging around Harding, South Carolina, was a mere detail, Ponce often thought pettily. *She*, certainly, would never have had the guts to leave and go to New York City. Then again, Dolores Tulp had loved her mama, and the idea of leaving her was as awful as her show-business dreams were fantastic. Ponce Porter, certainly, had no such problem. Yes, she cried at twelve when her daddy drove her to boarding school, but after a few days there she would look around and sigh with amazement not to find her mama hanging on to her, grasping her hand to inspect the state of her cuticles, coming up behind her with a brush to run through her pretty yellow hair, oh, just this once. The entire notion of mothers giving life to their children was lost on Ponce Porter. Her mother was hell-bent on stealing her daughter's life back for her very own self.

She had known this, Ponce used to think, as early as kindergarten. When her daddy had taken her to her first day of school, Ponce wailed mightily, like all the other children. But after the rest had dried their tears and been lured inside with the promise of brand-new crayons and graham crackers with milk, Ponce was still bawling on the playground. Bill Porter had never seen such dramatics, not even in a house where his wife read movie magazines all day and cried over nothing at all, where his three other daughters minced and shrieked over nothing at all but cheered "Daddy!" just as loudly as they could when he came home—well, living in a house full of females was a certain lot in life.

But this child was something else again. The first time

Ponce had seen a spider she must have been, what, three years old, and she carried on so insistently that he and Dolores had to change her bedroom, move the girls all around, because Ponce flat-out refused to set foot in that room again. He had never seen such an iron will, not even in his wife. And now he stood in front of the school as his daughter howled insistently, and the teacher, one hour into the job and already looking worn behind her small, square glasses, pulled him aside and murmured, "Mr. Porter, you know that in the state of South Carolina, kindergarten is still optional." And even though he suspected that she was telling him a convenient lie, he scooped up the squalling child and carried her right back home.

Dolores Porter was disconsolate. "Ponce cannot just sit in the house," she cried. "What will people say?" And indeed, if Ponce had been old enough to figure out that no school would mean more Mother, she might have reconsidered. Instead, she refused to leave her room and wouldn't mind her mama, no matter what, so each night at dinner there was a brand-new litany of Ponce's insubordination, until Bill Porter could stand it no longer. He called his old friend Chuck Crosby, who ran the one movie theater in Harding, and they worked out a deal: Every day, for a solid school year, after Bill came home from his hardware store for lunch, he would drop Ponce off at the Playhouse where she would sit through the same movie every day for a week, until it changed.

The very first afternoon, Ponce wasn't sure about her daddy just leaving her there alone and opened her mouth to cry. "You just remember, you are here because you are too special to go to kindergarten like the other children," he told her. "I'll be back for you in time for supper."

Well, free of her mama, free of school (and, Dolores was right, the scandalous talk of the town: *Whatever is the matter with the youngest Porter girl? Maybe she's mentally retarded. That must be it. Only she does have the loveliest manners, once you speak to her*), Ponce sat happily in the darkness, thrilling to the screen, near the back where the door opened, so that Mr. Crosby could always find her. Ponce loved Disney pictures like *Fantasia* and *Mary Poppins*, but *The Parent Trap* took her breath away. To be rid of your mother and then scheme to bring her back again? Ha! But so many times it seemed that even the newer movies never made it to Harding on time, so Mr. Crosby would play the Fred Astaire–Ginger Rogers films he kept around, and those were Ponce's favorites. She memorized every word and vowed right then that she wanted to go to New York City, preferably on an ocean liner, but however she got there, New York City was the goal, filled as it was with men and women dancing at elegant parties and falling in love. Never had a six-year-old been more content, or done a more knowing imitation of lighting a cigarette, than she.

Finally, after her year of special education at the Harding Playhouse, Ponce went to public school like everyone else, and it wasn't until the sixth grade that trouble started again. At the age of twelve, she showed the beginnings of turning from a beautiful child into a beautiful teenager, and Dolores Porter clamped down harder than ever. Even Bill Porter had to admit that his wife was going overboard, putting Ponce's hair up in rag curls every single night, smearing cold cream on her face "to protect her complexion."

Ponce had always been a finicky eater, and at that point, she practically stopped eating altogether. She developed an elaborate system of taking the newspaper that her daddy had thrown out the night before and folding a sheet or two inside her cloth napkin, where most of her food would go when her mother turned away to fuss over her sisters. Then, when Ponce cleared her plate from the table, she would slip her package underneath her shirt and run outside, pretending that she was going to play with the other kids in the neighborhood.

Instead, she would take her dinner over to Mrs. Van, a black widow who took in laundry and lived a few blocks away. Ponce always told Mrs. Van that the food was leftovers and that she hoped she would enjoy it. In Sunday school Ponce had been taught to help the less fortunate, and she had always liked Mrs. Van. Even during her moviegoing year, when everyone in town whispered and pointed at Ponce, Mrs. Van was kind to her. In the mornings sometimes, Ponce would tell her mama she was playing outside, then walk over to Mrs. Van's house. Often, the older woman would be out in her vegetable garden, and when she saw Ponce she never looked at her funny, the way other people did. She would just start talking to her, telling her about picking pea pods in the summer and planting yams for the fall. Ponce wasn't always sure what she was saying, but she listened. Most mornings, Mrs. Van would take a break and sit on her back steps with a knife and an apple, and first she would cut the peel in one long strip and then she would cut a slice for Ponce and before long, the little girl started following her inside to watch her work.

Ponce loved the smell of the laundry and was never scared by the hissing steam of the iron. Mrs. Van could take any crumpled heap up out of the basket, sprinkle some water on it, and right in front of Ponce's eyes white shirts appeared crisp enough for Fred Astaire himself. Ponce told Mrs. Van that her shirts were just like the ones in the movies, but the older woman laughed and shook her head. These were churchgoing shirts, she said. No movie stars here in Harding.

After the year she skipped kindergarten, Ponce continued

to visit her friend. Mrs. Van told the child stories about growing up in Alabama, and about her grandparents, who were
the children of slaves. But what Ponce liked best about Mrs.
Van was that she never once told her she was pretty. She told
her she was smart. She liked how Ponce was always
reading from a book—which, Ponce thought when she got
older, may have been the only reason she paid any
attention in school at all. In her sixth-grade year, she would sit
with Mrs. Van and read her lessons, then show her some
stories in the newspaper. Mrs. Van had learned her ABCs, she
told Ponce, it was simply her eyesight that stopped her from
reading. But the child figured out the truth, and after she had
laid out her uneaten dinner they would sit with the funny
pages and Ponce would read them out loud. Mrs. Van just
loved that.

Well, after the day in late April when a pork chop fell from
underneath Ponce's shirt and hit the kitchen floor, Dolores
Porter got wise. Ponce couldn't remember seeing her that
angry, ever. And once her mother discovered that this "catering service," as she called it, had been going on for the better
part of a school year, she vowed to stop it. It had taken forever
to disabuse the town of the notion that her daughter was
mentally retarded—just spoiled to death was the ultimate
verdict—and now to have this same child take up with the
colored laundress? Whatever was the matter with her? To
have all that beauty and so little sense.

So despite the awful cost, boarding school it was. Ponce
wrote Mrs. Van a letter every week and, when she came home
for Thanksgiving, went over to her house and read them all to
her. They kept that up every year Ponce was away, and when
she finally graduated and was ready to move to New York
City, having landed a modeling contract even before she got

there, Mrs. Van was so proud. She sat Ponce down and gave her a Bible that had belonged to her grandfather.

"I know all my Bible stories here anyway," she said, pointing to her head. "And you know about my eyesight. I always thought I'd have one of my own children to give this to, but Mr. Van died before that ever happened."

She and Ponce cried and embraced, and that was the last time Ponce ever saw her. When Mrs. Van died, two years later, Ponce got a package in the mail from the pastor at the older woman's church. Inside were all the letters Ponce had sent through the years, along with some pictures of her in one or two ads she had sent as well. After Mrs. Van died, Ponce didn't go back to Harding for five years.

Of course, distance didn't stop her mama from her nagging—or what she preferred to call "helpful suggestions." Since Ponce was already modeling in New York City, why didn't she become an actress, too? But unlike Dolores Porter, Ponce didn't aspire to stage or screen. She couldn't sing a note, and the only acting she was ever proud of was the moment she announced "Mother, I will miss you so" as her daddy started the car for the long trip to boarding school.

Dolores's pain at Ponce's absence was eventually obliterated when her daughter married Lee Morris.

From one in the afternoon until three each weekday, every housewife in Harding had always stopped whatever she was doing to watch Lee's shows, all three of them, in a row. If the men of Harding marked time with paychecks and football games, the women did the same with their "stories," as they called them.

Then, the children would come home from school, and the telephoning began. "Do you think she'll ever leave him? Do you think he loves her after all?" The kids would grab their cookies from waiting plates and slam the screen doors behind them while the women stretched the phone cords across their counters to peel potatoes as they marveled at the dramas of the day.

So when Ponce snagged Lee Morris for her very own, they all agreed there could not be a better husband. Never mind that he was a Jew. They all read *Life* magazine. Jews ran show business, anyone could tell you that.

From her bed, Ponce did a quick scan of the news channels, then realized she had better get up and get rid of her ruined clothes before Juanita found them the next day. She turned off the ringer on her phone—she had no intention of getting up one second before noon—and looked at her appointment book. It wasn't a court day, but she wanted to make sure she had canceled her trainer. The book fell open to the page for the previous week, when she had taken Rachel Lerner to lunch in the Grill Room at the Four Seasons.

She closed the book and smiled. She liked Rachel. Ponce almost never had lunch with anyone—it was a spectacular waste of time, in her view—but she wanted to get to know Rachel better. Honestly, though, the appetite on that girl! She ate a huge spinach salad and two crab cakes and had an eye out for dessert (though she skipped it), while Ponce pushed a plain, albeit perfectly cooked, omelet around her plate.

"I didn't see that on the menu," Rachel had said.

"It's not listed, but a good kitchen will always make it for you," Ponce said absently—one of the many facts of life she had learned from Lee. She gave a curt wave to Annabelle Gluckman, who, thankfully, was traveling with a group of suits into the Pool Room.

"Cleavage in midday, what a treat," Rachel said, watching her go.

Ponce smiled. "That look had a lot more mileage when Annabelle first came to New York," she said. "Before she met Walter, she had a reputation for being quite generous with her favors, if you catch my meaning. Lee said the men called her 'the British Open.'"

The conversation had taken off from there, and Ponce found herself telling Rachel things about her relationship with Lee that she hadn't thought of in years. She reminded herself that the point of the lunch had been for her to get to know Rachel better, but wasn't that always the way when you talked to a writer? You ended up spilling your entire life story before you even realized it. And Rachel was an eager audience. She couldn't get enough, and Ponce found herself enjoying the attention.

Yes, she said, she had been captivated by Lee, who was smart about so many things. Though marrying him, she added, was most definitely a career choice. She recalled how he used to ask her, mockingly, "Would you still love me if I weren't rich and famous?" To which she would reply, "Would you still love me if I weren't young and beautiful?" Ponce laughed. "That always shut him up," she said.

"But really, the jig was up for me," she went on. "If I didn't marry Lee, what was I going to do with the rest of my life? I hadn't gone to college, which was stupid. I know I should have been a better student, but I must say, where I grew up, being beautiful was more important than anything else. It meant that you would marry well and be taken care of for the rest of your life. So yes, I married for the money, but I was never bored. I learned so much on the job. And the minute I got sorry, I left."

Well, maybe not the minute, and she soon admitted as

much to Rachel. Lee, who had been in analysis for most of his adult life, had lobbied for years that Ponce go herself. Finally he insisted. But as decrees often do, that one backfired, serving to sow the seeds of his own destruction. Ponce's analyst, highly recommended by Lee's own, was an older Jewish intellectual—a fabulous woman with a beautiful face and an imposing bun—who was so horrified by her Southern belle client that after the second session she insisted that Ponce go out and buy a copy of *The Feminine Mystique*, incredulous that so many years after the fact she had to spell Betty Friedan's name for her. Then, for months, she berated Ponce for her disgraceful lack of education. Before long, Ponce enrolled at NYU.

"Once I read Betty Friedan, I got it," she told Rachel. "It took me a while, but finally I did. All those movies I watched growing up! All those elaborate parties I wanted to go to. That's what I thought was important. Well, I went to those parties *and* I went to school. I learned I was perfectly capable of doing both. And even though that marriage saved me from some real financial shit, I realized I was in it for more than the money. To this day still, Lee is the most interesting man I've ever met. And he surrounded himself with creative, talented people. Writers, actors, directors, I just loved them. That life of the mind was the draw for me. The lawyers? The Wall Street people? Bored me to death."

Rachel nodded. "Same," she said, in between bites.

"If I had really cared about the money, I would have had kids," Ponce went on. She turned to signal a waiter for coffee, but one was already at her elbow, setting her up. "Why, thank you," she purred, waiting for him to leave before she spoke again.

"Because, you know, there is no easier way for a woman to make money in New York City than to marry rich and breed," she went on. "With a good lawyer, you can make a living for decades. But I've got a missing gene, I guess. I never wanted a child. For some reason—my mother, most likely—I only see doors closing and windows slamming. I'd rather be shot."

Now Ponce set down her appointment book and looked at the clock. Nearly two a.m. She realized that she was hungry. Of course, she hadn't had more than four mouthfuls all night, worried as she was about keeping Jacqueline upright. In the kitchen, Ponce broke into the stash of cheese crackers filled with peanut butter that Rachel had given her. Rachel liked to shop for groceries on the computer, get those huge packages of things—like thirty rolls of toilet paper all at once—and under the table at the Four Seasons she'd presented Ponce with a shopping bag filled with forty-five individually wrapped packages of her favorite snack. "A lifetime supply," Ponce had joked, but now she was glad to have them.

On the way back to bed she walked into her darkened living room to look out onto Fifth Avenue. It was picture-perfect, empty, the bench in front of the Park lit by a streetlamp. This was exactly what she had hoped for, all those years ago at the Harding Playhouse. Of course, had she been just a bit smarter—as every woman she knew had told her incessantly—she could have had this view and so many more. But when it came to having a child, she just refused to give in.

Not that it mattered to Lee. Ponce was his fourth wife, and he'd already had four children, none of whom he particularly liked. Once he realized that Ponce genuinely didn't care about children, he let it go, though his awareness that such a vast revenue of potential control had been squandered continued to nag him. As Ponce enrolled in more and more classes and took up more and more hours with her studies, Lee became something of a child himself.

"I got sick one time," she told Rachel at lunch, "with a fever of 103. And Lee said, 'I don't care, I want to have sex. Right now.' And I said, 'Lee, I can't believe this. I am really, truly ill.' And he went right ahead."

"What a bastard!" Rachel exclaimed.

Ponce sighed. "Well, the more time I spent on school, the madder he got. I think he would have liked to have gone back himself and graduated high school, gone to college like all the rich kids had. But he was too proud for that. And too impatient, really. He could read fifteen books in a week, he'd never sit still for teenagers who were too busy partying to pay attention. Knowing something, learning something, those were life-and-death issues for Lee.

"Anyway, then he demanded I take tennis lessons. He decided I wasn't good enough and needed to work on my game. I told him I couldn't possibly read up on the fall of the Roman Empire, do the flowers for a dinner for thirty, and perfect my backhand all in one day. He told me I absolutely could. And you know what? I did. Whether I wanted to or not. You want to know why I always sleep late? I'm still exhausted from my marriage."

Rachel looked stricken, but Ponce laughed.

"I'm not being fair here, Rachel, only telling you the bad parts. Lee was actually quite proud of me—on his good days. I mean, the thing about him, for all his craziness, was that he so loved literature and art and history that I think he was glad I could finally appreciate how much he knew—if not the literature, art, and history themselves!"

Rachel shook her head, and Ponce could see she was riveted. It was so unlike Ponce, really, to talk so much about herself. But she found she didn't want to stop.

"We went along like that for a few more years," she continued. "I graduated from college and decided I wanted to go to law school. I liked the logic of the law, the reasoning behind it. But I took a year off first, just to get some rest, and then somehow—oh, I remember, I sat next to Mike Posner at a dinner party and he told me he was giving money to a literacy program up in Harlem. And I had known a woman when I was growing up who couldn't read, and just loved her—but that's a whole other story.

"Anyway, I went up there and volunteered. I worked with an Irishman named Joe Murphy who was almost sixty—he looked something like my granddaddy, truth be told. He was a janitor in the public schools. Well, I met with him three times a week for nine months, and I'll tell you, when he got his diploma, or certificate, whatever they call it, and he stood up and read a speech he had written thanking me, I just about cried for a week. It meant so much.

"But Lee didn't like it at all. He didn't like my going to Harlem. He said he'd be happy to write them a check without me wasting my time. He'd say, 'You think Mike Posner is spending five minutes up there? You and your strays, your hard-luck cases.'"

"Lovely," Rachel said. Her tone was harsh.

Ponce nodded. "I know. He wasn't really that way, it was just, well, he wanted me to pay attention to him, not to Joe Murphy. And once I got into law school that spring, things got worse. Lee had me throwing a party a week, which I went ahead and did, and I told him I'd be happy to keep it up right until the moment school started in the fall. But once it did, he pretty much left me alone. I mean, all our friends knew I was enrolled, so he had to lay off."

She actually ate a forkful of her omelet. "After I graduated, though," she said, "and started at Corning Hilliard as an associate, suddenly all he wanted to do was travel. He would just *have* to go to Paris, and he would force me to ask for vacation time I hadn't even earned. Well, we fought it out a while longer—we'd been married twelve years by then—and finally I left. I just packed a suitcase with none of my jewelry, none of the *stuff* he was always so afraid someone would take away from him. I didn't give a damn about that. I moved into a studio apartment, started an affair with a novelist, and that was that. I tell you, when I get done, it is so done it's ridiculous."

Rachel loved that line, laughing with delight, and Ponce had been amused. The girl's face was like a slot machine. You knew within seconds if you had won or lost.

"Of course, the divorce was ugly because Lee made it that way," Ponce said. "He didn't like being left, he was used to doing the leaving himself. The partners at Corning insisted I fight for more than I wanted—they were right, of course, I realized that in retrospect—but I wanted it to be over, and eventually it was."

The waiter arrived to pour more coffee. Ponce asked for the check.

"No, forget it, it's not over," Rachel said after the waiter left. "Gus said you were still friends after the divorce. What happened next?"

"You *are* a reporter," Ponce said, amused. "Let's see. About a year passed, maybe a little more, without our ever running into each other. Then one day, there he was right in front of me, at the Museum of Modern Art, of all places. I don't know which of us was more surprised. We went for a drink and ended up talking for hours, and incredibly enough, after that, we did become friends. Much more than when we were married. But by that point, life had changed for Lee. He was, what, seventy-three, and had no intention of remarrying. He dated plenty after our divorce, and naturally he found something wrong with every woman he met. So he didn't mind just having some company.

"We'd go to the theater together. Have dinner. When I saw the apartment I live in now and told Lee I thought it would make a good investment, he went ahead and bought it for me. He loved that kind of grand gesture—especially after our divorce, when he did things like insist I return the frame of the one painting that was actually mine."

Ponce smiled wryly. "He was still difficult," she went on, "no mistaking that. But when I didn't want to take his shit, I left and there wasn't a thing he could do about it. He wanted sex and I didn't? Too bad. That part of it was over.

"Then, a few years later, he got sick. Liver cancer. Within six months he was gone. Well, Lee hated being sick more than anything. I knew that, and for most of that time I never left his side. What's fair is fair. That man gave me a life I could only dream about back in Harding, South Carolina, and I've never spent a day when I've forgotten it.

"His children suddenly appeared—all grown, of course, some of them older than me—playing these big scenes about how he never loved them and never gave them enough money. On those days I would just hide in the kitchen with the cook. That was the last place anyone thought to look for me! I got him a platoon of nurses, just the nicest women alive, but he was convinced they were stealing from him, so I offered to stay over and sleep right next to him, keep an eye out."

Rachel nodded, and her smile was sad.

"I also took a leave from the firm, which I must say was the smartest thing I ever did," Ponce continued. "I never gave a shit about making partner, and quite frankly no one there did, either. They knew about my life outside the office, and even though no one ever came out and said anything, they resented it. They questioned my commitment, and they were right to.

"After Lee died, I quit altogether. It turned out that he had left me some money—which he said he'd never do, I'd gotten enough in the divorce. Then again, for Lee, it really was only *some* money. But it was enough so that if I invested it properly, I wouldn't have to work again. I bought myself a Metro-Card and started going down to the courts twice a week, doing pro bono legal work for a group that places children in foster care. I like it—the people I work for, the kids who get to go home with people who actually want them there. It's so much better than working at Corning. All those grueling hours just so one company could buy another, or some hospital could kill someone and get away with it."

"Absolutely," Rachel said earnestly.

"So these days," Ponce went on, "when someone like Jacqueline calls me in a frenzy, I'm available. That poor girl. I mean, she'll be okay. She said her lawyer thinks she might even keep half the places—but you know, that's not what she ever cared about. She really loved Mike Posner. If he had been happy to live in even one of those houses with her, it would have been enough. But he has that Wall Street mentality I never could stand—the rush of the buy, and the next and the next. Jacqueline knocked herself out to fill those places with everything beautiful, but as she said, the one thing in each home he never wanted was her." Ponce sighed. "That's why I'm helping her," she said. "One of my strays, as Lee would say."

She picked up her bag to dig out her credit card. "Also," she added, "working two days a week leaves me plenty of time to watch my sports."

Rachel's face fell, and Ponce laughed.

"No, no," she said. "For me that's heaven—watching the tennis and golf, football, baseball, basketball, as much as I want. Lee was bored to death by it. I learned to love it when I was growing up. Daddy and I watched all the time. It surely was another way to escape Mother, who just hated sports, but it was something I really enjoyed. And I liked my father. Oh, he was handsome! It's funny, that's not something I ever noticed until I got older and all my friends from boarding school would meet him and swoon. He was a quiet man, serious. Didn't talk much. But when it came to sports, he talked plenty, and I was the only one in the house who knew what he was talking about. And since he died—that was a year or so before Lee—well, it brings him back to me.

"I can also keep caught up on the papers now. You know, I'm a political junkie, just like Gus."

Rachel rolled her eyes. She believed that all politicians were liars, and whenever Ponce and Gus took off on one of their tangents, she glazed right over.

"But that's also where Red Evans comes in," Ponce said. "For that friendship alone, I'm grateful to Lee. Red is such a smart writer, with such a great political mind. And he's a genuine friend. Some days we talk for hours. I mean, obviously, he's still grieving. Cackie died, what, just a year ago?, and they were married for thirty-two years. She was a marvelous girl, you would have liked her."

Rachel started to say something, but Ponce cut her off.

"No, he's not coming to the Jacqueline dinner. He says he will, but I know he'll cancel the day of, so I've just let it go. I've tried everything to get him in from the country—to see theater or the Knicks—but he won't budge. He won't work, either. All he'll do is sit in that house in Connecticut where Cackie died, and drink and talk on the phone. The only visitors he'll allow are his kids." She shrugged. "He'll leave when he's ready, but I'm just grateful for the phone."

"You were really close friends with her, too, weren't you?" Rachel asked, and Ponce nodded.

"You know, the thing I find interesting about you," Rachel continued, "is that you seem able to have friendships with both people in a couple, which for everyone else is the hardest thing. Because there's always one person you like better, even though you're stuck with both of them."

Ponce signed the receipt. "I agree," she said. "And there are plenty of couples where I only see the person I like. But what I've found is this: Even people wildly in love, like you and Gus, don't always love to do the same thing at the exact same moment. Gus and I can talk politics for hours, which bores you. You and I can talk for hours about Lee and the horrors of Annabelle Gluckman, which bores Gus."

Rachel thought a minute. "Yes, but here's what's odd. You're a perfect audience to both sides, which is something men always expect but women never get because they're too busy doing it themselves. You're like a spare wife, even to the wife. Which is why the women are never jealous about your relationship with their husbands."

Ponce shrugged. "That may be," she said. "But I just like who I like. My friends are the most important thing in the world, and I have no room for any new people in my life. Well, besides you, of course. I've known Gus forever, and I told him not to marry Terry—"

Rachel's eyebrows shot up, but Ponce kept talking. "You never mind about that," she said. "That is for another day. But the point is, I have plenty of people to care about, whether they're married or not. And they care about me."

Rachel thought a while longer. "Were you ever *in* love with Lee?" she asked, still seeming dissatisfied.

Ponce considered. "I guess I never was *in* love with him," she said. "But I loved his mind, his energy, the world he gave me." She watched Rachel watch her, maybe even judge her, and sat up straight in her chair. "You're still young," Ponce said. "What are you, thirty-two?"

Rachel nodded.

"You don't know yet that falling in love is not a given," she went on. "Most people never fall in love. Some people never miss it. It took me a very long time to recognize that intimacy is not an easy fit for me. So goodbye, marriage. But without my friends, I'm not sure I'd want to stick around."

They got up then, and Rachel hugged her. They walked through the empty restaurant—it was past three-thirty—and Ponce stopped at the reservation desk. Rachel heard her confirm a table for Christmas Eve.

"You come here on Christmas?" she asked. "Why?"

Ponce shrugged. "Every year I take Lee's cook and his housekeeper out for Christmas dinner," she said. "One is a widow"—she pronounced it *widduh*—"and the other doesn't have any family here, they're back in Switzerland."

Rachel looked bewildered. "You mean, you spend the holidays with the help instead of with your own family?"

Ponce's eyes narrowed. "'Help' is the right word for those women, Rachel," she said in a tone that got the younger woman's attention. "When I was having a hard time in my marriage, trying to keep it together and go to school, all they did was help me. I learned a long time ago that the people who are kind to you, who love you and care about you, are not necessarily the ones you were born to or raised with. You learn to find your family in all sorts of places."

The younger woman nodded soberly and thanked her new friend for lunch. The two embraced before going their separate ways.

. . .

But that really was true, what she had said, Ponce thought, pulling back the bedcovers. And certainly, if her mama knew that from the very first year of Ponce's marriage to Lee that a high school senior from the Harlem public schools had gone on to attend four years of college, all expenses paid, under the Martha Van Scholarship, awarded annually to a young woman of exceptional promise, well, she would just spit, wouldn't she?

Ponce smiled and switched off the light. She was ready to sleep now.

Chapter Three

By ten o'clock on the Monday morning after New Year's, the *Boothby's* office was still empty. That wasn't unusual; the only day the magazine staff arrived early was Tuesday, for the weekly ideas meeting. The editors were a churlish bunch then, suffering leftover exam anxiety behind their sunglasses, toting extra-large coffees and bags full of newspapers and magazines. Except for Topher, Shawsie, and the managing editor, who had offices along one hallway, and the art and fashion departments, stationed upstairs via an open metal staircase that sounded like hell when the Manolos hit it, the majority of *Boothby's* staff worked in a big central square — the editors in glass-walled offices around the perimeter, their assistants pooled in the open middle. On Tuesdays the assistants kept to their cubicles, pretending not to watch their bosses grow ever more desperate, struggling to come up with enough ideas to prove to Topher that they were still creative, cutting-edge, smart, young — whatever he wanted at that particular moment, if only he would go on signing their expense reports.

Topher Bowles had been the editor in chief of *Boothby's* for almost ten years, having turned a forgotten title from the fifties, when the place had a brief life as a second-rate *New Yorker*, into the kind of magazine *The New Yorker* might be if it won the lottery and got a face-lift, a younger beau, and a place in Rio. The stories were smart, tightly written, well reported, and photographed by the best in the business. Sure, the emphasis was often on Hollywood or Madison Avenue, true crime or even the club scene in New York, but the high-brow treatment of intellectually low-rent subjects proved a winning combination, and *Boothby's* was the kind of success most editors never realize.

For Topher the victory was particularly sweet. His maternal grandfather, a bartender who worked at the same Irish pub on Second Avenue for almost fifty years, had had three poems published in the original *Boothby's* and, until the day he died, still aspired to *The New Yorker*. He started taking Topher to the pub when he turned seven, and the boy loved the scads of cousins, uncles, and aunts who would keep him company there or include him on trips to the playground, the movies, or the zoo. Topher's mother had made a brilliant marriage to a WASP from Greenwich who gave his wife everything she wanted on the condition that she spare him her unwieldy family. But as an only child, Topher was terribly lonely, and he could never understand why his parents chose to bring him to the country club for holidays like Thanksgiving, the three of them sitting alone saying practically nothing, while he knew the fun the crowd down in the city was having.

By the time he got to high school, Topher rebelled plenty. He and his best friend, Skip Shaw, were regulars in detention, and once they were almost busted after a party got out of hand and a cop spotted them smoking a joint near Skip's car.

Topher was terrified that his father would find out, but in the nick of time, Skip's older sister, Mary Elizabeth, whom everyone knew as "Shawsie," turned up and talked them out of trouble. It seemed she worked as a candy striper at the local hospital with the cop's daughter, and somehow, before too long, Skip and Topher were allowed to go, their biggest concern the confiscated dime bag they would never see again.

Topher had gone on to Yale, then fallen out with his father after refusing to take over the family's stock brokerage. After kicking around publishing for almost a decade as a writer and editor, he took loans from friends and revived *Boothby's*. About five years in, Arnold Rubinstein, owner of the powerhouse Rubinstein Publications, came calling with an enormous infusion of cash, and suddenly Topher was a publishing celebrity. He was *the* point person on the rich and infamous, but was clever enough to stuff each issue with incisive columns on politics and media and at least one long piece on some offbeat topic—say, the history of fringe in American costume—that invariably delighted everyone who read it. Like a terrific party, the unlikely mix made a genuine splash.

As was the case at all successful magazines, the editor in chief served as the benevolent despot, and Topher was alternately loved and feared by his staff for his brains, wit, and legendary impatience with laziness, stupidity, and pretense. Everyone was intimately acquainted with his schedule: They knew exactly when he saw his personal trainer, or Arnold Rubinstein, or even his accountant, which gave them a heads-up to try not to say or do the wrong thing, because at *Boothby's*, as at the White House, they all served at the pleasure of the president. Unlike the White House, however, the *Boothby's* staff couldn't just leave and make more money elsewhere. In publishing, this was as lucky as you could get.

Perhaps no one understood this more clearly than Babette Steele, which may have been why, at nine o'clock on the Monday morning after New Year's, she was the only assistant at her desk. Bent over her file cabinet with a roll of paper towels and a bottle of Fantastik, she cleaned inside and out, making lots of room in the top drawer for what she hoped would be notes on the many pieces she would write in the coming year. At least that was her New Year's resolution. All she needed to do now was convince someone to assign them to her.

She had pitched a number of ideas to the editors, but none had worked out. They would look at her, bored, asking the inevitable "Do you have access?" She sipped her double skim latte, feeling her familiar frustration rise. Did she have access to Bono and Britney Spears? As if.

"I'll take that, thanks," Babette said to the mail clerk, who was carrying in a colossal bundle. He dropped it gratefully onto her desk.

"*Boothby's*," she said, picking up the ringing phone and cradling it between her shoulder and neck as she snipped the confining strings and sorted expertly through the released mass looking for invitations.

"Yes, this is she."

French embassy. Engraved and addressed to an editor who had left for St. Barth the week before. She put it to one side.

"Yeah, that's great, I'll see her at one." She hung up. Annabelle Gluckman's secretary had the same high-toned accent as her boss, which, Babette couldn't help but think, was the most high-toned thing about her. Really, Annabelle could be so maddening! There was no denying that she and Walter were at the top of the social heap in New York— Annabelle talked constantly about the famous people they knew. But over the past year, Babette had come to realize that the connections were more Walter's than his wife's. He was a legend in TV news, and she was perceived as a pushy climber who had usurped the beloved Gerta Gluckman, salt of the earth and mother of Walter's children. People still invited Gerta, because they adored her—which made her, for Annabelle, the equivalent of a low-grade fever she could never shake. And while Annabelle had delivered on her promise to Babette and gotten her invited to a handful of cocktail parties, they were all press events. Not one in a private home. Well, okay, one. The Jacqueline Posner dinner.

Babette was especially miffed by Annabelle's Christmas gift to her: a small bag of obviously used Solange cosmetics, apparently left over from a photo shoot. Nothing like a pot of glitter eye shadow bearing some else's thumbprint.

Babette resolved to put that snub behind her. It was a new year, and somehow she was going to get Annabelle to fork over some contacts. After all, when Babette had been seeing Rolf, that chef in TriBeCa, Annabelle ate there free for months. She owed her. Babette had been at *Boothby's* for six months now, and her only assignments were two tiny pieces: three hundred words on an up-and-coming rock star, and another three hundred on a German model who had seemed pissed, quite frankly, that her big moment in *Boothby's* had arrived and this *clerk* had been sent to do the honors. The model made Babette cool her heels in the living room of her hotel suite for the two hours it took her agent to convince her to calm down and talk.

Babette glanced at the next envelope. Suba. A hip place downtown. And addressed to an editor with a six-month-old infant. She'd never miss it. Babette added that cocktail-party invitation to her pile and kept flipping. At twenty-five, she had been working in magazines since she'd graduated from NYU: two years as a temp, then in the beauty department at

Self. That hadn't been half bad, actually. Lunches about lipsticks, dinners about mascara—and not just in New York. Makeup companies would happily fly you to Anguilla to better appreciate the newest shade of coral blusher, seaside, and all you had to do was write a bouncy caption for a sundappled picture and everyone was happy.

But the truth, as at most women's magazines, was that the lack of a male population became a real problem. "You meet men through men," Babette's mother always said, and even though she could be a total pain, Babette knew to listen to her on that subject. Her parents' marriage had been a disaster—her father specialized in harebrained business schemes that succeeded only in failing—and they had split when Babette was five. He took off, and for the next few years checks arrived intermittently with postmarks from Tucson or Houston. By the time Babette reached junior high, he was gone for good.

But since then, Aileen Steele was rarely alone. She had always been a beautiful woman, and was something of a speed dater in her youth. After her divorce, she picked up where she'd left off. Thanks to her semi-deadbeat husband she needed to find a job, and eventually landed a steady one at the Riverdale branch of the New York Public Library. It was reasonably close to home, the hours were good and so were the benefits. She was able to put her daughter through NYU, as long as Babette commuted and pitched in on expenses by waiting tables on the weekends. Babette admired her mother's resourcefulness but wished that her taste in men ran less toward frustrated poets teaching English in private schools with six bucks in their pockets and more toward investment bankers with lavish expense accounts and Manhattan penthouses.

The most recent beau was a particular drag, Babette

thought. Seamus Ferguson taught English at Dogwood, one of the elite private schools in Manhattan, and in his youth in Ireland had even published a novel. A former runner, he had qualified to compete in the Olympics but had taken a bad fall and injured his hip, and in the years since had developed an addiction to painkillers. At Dogwood, after he missed first period at least twice a week for months, some of the parents complained—what were they paying top dollar for?—but the school let it go. Or had until Seamus gave two Harvard-hungry football players B's instead of the A's they expected. They were mediocre students, he insisted, showing the principal the papers the boys had written. If he were doing his job properly, Seamus added, he should have given them C's. The parents appealed, Seamus refused to back down, and one of the fathers pulled his donation. Practically overnight, Seamus discovered that the A's had been delivered, the donation had been reinstated, and he had been terminated.

In the jobless six months that followed, Seamus swore to Aileen Steele that he would stop his pills cold turkey or look into rehab or twelve-step programs. He did none of those things. Babette counseled her mother to break it off, but Aileen believed that she could fix anyone if she put her mind to it—her vanished husband aside—and when Seamus took on some freelance editing, she only encouraged him. He would sit at Aileen's kitchen table, ranting about never teaching the brats of those rich fuckers again—before exhausting himself into his next phase, which was getting weepy about his plight. He would call Aileen his "rock" and his "dear one" and kiss the backs of her hands as Babette squirmed, her eyes on the clock.

Babette's own track record with men was somewhat more successful, she told herself. Okay, so she had started with the requisite older man, an Argentinian banker she met at a hotel bar who had one little quirk: He liked her to pee on him. Each time she did, he bought her a piece of Louis Vuitton luggage. The memory still made her laugh—for a complete set, it had been a small price to pay! But he really was too gross, so she resolved to find men closer to her age, with more sanitary habits. There were a few investment bankers who liked going to showy restaurants like Balthazar, where they would order expensive champagne and spend hours making out with her at the table. But when it came time to go home, they were half in the bag and usually fell asleep in the taxi.

Having determined that the financial markets opened too early for her interest in nightlife, Babette found a local anchorman instead. He was something of a confirmed bachelor and a lot of fun. They had great sex, he knew tons of cool people, including the mayor, and they were invited to some really happening parties. She had a total blast with him, right up until the moment he called to tell her he was engaged to an heiress to a pharmaceutical fortune.

That threw her, she had to admit, and she didn't date anyone at all for, what, at least three months. Then there was a lawyer, nice but a snooze; a divorced screenwriter who was a great lay but spent every weekend with his young children, which was a total drag so she dumped him; and a hedge-fund manager who after a few weeks told her she was just too tall to sleep with and he dumped her.

Well, maybe her track record wasn't that much better than her mother's, once she'd stopped to look at it. So it was the promise of men—more men, better men—that had spurred Babette to hound the secretary in Rubinstein human resources to get her seen for this job, and she had tried not to waste a moment since.

Babette tucked that day's selected invitations into her top desk drawer; it was still too early to RSVP. She would wait until after lunch, when the assistants were all sure to be in their seats. She would call on behalf of the person whose name was on the envelope, then, on the day of the event, show up and announce herself as the person invited. In four years of playing this game she had been challenged only once, by two assistants huddled at a table in a freezing draft near the front door of a chic new museum. Babette leaned in and explained, sotto voce, that her boss couldn't make it at the last minute and sent her instead, just for fun, and the girls nodded understandingly and waved her right through. Truly, with just a little planning, you could go to great places in New York every night of the week. It was how she'd met Robin Brody, after all.

Babette turned back to the mail to consult the press releases in her hunt for story ideas and soon spotted one from a hot fashion firm. "Carmen is the most exciting new talent on the Chicago fashion scene," it read. "She is a young woman who channels the spirit of her native Cuba, combining the traditions of her tropical childhood with the energy of her adopted American city, which results in a unique design style all her own."

Babette looked at the pictures. Skimpy tops. Skimpy bottoms. Bright colors. She read the bio: "Carmen and her mother, Rosa, were tragically abandoned by her father even before her birth. For years, Rosa appealed to her extended family in America for help. They struggled to save some money and finally, when Carmen was eleven, mother and child made the terrifying escape from Cuba, hidden away on a supply boat. Incredibly, they got to Miami, where a cousin drove them to Chicago to join the family. In the bitter cold weather and without the language, it was difficult for Carmen. But her family's history guided her always. In the most unforgiving of Chicago winters, her passionate use of island color warmed everything she touched." Then there were pictures of cashmere tank tops in shades named mango, guava, and pineapple.

This was it. Babette could just feel it. What a story! The hardship of Carmen's childhood, the father she had never known, the struggle to be free. It reminded her of her own childhood, truth be told. Well, sort of.

Not to mention the fact that if she wrote this piece well, Topher might let her carve out fashion as her beat. Babette had given this a lot of thought since Ponce Morris asked her if she covered fashion. Frankly, it had never occurred to her. She figured that at a place like *Boothby's*, the thing to be was literary. But maybe she wasn't that great a writer. That's what Topher seemed to imply, anyway, the one time they met for drinks and he had downed two martinis in half an hour. He didn't come right out and say it, but every time she talked about her writing ambitions, he talked instead about her great visual sense. She wasn't sure how he knew she had one, exactly, but fashion was visual, and it was fun. It changed all the time, and no one seemed to take it too seriously. Compared to the heavy-duty political columns *Boothby's* ran or the intense personality profiles someone like Rachel Lerner wrote, getting famous people to cry about their lost life choices, well, fashion seemed a lot easier. Besides, despite a perpetually limited budget, Babette had always been a good shopper. She knew how to wear clothes.

That's what Robin Brody told her, anyway. Babette glanced furtively in the direction of Shawsie's office. She had never meant to get this involved with Robin. Really. It had started a few weeks before Thanksgiving, when she had gone to a party at Barneys (using an invitation meant for a senior editor who was on a shoot in Madrid). It was for a perfume launch, and models taller and younger than Babette had walked around the store in elaborate evening gowns, giggling and spraying the cloying fruited scent on everyone, even the men, while a string quartet played near Women's Shoes.

Babette took a glass of red wine from a tray, and Robin had come up behind her. "A vintage year for a vintage beauty," he said. She laughed, recognizing him from pictures, and he talked to her for a long time. She knew he was married to Shawsie, but she also heard that he told people his marriage was "open." It remained unclear whether Shawsie knew it was.

Robin had complimented her on her outfit, a clingy red cocktail dress that showed off what little cleavage she had. She found him absolutely charming, and when he suggested they go downtown and drop into Butter, a happening restaurant where he knew one of the owners, she said sure. He kissed her in the cab, which took her by surprise, but he didn't push it, and she liked that. At Butter they nibbled on hors d'oeuvres and drank cosmopolitans. Then they got into one of the waiting limousines and were driven all over New York for the next two hours while making passionate love in the back.

She felt her face flush just thinking about it. It had been so great, she told her friends, she couldn't believe it. "I mean, he must be, like, forty, right?" she said, "and he was *so* much more fun to fuck than the guys our own age. Isn't that hilarious?"

Less hilarious was the fact that somewhere along the way she lost one of the crystal chandelier earrings she had borrowed from the *Boothby's* fashion closet. She spent most of the next morning on the phone with Barneys and the limo company, but no one ever found it. And despite tearful pleading with the fashion girls, her borrowing privileges were revoked. Those were the rules—you lose the goods, you lose your privileges—but at least no one had asked her to pay for it. If she went to work in fashion full-time, though, she hoped they might give her a second chance.

Anyway, things with Robin had been terrific—or as terrific as they could be, considering Babette was sleeping with the executive editor's husband. Not only was Shawsie one of Babette's bosses, but she was always so nice to her—not at all like the other top editors, who grunted their orders and rarely made eye contact. Shawsie always stopped to say good morning, ask how Babette was. Babette felt terrible about this, really she did. Or at least she did when she was at the office. It was just, well, in any moment she spent with Robin, whether it was in the stall of a ladies' room at a club downtown, in the backseat of a car, or even in the living room of the apartment she shared with two friends, if she stopped to think about it at all, she could never quite remember what Shawsie even looked like.

And if that wasn't enough of a dilemma, along came Montrose Merriweather. His Wikipedia bio said he was fifty-five, old enough to be her father and then some, but Babette found herself bowled over. Really. She liked the way he looked at her—studying her, almost—and she liked his elaborate manners, and she especially liked the way he smelled, from cigarettes and some kind of cologne, but not too much.

Babette was no stranger to older men certainly, including the Argentinian banker. They were so easy to please! Grateful and generous. But there was something about M that was different. Never leering or overbearing. Serious but still fun. Comforting, in that he always had a plan. Doubly comforting in that whatever the plan, he could always afford it, even if it was going to Paris for lunch. (Jacqueline Posner told Babette at the party that one night when she was in Georgia working on the restoration of M's house, he talked at dinner about a langoustine salad he loved at a particular Parisian bistro and by the end of the meal he had piled her and his then-wife onto his plane. After a brief pit stop at the Ritz to freshen up they'd gone straight to lunch where M had eaten three of the salads. Then they'd flown home. He had an important meeting the next day.)

Babette loved that story and she didn't care if liking that about him made her shallow. As someone who was never even allowed to buy a book growing up—she had yearned to write "Property of Babette Steele" on the inside covers of the ones she liked at the library but knew her mother could be fired if she did—she found M's particular worldview exceptionally attractive.

After Jacqueline's party—was it only a month ago?—M had taken Babette to the Carlyle for a nightcap, where they sat next to each other on a small couch—cuddling, sort of. Though truly, he was so tall his knees seemed to be everywhere. But they kissed and talked and held hands, and she would have gone upstairs with him, but he said he had to leave town early the next morning and would call her when he was back. Which he did.

When she saw him during Christmas week he rented one of those horse-and-buggies to go through the Park, and they sipped whiskey from a silver flask. He held her close, and when he felt her garter through her skirt—what the hell, she had pulled out the stops—he stroked her thigh in a lazy way until finding the bare flesh beneath it. Oblivious to the cold, she turned toward him, not giving a damn about the driver, but M would go no further. He caressed her skin slowly and casually as he kissed her, and by the time they got back to his hotel she could barely walk to his room. She had never been that jazzed to sleep with someone in her life, not even Robin Brody. Sure, being with Robin was fun. But it was more like gym. M was a grown-up with a goal, and that goal seemed to be making her sublimely happy, repeatedly. And the diamond stud earrings he presented her with afterward both surprised and delighted her.

The following day Babette called her mother, sparing her the details but telling her that she had met Aileen's onetime dancing partner. Aileen was genuinely excited.

"Honey, I remember him just a little bit, but everyone knows him now," she exulted. "Sure, he's older than you, but there isn't a better education for a girl than an older gentleman who has seen the world."

That made Babette roll her eyes. (Thank the Lord she had never mentioned the Argentinian banker—and that she and her mother never traveled together.)

But education aside, the biggest problem with the older gentleman in question was that he didn't yet live in New York. Although Jacqueline's apartment was in mint condition, M didn't like the bathrooms and insisted on replacing the marble before he moved in. The shipment was delayed in Italy, and who knew how long it would be before that work even began, much less was finished? M was also still enmeshed in divorcing the third Mrs. Merriweather, and Babette knew there was a very real possibility that he would wake up one day and decide that three was enough. And, he said, his business interests in Europe and Asia were why he had to travel so much.

Babette was philosophical. If things were meant to work out between them, they would. Still, she couldn't help but wonder what might happen when he did move to New York. She tried remembering all the details about Jacqueline Posner's apartment, but there was just too much of it that she hadn't seen. All she really had a picture of was the dining room and the front hallway. So in the countless hours when she sat at her desk, doing something like hanging on hold forever trying to get someone on the other end to take a lunch reservation for one of the editors, Babette would think of Annabelle's place instead. That was the closest she had come to getting familiar with a big-deal Manhattan apartment, even if the Gluckmans' place was on Central Park West and about a third of the size of Jacqueline's. It had a grand hall-way, though, and a dining room that seated forty and a view of the Park, so it wasn't bad at all.

She imagined herself there with M, throwing a dinner with Ponce Morris's help, the two of them side by side, greet-ing guests. M would welcome everyone and make a toast to announce how he finally had the home he'd always wished for, and Babette would just shine—and so would her wrists and fingers and throat, and everyone in New York would talk about all the beautiful jewelry M had bought her. And the sound of champagne corks popping would punctuate the string quartet, and there would be giant bowls of caviar—people had devoured it that night at Jacqueline's—and Babette would make sure that M flew in the chef from Paris who made the langoustine salad he loved. Ponce would make her own toast then, to say that it was Babette's idea to do that and wasn't M lucky to have her? And the night would pass with everyone talking about how extravagant it all was—but sweet, really, because M only wanted to make her, Babette, happy.

Then the person on the other end of the reservation line would pick up and Babette wouldn't remember why she had called, and after having to call back and getting yelled at by whichever editor had asked for her help, she would remind herself that M aside, her first priority had to be getting her career in shape at *Boothby's*. If she had learned anything from her mother, it was the necessity of having something to fall back on.

To that end, Babette forced herself to concentrate on the press release about Carmen. If *Boothby's* would give her an assignment to go to Chicago and do this piece and they actually liked it, maybe she could get them to send her to the collections, too. In Europe. She could write about some new designers, try some in-depth interviews. If the fashion editors liked her, well, anything could happen. No, she didn't speak French, or Italian, but everyone these days spoke English, didn't they? It would be fine. All she needed to do was get this assignment.

She thought again about Ponce Morris. It was she whom Babette had to thank for this idea. When Ponce had asked Babette about fashion, it was almost as if she sensed that this was the right way for her to get properly launched. Babette needed to see her again, maybe establish the kind of relationship where Ponce could be her mentor. Yes! How much better would that be than relying on Annabelle? Considering the possibility, Babette grew excited. It was fate, really. All those years she had spent following the former model's glamorous life—and Ponce had really liked it when Babette told her she'd noticed how Ponce never hogged the picture! That was the kind of woman to learn from, the kind who didn't chase the camera.

And now that Babette had succeeded in getting herself this great job in magazine publishing, this was the moment to learn everything there was to know about the social New York she had dreamed of for so long. She felt the twinge of a reality check. Well, maybe hers wasn't the greatest job, especially compared to Shawsie's. And as Ponce seemed to have become quite close to Rachel Lerner, maybe her mentoring plate was full. Babette felt deflated suddenly, and sighed at the injustice of it all. Ponce Morris might as well live in Alaska, that's how far away she was! And Babette knew that

Rachel would be no help. She just didn't like her, Babette could tell. She would have to be patient and rely on Shawsie's good graces instead.

By noon, the office had filled not only with Babette's co-workers but with the unmistakable scent of defeat. Yes, some faces were tanned, and one or two were still swollen ("You look so *rested!*"), making it clear they hadn't traveled farther than their plastic surgeon's offices. But the pre-holiday giddiness, the promise of redemption that had lifted the spirits of the place up to bursting before the holidays, had flatlined. No marriage proposals. No dream job offers on the slopes or on the beach. No love affairs that lasted even long enough to mention. People mumbled their good mornings, but there was little eye contact as they phoned their shrinks for catch-up appointments and swallowed Excedrin with the dregs of their morning coffee.

"Did you have a nice Christmas, Babette?" Shawsie stood in front of her.

"Oh, yeah, great. And yours?" Babette stood abruptly, and her chair, on wheels, flew backward and slammed into her desk, sending the mounds of mail into an avalanche. She turned and grabbed at them.

"Nice. Quiet, actually." Shawsie helped catch the piles and watched as Babette straightened them. "Why do you have everyone's mail?" she asked, seeing the names on the envelopes.

Babette smiled easily. "Well, two of the other assistants are still out on vacation, so I told the mail guys I'd be happy to help do the sorting."

Shawsie smiled too. "That's awfully nice of you."

"No big deal." Babette blushed.

"So have you gotten any more roses?" Shawsie asked playfully. The day after Jacqueline Posner's party, M had sent

Babette three dozen in a long white box. Everyone in the office had gathered round and counted.

"No, but he did give me diamond stud earrings for Christmas, and then to say 'Happy New Year' he sent me an ankle bracelet with my initials all in diamonds."

Shawsie gasped. "Really?"

"Well, not big ones or anything. They're like little chips all smashed together. You know what I mean?"

Shawsie walked around the desk to get a look at Babette's ankles, and the younger woman blushed again. "I had to take it to the jeweler to be enlarged," she said. "It wasn't big enough. Isn't that hilarious?"

As Shawsie nodded, Babette rushed on, "I've actually been meaning to tell you that I'd love to get to know Ponce Morris better. I mentioned that night at dinner that she should come down here and visit us sometime, and she said she would. Do you think that maybe the three of us could have lunch?"

Shawsie laughed. "Ponce only gets out of bed before noon on the days she has to be in court," she said. "She doesn't do lunch."

"Well, drinks, then?"

Babette was a nervous girl, Shawsie thought. In the few minutes they'd been talking, she had swept her hair up into a ponytail, taken it down again, shaken it out and hooked it behind her ears, then scooped up a headband from somewhere underneath all that mail and pushed it over the entire mess. Shawsie wondered if she had ADD—or maybe one too many cans of Red Bull for breakfast. The girl burned more energy than a furnace.

"I'll ask her," Shawsie said as one of her assistants suddenly appeared.

"It's the Jessica Simpson person you were waiting to talk to," the assistant told Shawsie, who was halfway down the hall before Babette realized their conversation had ended. She was still staring at the spot where Shawsie had been standing, when her phone rang.

"*Boothby's.*"

"Hello, beautiful." The voice was deep and sultry.

"Well, hello." Babette's tone was equally throaty.

"My darling, I have dire news, simply dire."

"What? What's the matter?"

"I can't see you tomorrow."

"Why not?"

He sighed.

"Is it another woman?"

He sighed again. "Actually, my pet, it is."

"Thom!" Babette started laughing. "What do you mean?"

"Well, my sweet, I have been given as a Christmas present to someone—ten sessions—which I don't have to tell you means a thousand smackeroos for the Thomster, Personal Trainer to the Stars of Tomorrow. And the only time she can make it is in your slot."

"And who exactly are you throwing me over for?"

"Um, let's see, I can't even remember her name, now that you mention it. Wait, wait, here it is. Rachel Lerner."

"What? That girl looks as if she's never lifted more than a pencil. Or a sandwich."

"Meow, meow, kitten. Now you know that Thom thinks every human body is a work of art waiting to be realized. And besides, the person paying is Ponce Morris. So what can I say? Anyway, tell me everything. Is she fat?"

"Well, no."

"So what's with the sandwich?"

"Oh, I don't know. She's one of those people who's really smart but she never says hello and I can tell she doesn't think I'm smart and she's never nice to me."

"Well, pussycat, she sounds fat to me."

They laughed. Babette rescheduled her appointment, hung up, and kept sorting the mail. She just loved Thom. She had met him at *Self* when they were shooting a piece on personal trainers, and the lawyer Babette was dating at the time ponied up for ten sessions as a birthday gift. She'd used them up long ago, of course, but still scraped together the money to see Thom once a month. He could lay his hand on her ass and tell immediately what she needed to do more of.

She glanced at her watch. She would have to leave soon for her lunch with Annabelle, who, granted, was no Ponce. But at the moment, Babette knew, it was all she had.

Ponce walked into her apartment and threw her keys on the table as the phone rang. She looked at the caller ID. Shawsie. She picked it up. "How *are* you?"

On the other end of the line, Shawsie smiled. Ponce had that way about her, for the people she loved, of sounding absolutely *delighted* whenever they called.

"Well, just fine. And you?"

"Fine now that I'm home. I had one of those dreadful mornings in court, so I'm glad I'm out early. I tell you, I don't think half these judges should be on the bench. The one I had today was not remotely prepared."

"Well, I'm about to offer you some fun instead. Come have a drink with me and Babette Steele this week."

"What?" Ponce was surprised. "Whatever for?"

"Oh, she's a nice girl, Poncie, and she seems to idolize

you. You were so sweet to her at the party and everything. She's trying to make friends, that's all."

"For heaven's sake, Mary Elizabeth, if I had to have a drink with every person I said hello to at a party, I wouldn't have time to do anything else." She paused. "Sorry, long morning. Look, if it's important to you for work reasons, I'll do it. But if not, I'm inclined to skip it."

"So you're saying no?"

"Well, yes. If you like her so much, why don't you do something to help her at *Boothby's*? There's certainly nothing I can do for her."

"Okay, okay. So what are you doing tonight?"

"Well, he made me promise not to tell you, but Red's in town."

"He is? That's amazing. Why?"

Ponce hesitated. "He called me on Christmas Day and asked if I'd gotten everything I wanted from Santa Claus, and I said no, I hadn't, but if he came down here from Connecticut and had a hamburger with me, then my list would be complete. He just laughed, and we didn't mention it again, but when he called to say 'Happy New Year' he said that it was Santa calling, and as long as he didn't have to have it any-place where he would know somebody, he was ready to come to New York and eat his hamburger."

"Good for you, Poncie," Shawsie said. "You'll be a tonic for him. And he's smart to do it this way. If the family gets involved, everyone will start crying, but the two of you can just talk each other into the ground the way you always do. I personally am delighted to miss three hours' worth of basket-ball scores. But the fact that he's leaving that damn town for the first time in a year, that's a major step. Where are you going to go?"

"I apologize, Mary Elizabeth, but he knew I'd break the promise about telling you he was coming, so he made me really promise I wouldn't tell you where we're eating."

"Fair enough. Is he staying over?"

"He is. The Yale Club has that quiet room he likes, so he doesn't have to rush for the last train."

"Oh, this is such good news! Will you call me tomorrow and tell me every last thing?"

"Of course I will."

"You are a true friend, Ponce. Send him my love, will you? And tell him no hard feelings."

Ponce hung up. She was glad Shawsie was pleased. She herself was surprised that Red had given in. Over the last year, she'd lost count of the times she'd begged him to leave that house and come to the city. Hell, she'd even offered to go up there. That made Red laugh. He knew how much Ponce hated the country. "I only need to see a backyard," she would say, "and the first thing I still do is figure where in it I can hide from my mother."

So Shawsie was right. That he was getting out of Connecticut was a very good sign, indeed.

Ponce's warm thoughts of Red lasted about five more seconds, until she recalled her dismissal of Babette Steele and felt slightly ashamed of herself. There was no good reason not to have a drink with the girl, certainly. But Ponce had long ago discovered that her entire life—if she let it—could be consumed by "shoulds." Yes, she should do about a million things to prove to the world that she was a good and generous person, like spending an hour listening to the hopes and dreams of a twenty-five-year-old she had met once for three minutes and had no reason ever to meet again. So she had resolved to banish the "shoulds" and stick to the "have to's" (getting out of bed at six a.m. on court days) and the "want to's" (seeing Neil Grossman). If her theory didn't always make her life easier, it certainly made it less crowded.

Anyway, Ponce knew, Shawsie would make it up to the girl. No one was more fair-minded. Ponce had adored Shawsie from the moment she walked through the door of one of those ratty First Avenue apartments, the *Village Voice* ad for a roommate still in her hand. She remembered thinking that Shawsie actually looked the way Katharine Hepburn sounded: a stand-up New Englander, always in charge, who once she made up her mind about something never gave it a second thought. Shawsie was the kind of girl men used to call a "gal"; she had that tousled head of auburn hair, she always wore slacks (her legs couldn't carry a skirt), and her pockets were full of quarters and Hershey Kisses for the kids on her block back in Greenwich.

Ponce remembered the time, not long after they started rooming together, that she brought home another model, a girl so drunk Shawsie had to come downstairs to help haul her inside. Ponce and the girl were set to shoot a liquor ad the next day, some sort of gin, and the label had thrown a party that night, a promotional thing at the "21" Club. Though Ponce knew better than to drink the night before a shoot, the other girl didn't, and she had already, in the cab, thrown up on herself twice. Ponce was in a state, but Shawsie remained unflappable.

"You'll get into the shower and then straight into bed," she told Ponce, who protested heatedly. "Mrs. Ford will kill you, and you know it," Shawsie warned. "Not only if you stay up all night and can't go tomorrow, but if you go looking puffy and exhausted. She won't use you for months. No. I will deal with this, and that's that."

Ponce, who prided herself on listening to no one, stripped, showered, and climbed straight into bed. She took a pill and went right out, while Shawsie managed to take off the girl's clothes—wasn't it incredible that Ponce simply could not remember her name?—and drag her into the shower stall. As soon as the water hit her, the girl started coming to, and when she realized what had happened began to cry. Afterward, Shawsie poured her a cup of tea, gave her a robe and an ice pack, and then sat with her to make sure she kept it on her eyes.

When Ponce woke at seven a.m., Shawsie was still fast asleep, but the other girl was awake and ready to go. Shawsie had left Ponce a peanut butter and banana sandwich on white bread—one of the only things Ponce liked and would actually finish—cut into quarters and wrapped in a Baggie with a little note: "Don't wake me. My boss is on vacation, so who cares?"

Ponce made it her business after that shoot to get a case of the gin delivered to Shawsie, along with some gold hoop earrings from Tiffany, and the girl sent over two cartons full of Pappagallo—purses, shoes, scarves, belts. Ponce was irritated—obviously she had done another shoot and committed grand larceny—but Shawsie always saw the better side of people. "Ponce Porter, these shoes are 9AA, do you have any idea how hard it is to find that size!" she exulted. "I don't care where she got them from."

Frankly, Ponce couldn't believe that the girl had even noticed a shoe size when she could barely sit up. "I suppose she spent enough time down on the floor to find it out" is all she would allow. But Shawsie had worn that stuff for years. Hell, she might still be wearing it, now that Ponce thought about it.

She smiled. What a character her friend was. A completely good egg who always came through, no matter the pinch. And that included Babette Steele, certainly. Babette was someone Shawsie could manage all by herself.

. . .

Shawsie pulled on her coat and threw a few things into her bag.

"Hey, heading out?"

Topher Bowles had stuck his head into her office.

"To the Fabiano spring shoot."

"Right." He handed her a sheaf of papers. "Would you mind taking a look at the Miramax piece? I want to be sure we're not missing anything."

"Sure." She slid it into her bag.

"See you at the Acorn tonight?" Topher asked.

Shawsie looked blank.

Topher smiled. "Our party for Michael McMurtry? Hunky February issue cover boy with the open shirt and six-pack abs? Skip said you and Robin were definitely coming."

Shawsie sighed. "I forgot all about it. We've got another appointment with Neil, at six, and I get so bummed after those meetings, I doubt I'll be up for it. But never fear. I'm sure Robin will party for the two of us."

"Okay. Later."

Whenever the talk turned to her fertility problems, Shawsie had noticed, Topher seemed to take off. Maybe it was because he and Anne had had three kids, no problem. Maybe it was because his divorce from Anne, who had taken those three kids with her back to her family's home in Maine in spite of his wishes, was still a very sore point.

Down on the street, Shawsie picked out the right car from a blockful of idling black sedans and ducked into the backseat. She was glad that the Acorn had proved such a success for Skip, a perennial screwup who had always smoked dope the way their mother drank. Named for the children's dining room at the country club they'd gone to growing up, Skip's nightspot had been super-hot when it opened three years before. Like most of those places, it started as a hangout for models and the men who covet them. But unlike most, which close within months, the Acorn had settled into a happy middle age, where people met late for burgers and drinks or used the two-level space for private parties. Even though other places were much hotter now, Topher, for one, continued to give Skip the magazine's business.

Sweet man, Shawsie thought, staring out the window. When she noticed that the car was scarcely moving, her warm thoughts turned to irritation. She directed the driver west—for heaven's sake, that's where they were going, weren't they?—and after mapping out the route settled back in her seat, forcing herself to calm down.

What would happen with Ponce and Red that night, Shawsie wondered. Ponce really had her hands full, trying to lure Shawsie's uncle back to the land of the living. But for him to volunteer to come to the city at all was so encouraging. Shawsie thought of calling Red's eldest, Sally, who worried over her father as much as Shawsie did. No, she should wait to hear from Ponce about how it went. She had to stop trying to *manage* everything, she thought, for maybe, oh, the millionth time. If she only had a child to focus on . . .

She dialed Robin on her cell. No answer. He was supposed to have been working today, trying to get an outline together for a new novel. Of course, that's what he was supposed to have been doing most days for the last three years now. She hoped he remembered their appointment with Neil. She knew he would remember the party for Michael McMurtry.

"Shawsie! Hey!"

When she entered the studio, she got the greeting she always got: one assistant acknowledging her loudly enough for the other assistants to hear—because if any of them were in the next room pilfering cheese from the buffet or trying on extra pairs of shoes that were meant for the model, there would be hell to pay.

What she didn't see were the fashion editor and the stylist in charge of the shoot, who were hidden away popping Xanax and steeling themselves for her onslaught. Whoever heard of an executive editor supervising fashion shoots? The whole point of being that high up was you didn't have to do crap like that anymore. Even the fashion director didn't bother showing up half the time. But Shawsie was some Type A nightmare who couldn't let one thing go. Managing shoots had been her old job, and when she got her new job, she just held on. Maybe she wanted something to fall back on; maybe she just loved having every agent in Hollywood begging for her meticulous attention to how many shrimp were on the buffet platter. For heaven's sake! As much as *she* wished she would have a baby, it was nothing compared to the rest of the staff.

The star of the spring fashion spread was Tikka, an Indian supermodel who was absolutely it at the moment. Hopefully, her itness would last until April, when the issue came out. Shawsie entered the dressing room and found the girl sitting in the makeup chair. "Tikka, hi, I'm Shawsie, and I'm so glad you're here with us today," she said cordially. The makeup artist stepped back to make room for her but the model kept her face upturned. She moved her eyes from the ceiling to Shawsie's face.

"Hey," she said absently.

Shawsie smiled. She had long ago gotten used to the fact that half the talent had no idea who she was. But Shawsie wasn't worried. This model might be burning hot, but as recently as two years ago she and her family had been out on the street in their native country, and the girl was too smart to blow her good fortune with temperament or rudeness.

Shawsie then whipped through the racks of clothes with the fashion editor and the stylist, smiles plastered on their faces as she double-checked that the shoes, bags, and scarves were all accounted for and that anything missing was noted early enough to be brought in fast. Nothing was missing, in fact. Usually she thanked them profusely, but today she didn't even seem to notice.

Out in the studio, she found only one of the star photographer's six assistants, busily trying to hide behind a pile of camera equipment.

"Hello there! Where's Fabiano?" she called.

The boy looked nervous. "I, I don't know," he stammered.

Shawsie started toward the men's room.

"No, no, I'll get him for you!" the assistant yelped, zooming past her.

Fabiano was an incurable coke addict, Shawsie knew, so she always tried to arrive at shoots early enough to prevent him from doing too much damage.

Within seconds he emerged. "Ciao, bella!" he boomed, kissing her on both cheeks. His face was still damp from the tap.

Shawsie's hello was effusive and sincere. Fabiano was extremely talented and usually did top-notch work. (The fashion girls' gripes about Shawsie aside, none of them could ever control him. They'd give her that.) The two walked arm in arm to check on Tikka's progress, and soon enough Shawsie was sitting in a folding chair on the far side of the studio watching Fabiano croon at his subject. Tikka's ennui, so off-putting in real life, combined somehow with the lights and the camera to replace her air of vacancy with one of mystery. All was well.

Shawsie sipped from a small bottle of cranberry juice and relaxed, or tried to, thinking again about her appointment with Neil Grossman. She had never imagined that getting pregnant would be this hard. Yes, at forty, she was old—ancient, really. Biology dictated that she should have done this twenty years ago, but twenty years ago she had had no one to do it with. Most things had come late to her; she often ruminated on the fact that she had never been lucky. When her dad died, it seemed that everything in her life stopped functioning. Everyday living was too much for her mother, as it was for Skip, so she took over. But what did she know? She was just a kid. Still, she was smart and organized—her mom often told her so, as grateful as she was guilty that a thirteen-year-old was doing the marketing and supervising the gardener while she herself had a cocktail hour without end in front of the television set. "You are your father's daughter," she would tell Shawsie, by way of encouragement, while neatly absolving herself of any responsibility.

Shawsie had taken her own responsibilities to heart. Instead of going to Duke, which she had yearned for, she chose Connecticut College, so she'd be close if her mom needed her, which she invariably did. Skip, by that point, had been shunted off to boarding school, but their mother couldn't seem to do the most basic things—pay her bills on time, even turn up at her psychiatrist's office when she was supposed to. If it hadn't been for her uncle Red, Shawsie would have lost her mind entirely. He was such a decent man. He had encouraged her to go to Duke, reiterated what the shrinks said about enabling her mother, repeated the benefits of leaving her sufficiently stranded so that she'd have to do things on her own. But Shawsie refused. She had already lost one parent. She didn't want to lose the other.

That blind spot aside, however, Shawsie had always been a realist. She knew she looked nothing like the skinny blond-haired blue-eyed Greenwich ideal. Everything she ate went straight to her hips, and after years of sailing with her dad, her skin seemed to defy sunscreen, looking chapped and parched no matter the moisturizer. She had little taste for tennis or golf, much preferring to spend a Sunday in bed with a book. She had acres of friends, pals, acquaintances. To know her was to love her, she often thought, ruefully. Only she was lonely. She wanted a family. A whole family. Not like the one she had.

After graduating from college, she got a job in book publishing, as one of two assistants to a famous editor, and that's when she had moved in with Ponce. Shawsie liked her immediately, especially the clear-eyed way she saw the world. She found Ponce's modeling as exotic as Ponce found book publishing, but there was a comfort between them from the start. It was Ponce who encouraged Shawsie to leave the famous editor after she'd endured three long years of his treating her like shit.

Shawsie had an opportunity to go to *Esquire* and work for the editor there who arranged the cover shoots and the big celebrity stories. She was an instant hit. The guys in the office all loved her—not to date, but to nurse a hangover with, tell their women woes to. When Shawsie turned up at a shoot, she had the knack of putting everyone at ease, and this went a long way with the Hollywood types. Six years later, when her boss left, she got his job, and two years after that Topher stole her for *Boothby's*.

"I can match your salary but I can't give you a raise," he told her, as the magazine was still in its pre-Rubinstein phase. "If you do the celeb stuff and also edit some pieces for me, I'll make you executive editor." That wasn't exactly altruistic, he knew. Shawsie was a terrific editor. She had voluntarily pitched in on some of Topher's early issues and managed to turn some real messes into graceful prose, practically overnight. Once Rubinstein came on board, Topher put her compensation package on the table alongside his own. She meant that much to him, he told the new publisher. And she did. From the day she'd talked him out of his trouble with that cop in Greenwich, Shawsie had been a light in Topher's life.

The light for Shawsie had come in the person of Robin Brody, whom she'd met at an *Esquire* Christmas party her first year there. They'd become pals—what else is new? she'd despaired at the time—but she stuck it out because she liked Robin and loved his writing. They could talk for hours, meeting at Fitzer's, an Irish bar near Fifty-seventh Street. They talked about Robin's endless book tours and about his plans for his next novel. He so looked forward to that, he said, to finally have the chance to think about a different story! He talked about his aging aunts in Staten Island who raised him and how they couldn't appreciate his success. They'd read his book and lamented the curse words, he told her, trying to laugh, though he was obviously hurt. When he sent them his good reviews—glowing reviews—he got no response at all. They'd wanted him to go to law school, make something of himself. This writing thing just wasn't the same.

Shawsie reassured him, praising his talent and empathizing with his being so out of sync with his truncated family. She told him her own story and he was just as supportive of her, condemning her selfish mom and her absent brother (at least until he actually met Skip; then he became his best customer at the Acorn).

Robin smoked Dunhills, and in spite of herself Shawsie fell in love with the smell. She also loved the way he turned up the cuffs of his shirt when he took off his jacket and the way he made it a point never to let his glance follow another woman's behind when he was with her. He sent her funny cards that he thought might amuse her (they did) and extravagant amounts of flowers on holidays like Presidents' Day, just for a laugh. He called her at midnight from Cincinnati or Milwaukee or wherever he was selling his book, and they'd talk into the New York dawn. Shawsie knew his reputation, and he lived up to it: Weeks would pass when she wouldn't hear from him at all, and she'd know he was involved with a woman. But she didn't care. No one else made her feel the way he did.

Then one day, long after she'd moved to *Boothby's*, he'd come to meet with Topher, and on his way out stopped into her office to say hi. They'd gone to Fitzer's for a beer, got hungry for dinner, and crossed the street to the Palace diner for cheeseburgers. Then they went back to Fitzer's for a nightcap and ended up at Shawsie's apartment, where they stayed for the three most exhilarating days of her life.

The following Monday morning Shawsie walked into Topher's office to tell him that she and Robin Brody were getting married. They were leaving that afternoon for Nassau, and Shawsie's paternal grandmother, who had washed her hands of her ruined daughter-in-law and left her to Shawsie's care for all those years, was arranging for them to get married on the beach.

Of course, Gammy didn't tell her granddaughter that she had heard about this fellow's reputation from her friends in New York, and as soon as she laid eyes on him, she could see he was an operator. But so what? Shawsie was pushing forty, and as far as her grandmother was concerned a talented ne'er-do-well was better than no man at all. Life wasn't perfect, not even close. So if this granddaughter of hers, who had spent years without a dose of joy for herself, was blissful with this cad for even a year, could get one child out of it and move on, well, that was no small feat either.

And Shawsie had been blissful. Maybe not for a year.

Maybe for only six months. She was so in love with Robin she couldn't believe that their relationship was actually happening to her. When it came to sex, nothing much had ever registered with Shawsie; she hadn't been sure what the fuss was about. But Robin! He was a marvel, in every way. She had never felt so alive, so filled with pleasure and hope—so, well, madly in love. The two of them seemed to agree about everything—in the beginning, at least. They both wanted a baby and spent all their time trying.

"I've never been this happy," she confided to Ponce those first few months, while Ponce kept her sense of doom to herself.

"Isn't this a bit sudden?" she'd asked on the eve of Shawsie's departure for Nassau.

"Well, yes and no," Shawsie had said. "I mean, we've known each other forever, it seems, and we've been friends for so long. I think we're both at a place in our lives where the parties and the shoots and all the public showing-up is wearing thin. When we have a family, we can stay home more and Robin can write again. He's been blocked for so long because he's been so distracted. How could he not be?"

"Mary Elizabeth Shaw, I can only imagine you know what you're doing," Ponce had said finally. "And if you don't, you'll find out soon enough."

Ponce had been right, of course. Those first six months of staying home and staying in bed and finding that she still wasn't pregnant put something of a damper on the good time. Shawsie went to her gynecologist, who told her it was customary to wait a year before seeing a fertility specialist, but she insisted that at her age she didn't have that luxury and went straight to Neil Grossman. His waiting list was endless, but Ponce pulled some strings. Ponce had met Neil years before—Lee had been chairman of the board at Carnegie

Hill Hospital, and Neil was one of that institution's shining young stars—and the two of them had become friendly on the dinner-party circuit.

On Neil's recommendation, Shawsie and Robin started in vitro fertilization right away. She had blood tests of every sort and shot herself full of hormones on a rigid schedule—Robin had no stomach for it, he just couldn't give her the shot himself, no matter how together they were supposed to be on this thing. But he dutifully showed up at Neil's office on the appointed mornings at six a.m. to hole up in a room with a television and some porn tapes and produce something to send to the lab. He and Shawsie made jokes about it, but Robin soon found himself avoiding their apartment and avoiding his wife who, in spite of being told to relax, seemed to be living in a frenzy of anxiety and self-loathing that never quit.

When the procedure didn't work the first time, Shawsie was devastated. She and Robin agreed to Neil's suggestion that they take a break for three months before trying again. They were supposed to "do what comes naturally," so they resolved to spend every extra minute together. But soon enough, Shawsie had three cover tries shooting in Los Angeles and was stationed at the Chateau Marmont for weeks. And although Robin vowed to accompany her, he decided at the last minute to stay home and use the time to start his new novel in the office they'd set up for him in a studio apartment downstairs in their building. But somehow he never got around to it. There was a wine tasting or a cigar night or a book party for a buddy he just couldn't let down. And when a friend landed two tickets to the Victoria's Secret fashion show at the Plaza, well, what was he to do?

After the second IVF failed, their home life became all but intolerable to Robin. Shawsie was such a good girl. He had always admired how comfortable she was—or had been until now—in her own skin, how her sense of the world and its rights and wrongs led her like a compass through every "might" and "maybe" that caught him round the knees and brought him down. But their dream of a house and a couple of kids, a life Shawsie would orchestrate as smoothly as she did her job—Robin knew this and drew comfort from it—was simply not coming true. It felt almost biblical to him. Neither one of them had a family with everyone intact as they were meant to be. Maybe they were cursed. Maybe they weren't meant to have children because no one had ever taught them the proper way to be adults. Well, that last part would apply to him, not Shawsie.

He did try. They stopped going to Fitzer's—she couldn't drink, what was the point?—but they went to nice restaurants for romantic dinners and returned home to try to still enjoy doing what came naturally. They taped a bunch of old movies and spent one rainy Sunday in bed watching them. They ordered in pizza, Robin opened a bottle of wine, and they started having sex—he always enjoyed sleeping with Shawsie—but halfway through she burst into tears and couldn't stop. She wouldn't let him hold her or comfort her or even talk to her. She just locked herself in the bathroom and sobbed.

That had been it for him. He stayed out even later. And one of those nights, when he felt the fingers of a very tipsy model working themselves from the base of his neck up through his thick hair, grabbing it full in her hand and pulling him toward her . . . well, he woke up in a hotel room the next morning about as sorry as a man could be.

He told Shawsie he thought he should leave her. She wept. He said he would stay but suggested they give up the idea of having kids. She refused. He tried to convince her that he just wasn't like her, didn't have the stuff to keep at something like a dog with a bone. It was breaking his heart to see her like this. It was driving him out of the house.

Shawsie knew what that meant. All of it. She had picked up anonymous voicemail messages at work, always left in the middle of the night, from a woman with a Russian accent assuring Shawsie that her husband didn't love her anymore and she should let him go.

But Shawsie loved him. And she was not about to give up her dream family. After the procedure failed a third time, she really didn't know what to do. Robin was hardly ever at home. The new book was forgotten, and when Shawsie insisted that he do some work—anything—he signed up for a few freelance pieces at *Him*, one of those vulgar new men's magazines Shawsie hated, so unlike the elegance of *Esquire* when she had worked there. He was writing something about premium vodkas and something else about iPods, and she didn't care what it was so long as he had something to focus on besides going out at night. They had come to an uneasy truce where neither was happy. But Shawsie wouldn't quit. Not yet, at least.

"Yes, Shawsie? You are happy, no?"

It took her a moment to focus and remember where she was. Fabiano was beaming at her from across the floor, and Tikka was already wandering off toward the dressing room.

Shawsie stood quickly and assured Fabiano that yes, she was deliriously happy and he was the greatest photographer who ever lived. She embraced him, intercepted Tikka on her way to the shower to thank her, and got back into her waiting car just shy of six o'clock. She only hoped Robin would remember to show up.

Chapter Four

"And two more, come on!"

"No! Oh, I hate you so much!"

Babette dropped the weights and shook out her arms. "God, that killed," she moaned, pacing back in forth in front of the mirror, trying to ignore the muscleheads gathered at a nearby machine, checking her out. Who *were* those guys lifting weights all day? Did none of them have jobs? It seemed that no matter what time she had her monthly appointment with Thom, there was always this bunch of thick-necked creeps wearing little black gloves strutting to and from the water fountain.

"We must suffer to be beautiful, buttercup." Thom came up behind her. "Look at that definition. Bring on the sundresses."

She rubbed her left upper arm and wondered which part of the sticks he had come from. No one in New York had uttered the word "sundress" in decades.

"It feels like getting a shot," she complained.

Thom ignored her cranky tone. "Okay, now, fifty sit-ups. Come on, lie down and I'll hold your feet."

"No, Thommie, do we really have to this minute? Can't we take a break?"

"No, we cannot." He looked at her face and regretted his tone. He knew that it was a struggle for her to pay his fee and that their sessions were important to her. Not only the exercise but his advice, which she sought on everything from guys to flea-market purchases. Oh, what the hell. She was twenty-five—his youngest client—and already in great shape.

"All right, just lie down and we'll talk for two minutes."

She brightened as he sat cross-legged next to her.

"So how was Rachel?" she asked.

He shrugged. "Not half as bad as you made her out to be. She told me right up front that she hates being told what to do, that she hurt her wrist once lifting too much weight and had no intention of doing it again, and that what she really needed from me was to figure out some programs for her to do once our sessions were over. I mean, at least she had a plan. So many people—not you, my pet, naturally—think Thom is here to reverse centuries of bad behavior."

"I don't care about her workout! What did she say about me?" Babette asked impatiently.

"You?" Thom raised his eyebrows. "I can't say the subject ever came up."

"It didn't?" She looked hurt. "Well, why not? She knows I work at *Boothby's*, too."

"Well, maybe she doesn't know that you train with me."

That possibility had not occurred to Babette. "Well, then, what did she say about Ponce?" she pressed.

"Well, we certainly are Miss Nosy Pants today, aren't we?" he said lightly.

"No, Thom, seriously, I want to know. I think that she and I could become really good friends."

When he just nodded, Babette crossed her arms. "That was the moment when you're supposed to say, 'Of course, you guys would be great friends, why don't I mention to her that she should get to know you better?'"

Thom shook his head. "Whoops! Sarcasm costs thirty seconds of rest time. Do your sit-ups, angel."

She got into the proper position and began to raise and lower her torso, face set. As he grasped her ankles and counted out loud, Thom Johnston silently bemoaned his fate. Being a personal trainer in New York City was a balancing act, and a single misstep could cost you your livelihood. He worked mostly with women—rich, socially powerful, or sometimes just socially ambitious women—who all had secrets and big mouths. About a third of them actually knew something so good, so dangerous, that if he flapped his own mouth and someone traced it to him, he'd be back in Apalachicola quicker than lightning, praying the Wal-Mart would hire him.

Why, just two days ago he'd been told about a Park Avenue matron who'd walked in on her new husband having sex in the shower with her teenage daughter. As the husband ran through the apartment, naked and streaming water on the Aubusson rugs, the wife took after him with a hammer—only the maid got in the way and ended up in the hospital with a broken jaw. By this morning, Thom knew which New England boarding school the daughter was starting—next week—which lawyer the wife already had working on the divorce settlement, and which Caribbean island boasted the happiest real estate agent in history after an entire block of houses, enough for the maid and twenty of her nearest and dearest, had been bought and paid for. He would take it to the tomb, he'd promised his source. And meant it.

The key to success, Thom had discovered, was never to tell anything really important, only to repeat the same groundless gossip everyone else knew. Public domain, as it were. And, as if it really meant something, make the client swear on a stack of Bibles never to tell. He kept the high-grade crucial stuff completely to himself.

For instance: What he hadn't told Babette was that Rachel Lerner was a much tougher nut to crack than he'd let on. She didn't seem to know—and Ponce hadn't seemed to have told her—that the unspoken rule of the personal trainer sweating over the deeply imperfect body of the client included the quid pro quo of serving up some dish to make it worth the trainer's while having to endure the heinous sight of cellulite (a rare occasion, happily, in the winter months) or feel the rolls of fat sliding languidly up and down the midsection while trying to impart a lesson on the body's core.

Granted, Ponce Morris, a client of his for years, provided almost no gossip at all. But she was such a good ol' girl, with her array of Southern expressions—which made him just a bit homesick, he had to admit—that she was up and gone before he'd realize that she hadn't spilled an ounce the entire hour. And of course he could never ask. He could only fish.

Rachel Lerner was significantly less enchanting.

"Christ, was that necessary?" she had huffed after fifty sit-ups. "I mean, I'm just starting out. Isn't there some grace period or something?"

Her annoyance was so deep, so real, that Thom was thrown. Yes, *he* knew about Babette and Robin Brody— because Babette was so guilty she was dying to tell someone, anyone, and had spilled her guts during their previous session the moment she'd walked in. But he was dying to know if Rachel knew. Or if Rachel knew whether Ponce knew.

But the puss on her after those sit-ups! Usually, women fawned all over him, begging him for mercy, apologizing for being so revoltingly out of shape and making him work so hard.

"Look," Rachel had said, wincing as she sat up. "Ponce Morris is a lovely woman who thinks she is doing me an enormous favor, and for all I know she is. But I'm not an actress or a dancer or a movie star. As long as I'm healthy and fit into my clothes, I don't give a damn if my bikini doesn't look hot on spring break—because I've been too old for spring break for ten years now. Do you follow me?"

He nodded and smiled and at that moment gave up all hope of ever securing one shred of information. Rachel Lerner was like the Wall Street guys Thom worked with: in, out, goodbye. But for a female client, it was definitely a first. What he didn't realize was that Rachel had arrived knowing full well that Thom trained Babette Steele and was determined not to say a word he could repeat to her.

"Fifty. Perfect form! You rule!"

Babette groaned and rolled onto her side, clutching her midsection. "Thanks," she panted. "Now listen," she went on once she'd caught her breath. "Here's the thing. I'm still seeing Robin, but I met this older man who I really like and maybe I won't see Robin anymore. I don't know how it's going to work out yet, but I asked Shawsie if she could set up a drink with her and me and Ponce, and when that happens, do you think I should bring up her trying to have a baby? Because even though everyone in the office knows about it, maybe I'm not close enough and maybe I shouldn't know."

Thom was taken aback. "Well, you certainly have been busy," he said. "I . . . I guess I don't know, Babette. Don't you think you should wait to have this drink until you've, uh, resolved your status with Robin? I mean, what if Shawsie finds out?"

She shrugged. "I don't think she will. I mean, she hasn't caught on to anyone else. Why would it be different with me?"

"She hasn't found out as far as you know. But if you want my advice, cupcake, ditch the drink until you've got your ducks in a row, if you know what I mean."

Babette mulled that over while Thom straightened out her mat.

This was exactly why he was a trainer, he thought. From the neck down, when the body did what it was told, you could see the results almost immediately. People would be so much better off if only they didn't have heads.

"Maybe I should mention the baby thing to Ponce instead," Babette went on. "Like if we had a drink together without Shawsie. Because she probably knows more about Shawsie's condition than anyone but Neil Grossman."

Thom felt it best to say nothing about the likelihood of Babette's having a drink alone with Ponce. An editorial assistant meets a New York social icon in passing and expects the woman to become her best friend? Ridiculous.

"What's the big push on Ponce?" he asked. "Maybe you should find someone else to bond with, my sweet."

Babette shrugged. "Maybe I should. But when I think about the life I'd like to live, Ponce Morris is a perfect example."

Thom snorted. "You mean you'd like to be a middle-aged divorced widow who, no matter how rich, still didn't get nearly as much money as she could have, does volunteer work for a city agency, and stays home most nights?"

Babette didn't laugh. "Not exactly," she said. "Ponce is someone with genuine access to anyone in this city with power and money. You know Annabelle Gluckman, right?"

Thom nodded. And from what he'd heard about her, he was thankful he knew her by reputation only.

"Well, Annabelle is someone whose access comes entirely through her husband. And even though that's how Ponce got hers originally, she's made it her own. People really like her. Respect her. So, the way I see it, I've met her, she liked me, and she's best friends with someone I work with. Access leads to access. Right?"

Thom considered. "I would say that if you do see Ponce without Shawsie," he said, "you might still avoid the baby issue. I think she has her own issues to worry about on that front."

He watched the girl rise immediately to the bait. Thank heavens she could only afford him once a month. She was too much effort for too little return.

"What do you mean?" Babette leaned forward eagerly.

He took a breath. "Well, you know that Neil Grossman's office is in Chad's neighborhood," he said, referring to his boyfriend, the investment banker, who everyone assumed looked like Cary Grant in his prime (because that's how good *Thom* looked), though truth be told, Chad, however sweet, devoted, and, yes, obscenely rich, really looked like a young Vincent Gardenia. "Chad has seen Ponce going in and out of Grossman's office at all hours," Thom reported. This was entirely in the realm of circulated gossip: A number of Chad's neighbors had discussed it at a recent co-op board meeting when they needed a break after an unpleasant dustup about the wretched condition of the children's playroom.

Thom lowered his voice so that no one else in the gym would overhear him. "Chad thinks Ponce is trying to get pregnant too, before it's too late. She's a little older than Shawsie, and Chad thinks that since she's alone now, spending all that time helping kids, she's going to try to be a single mother and keep Shawsie company. I mean, she can certainly afford it. It makes sense, doesn't it?"

Babette nodded gravely. "Wow," she said. "It would be great for her and Shawsie to do it together, being so close and everything. I am so glad you told me."

"Babette, I told you nothing." The edge in his voice was real.

"No, no, I would never, ever say anything about you. Of course I wouldn't! But it does make perfect sense."

"Well, you just keep your eye on your triceps, my sweet. He who giveth perfect definition can also taketh it away."

She reassured him some more, and he knew that she meant it. Although he had given her only meaningless information, she wouldn't betray him. She was still too young and had too little. Not until she had lost something really important would she become as threatening as the rest of his clientele. She kissed him on the cheek, then turned and bounded past the preening musclemen.

Babette smiled benignly at the lot of them as she toweled off on her way to the locker room. What scoops Thom had! Truly, the money she paid this guy was so worth it!

It was the kind of punishingly cold January night that was made for staying in bed with a bowl of soup, Ponce thought, hunching her thin shoulders against the hard wind as she struggled down the block. She had on earmuffs, one pashmina shawl tied around her neck, another wrapped around her head, and still the tears flew back onto her temples. When she had set out from Fifth Avenue, it hadn't seemed this bad.

Only for Red, she thought, finally pushing open the door of Marshall's, an unglamorous hole-in-the-wall near the East River. The restaurant was on a block filled mostly with parking garages for the high-rise apartment buildings that crowded in around it; Marshall's had been owned by the same family since the fifties, and what people liked best about it was how it never changed. Ponce had discovered it in her modeling days and had been going ever since.

New York was full of places like Marshall's: a dark wood bar up front with a neighborhood crowd watching TV, wooden tables and vinyl booths in the back, with daily specials posted on a chalkboard. Quiche lorraine had been a special every night for thirty years, though these days, since one of the family's younger members had joined the business, it was called Alsatian tart.

"No one ordered it then, no one orders it now," the bartender joked with Ponce one night, and the regulars all laughed. They mostly recognized one another by sight rather than name: The older, still elegant men with meticulously trimmed mustaches who looked as if they'd been in fashion or advertising in a more glamorous day, sitting alone in their booths, reading a newspaper and sipping a single martini until their chopped steaks arrived. The younger men with loud voices and loosened ties, divorced fathers who had just endured an early dinner with children who refused to eat their chicken fingers and cried when they were returned to Mom. Those men sat up front, bantering with the bartender and drinking steadily, watching sports on television. They talked with their mouths filled with strip steak, and when the other team scored, they wadded up the aluminum foil from their baked potatoes and threw it at the screen. For the most part, women came in pairs and spent hours huddled in conversation, finally splitting a dessert, then the bill, with the aid of a pocket calculator.

Ponce and Shawsie had come here plenty through the years, and Ponce had brought Gus and Rachel, and Red and Cackie, though sometimes she just brought a book.

"Hey, how are ya?" The bartender greeted Ponce as the door blew shut behind her.

"Frozen," she said, unwinding the scarf from around her head. "I can barely feel my face."

"Go on back, Gigi'll seat ya," he replied. "Pinot Grigio, right?"

"Yes, thank you."

Ponce hung her coat on a hook and saw that all the booths were taken. Honestly, at six-thirty on the Monday night after New Year's! You would think everyone would be home, glad to be done with the holidays, or off on vacation somewhere. Then again, this kind of crowd didn't have the money, generally, for lavish holidays. And for single people without families, coming back to a place like this on a regular weekday probably felt better than anything they had done since before Christmas Eve.

Ponce headed for a table and Gigi intercepted her. She was a matronly woman with upswept coal-black hair, bright red lipstick, and white face powder, a look she had contrived at seventeen and never forsaken.

"Hiya, hon," she began.

"Happy New Year," Ponce said.

"Don't you see your guest, sitting there waiting for you?"

"What? Where?"

Ponce followed the waitress's pointed finger to a back booth where a man was staring at her, somewhat embarrassed.

"Jeez, Poncie, it's only been a year," Red said.

Ponce stood a moment, gaping. "I am stunned," she said. Though Red had never been her type—which Shawsie succinctly defined, when Ponce was still married to Lee, as "short and insane"—he was a dish from the old school, tall and broad-shouldered, with his thatch of auburn hair. Even when he was younger he had the worn air of a deadline hound: slightly sleepy, slightly amused, his dark brown eyes no less penetrating for the way they crinkled when he smiled. On the weekends when Shawsie went to meet him at the Yale Club, she laughed at how many of her girlfriends wanted to catch the same train home, so they might be invited up to join them for a last round. Red cut quite a romantic figure, Shawsie said, in his worn leather jacket, smelling like soap and cigarettes and, by that time of the day, gin. Each of her friends looked at him with a heady combination of shyness and excitement, which, Ponce knew, was the same way he looked when he'd see his own wife.

"Why don't you try being stunned sitting down?" Red asked, flushing, as Gigi took in the scene until, mercifully, Ponce sat.

"Red Evans, how much weight have you lost?"

He looked away.

"I asked you a question."

"Fifty pounds. But you know, I needed to lose at least thirty anyway."

Ponce folded her arms. His hair was streaked with gray, that was nothing new. But he looked bone-tired, as if he hadn't slept in months. His skin was sallow, the bags under his eyes practically purple. He looked nothing like Red Evans. At sixty-two, he looked like an unhealthy old man.

"Pinot Grigio?" Gigi set it on the table.

"I'll have another one of these," Red said, holding up an empty martini glass. "Three olives."

Ponce sipped her wine and tried to regain her composure, which meant she was quiet for longer than she meant to be. "If Cackie could see what you look like, she would kill you," she said finally.

Red nodded. "I've thought about that myself," he said. "And you know, the hell of it is, Ponce, that sometimes when I look in the mirror I see her looking back at me. The her who was dying. 'Cause this is sort of what she looked like at the end. Wasted. Yellow. Half dead. It's morbid, I know, but it makes me feel closer to her, seeing myself this way." He ran his hand over his face. "I stopped shaving for a while, but I found it ruined the effect."

Ponce just stared.

"When I talk to you on the phone, you sound just like yourself," she said. "I never dreamed you were in this kind of shape."

He motioned for Gigi to bring Ponce another glass of wine, even though her first was still full.

"Well, Poncie, you can see why I came, then. It was clearly time for a hamburger," he said gently, as gently as if he were speaking to Shawsie when she was younger, or to one of his own kids. It worked. Ponce looked over at him, really looked into his eyes, and her own filled with tears.

"Red, I am so sorry. To be in this much pain. I should have just—"

"You should have nothing. I wouldn't let you. I couldn't. I mean, you know how it was with Cackie and me. I never thought she would die first. She was five years younger, for Christ's sake. What the hell is that?" The storm that swept his face was instant.

Gigi returned with the martini and the wine. "Pork chops tonight," she told Ponce, who nodded distractedly.

"Red, you need to speak to someone." Ponce's tone was urgent.

He sighed. "I suspect you're right. That's what my kids tell me, anyway. And the minister at my church." He looked down at his hands gripping the edge of the table, then smiled. "But you know, the cashier at my local A&P thinks I look fabulous. Lovely woman, must be three hundred pounds herself. And every week, when she sees me, she says, 'Honey, you got that Atkins thing *workin'* for you! You look mmm-mmm good!'"

Ponce laughed. Red felt himself breathe again. "Shall we order?" he asked. "I believe I have an appetite."

Ponce motioned for Gigi, who circled back in record time. "Two pork chops with everything," Ponce said. "Even better than the hamburger," she assured Red.

Gigi nodded. "I already put them away for you," she said comfortably.

"Why, thank you," Ponce said.

Red smiled again. "It's good to be a regular."

Ponce looked at him and made a decision. There was no point in ruining the night, no matter how shocked she was to see her friend this way. They needed to move forward. She smiled too. "It is indeed," she said. "So, how about those Knicks?"

Red leaned back in the booth. "Well," he said, "I thought you'd never ask."

When they were through, around ten, Red pointed out a Bulls score on the television up front, and Ponce realized that the restaurant was empty save for two men at the bar. What the hell, they figured. Why not have a nightcap?

"Do you remember the time that I went with you and

Cackie to that Shakespeare play?" Ponce asked. "I can't for the life of me remember which one it was now, but you know, it was that big-deal one at Lincoln Center, and we were all so bored and Cackie got the giggles and you and I caught them and none of us could stop laughing, and then everyone around us started shushing us?"

Red laughed, his face buoyed by the memory. "And the minute the lights came up for intermission, we escaped to the Ginger Man?"

Ponce nodded. "And that time at the Knicks game when they were behind by two points and the guy next to you started screaming for the other team to win? And you started swearing at him, and he lunged for you, and Cackie got in the middle and stomped on his foot, and he started screaming that she'd broken it and he was going to sue you and you told him to fuck off and stop cursing at your wife?"

"Boy, was she mad! I thought that guy would never walk again." He wiped his eyes. "What a gal."

"She sure was."

He drained his drink. "I should thank you, you know. For going to the ballet with her all those years so I never had to. I owe you for that."

"Hell, Red, you owe me for nothing. I would have run barefoot over glass if Cackie wanted me to, because I'd know if she suggested it, somehow I'd have fun."

They both got weepy then, she told Shawsie the next day. But the place was closing—in the nick of time, it felt like— and amazingly, they got a cab right away. Yes, Red had eaten every bite of his dinner, whether he wanted to or not. And yes, they had talked sports—forever, by Shawsie's standards. Also politics. He hadn't lost a step, except he clearly believed that he had. And no, he never once mentioned going back to work, and neither had she. There had to be some benefit to having dinner with a friend who knew better than to raise a subject like that—a family member would have bothered it like a loose tooth.

But the two most important things, Ponce told Shawsie, were that he had promised to get some counseling and he promised to come back to the city again for dinner. Soon. He didn't say when. Only soon. And she believed him, Ponce said. He'd dropped her at home before going to the Yale Club. There was a moment right before they got to her block when it seemed they would both start talking about Cackie again, and that he might tell her everything that had happened to him for every hour of every day of the entire year since she died—but they just hugged instead, and said goodbye.

He will come back, Ponce told Shawsie. In his own time, when he's ready. The rest of them could only wait and see.

Chapter Five

Shawsie shoved at the front door of the brownstone which seemed stuck—Damn! What was she doing wrong? Suddenly, it flew open, and she almost fell through the doorway. She ran inside, down the hall. Robin looked up from his magazine and half smiled.

"Hey, kid, I thought you forgot," he said softly. The other couple in the waiting room grinned and rolled their eyes. What a joker. Like any of them could forget an appointment like this!

Shawsie looked at her watch, even though she had looked at almost nothing else for the past half an hour: 6:20.

"Did they call us already? Does Neil know I'm late?"

Robin put down the magazine and took her hands in his. They were ice-cold and trembling. "Shawsie," he said, keeping his voice low and turning his back on their audience. "You have got to calm down. It's not a date with the executioner. It's a doctor. He has no idea you're late. The fucking door hasn't opened once since I got here at five-thirty."

"It hasn't? Oh, gee, that's good news!" Shawsie unbuttoned her coat and hung it on the wooden tree in the corner. She glanced toward the reception desk.

"No nurse?"

Robin shrugged. "Maybe they don't get paid overtime. Or maybe there's one in there with him. But I haven't seen anyone. Come on."

He reached over and pulled her into the chair next to him. "Now, since we have a moment, I think we should take a close look at your competition." He pulled a stack of magazines onto his lap. "For starters, why didn't you guys come up with this?"

He opened a magazine for younger men to a cheesy-looking spread featuring two bottle blondes hanging on a guy with enough bulging muscles to be a float in the Macy's Thanksgiving Day parade. She smiled tentatively.

"Or this?" He went on, through the entire pile, showing her amateurish photo spreads, or third-choice subjects given third-choice treatment, and soon she was laughing and leaning closer to his chair and inhaling his cologne and wishing they could go to Fitzer's for a beer. How long had it been since life was that simple?

An inner door opened. "Mr. and Mrs. Brody?" A nurse held a thick folder in her hand.

The other couple smiled their encouragement. "Good luck to you!" the man boomed. "We're not till six-thirty, so he's practically on time!"

Robin and Shawsie followed the nurse down a silent carpeted hallway into Neil's office. "He'll be with you shortly," she said, depositing the folder on Neil's desk and leaving them to sit, small as children in the oversize leather chairs. The walls were paneled in dark wood, and all but obscured by Neil's numerous framed degrees. The bookshelves were bulgingly full, and the silver picture frames that lined the desk boasted shots of Neil with Sari and the kids. They were all tanned, all in T-shirts. White teeth flashed. Shawsie wondered who their dentist was.

She focused on a recent picture of Neil on the *Oprah* show: smiling, relaxed, looking very much like the ex-hippie he was, with his too-long hair and a gold earring glinting in one ear. Like a latter-day Jesus, Shawsie thought. A fertility messiah, holding his palms open over barren women, willing them to bear fruit. She glanced at Robin, sitting in his chair facing straight ahead, sweat glistening at his hairline.

The door opened. "Robin, Shawsie, thanks so much for waiting!"

They both jumped to their feet, effusive in their greetings.

Standing ovation acknowledged, he motioned them to sit. They sat.

Neil opened their folder and turned the pages, scanning wildly, bringing himself up-to-date. He leaned back in his chair. "Some people would say three strikes and you're out," he said, looking at them meaningfully. "Have you considered adopting?"

Shawsie felt as if he had punched her. "*What?*"

Robin reached for her arm, which she snatched away.

"Adopting? After forty-five thousand dollars and almost two years of hell? Are you out of your *mind*?" As if from a distance, Shawsie heard that she was shouting. Probably shouldn't do that, she thought. Too late now.

Robin grabbed the arms of his chair. He hadn't felt this kind of panic since he was a kid and his father would wake him, shouting, when he came home drunk in the middle of the night. It wasn't the words, necessarily, it was the noise, the sudden terror it brought. He had never heard Shawsie raise her voice, he realized. In all those years, even when they were just friends. Not once.

Neil grew still. He waited. Robin stuttered an apology. Shawsie tried catching her breath. "No," she said. "No. No. You are such a great doctor that you go on *Oprah* and tell women you can help them? Then help *me*. God damn you."

The silence was awful. Robin wiped his face with his sleeve. "Neil, I'm sorry, man. Really."

Neil nodded, but his eyes were on Shawsie. "What do you want to do?"

She stared. "I want to have a baby is what I want to do. And if I have to do this ten more times, I'm going to have one. And you're going to help me. That's what."

Neil turned to Robin. "Do you agree?"

Robin looked at Shawsie, nodding vigorously. "Of course."

Neil closed the folder. "Then we go on," he said briskly, standing up. "Call Dorothy and make the arrangements. This time, though, I'd also like you to see an acupuncturist I've been working with. We're doing a study on blood flow to the uterus, and I must say, even though it sounds a bit out there, we've been seeing some real benefits."

He shook Robin's clammy hand and turned toward Shawsie, who looked up at him, her face red with shame. She opened her mouth, but he spoke first.

"It's okay, Shawsie. This process takes a terrible toll, and I know it's not personal. Really." He hugged her. "You're doing great. You both are. This is the hardest thing two people ever have to do together. You both deserve a round of applause." His smile was small but real. "Go out and have a drink or something tonight."

Shawsie's eyebrows flew up, but he shook his head. "One

drink, one night, you're not even taking anything now," he said. "Give yourselves a break. And you don't even have to do what comes naturally when you go home. Just get some rest." With that, he was gone.

Shawsie looked at Robin and sank into her chair. "I shouldn't have," she said weakly.

He sat back down, too. "Come on, Shawsie, Neil knows you're just stressed. And I think he gave us some good advice, eh?"

She looked into his face. He looked winded and moist, like he had just run a great distance.

"Let's go to Fitzer's," he said. "I'm buying. Okay?"

He stood and extended his hand. She took it, although she couldn't see it through her tears.

"Okay," she said. She stood, and he held her while she cried, and after what seemed like a very long time they gathered up their coats and walked down the hall—from the inside, at least, the front door opened just fine—and they went out into the night to sit together and have a beer.

"Sweetie?"

"Hmmm."

"I'm hungry. Are you hungry?"

"Hmmm."

"I should have known. When are you ever hungry?"

Neil switched on the bedside lamp, and a golden light warmed the chintz drapes and the red carpet. He walked over to the desk and rummaged through the drawers for a room-service menu.

"Yes, good evening. I'd like to order some dinner."

Ponce picked up her head and squinted at him through the light.

"A Caesar salad, the roasted salmon, two vodkas, neat, a bottle of Pinot Grigio, and a club sandwich. What?" He listened a moment. "Yes, please."

Ponce smiled and put her head back on the pillow. "They asked if I wanted mayonnaise?" she asked after he hung up.

"They did. You do. It's coming." He smiled at her, still holding the phone to his ear. "Checking my service," he said.

Ponce swung her legs over the side of the bed. She knew that next up was the call to Sari. "I'm getting in the shower now," she said, closing the bathroom door behind her. She glanced at her wrist, suddenly curious about the time, but realized she had left her watch on the bedside table. Never mind. She wasn't the one who had to be anywhere. He did. And not until the morning.

She loved escaping with Neil for these out-of-town medical meetings. They usually lasted only two nights, but Ponce appreciated a good hotel and they always stayed in one, away from the convention-center barns where the meetings took place. Utter privacy, and no one was the wiser. It was Ponce's routine never to leave the room, except for an hour or so in the morning so the maid could make it up. Then she would go back and read, nap, maybe call a masseuse. Neil would come in and out, depending on his presentation schedule. All in all, these trips were like forty-eight-hour retreats, a chance to leave the real world behind. Half the time, Ponce couldn't even remember what city she was in. It wasn't the point.

How long was it now, three years with Neil? They had known each other much longer, of course, from when she was still married to Lee. Sari wasn't much in evidence then, staying home in Brooklyn with her babies and her brand-new clinic. Which made Neil, a hot young doctor at Carnegie Hill Hospital, whose board Lee ran, a very useful extra man at dinner parties. Though by Lee's standards, he was unaccountably bohemian. His hair was too long, he wore an earring—years before it was fashionable—and almost never wore a tie.

"What the hell is wrong with him?" Lee asked Ponce one night. "Shouldn't someone tell him that the sixties are over?"

Ponce only laughed. "He's a free spirit," she said.

"Nothing is free," Lee had grumbled in return.

What Ponce liked about Neil from the start was that even though he was obviously smart—brilliant, some people said—he never showed off. His emotional connection to his work, why he did it and how, was as important to him as the science behind it. And he was so patient! No matter how many screaming, sobbing women he would see, he seemed never to lose his temper or get a headache or be fed up. When she spoke to him during the day he was always calm. Focused. He sincerely wanted to help them. That wasn't something you could fake.

Neil was exactly Ponce's age, and had grown up in suburban New Jersey. His father was a pediatrician, his mother worked as his nurse (and had painted all the pictures on the office walls), and they practiced out of the house where Neil and his three older sisters grew up. Neil was the object of scorn and pity among his high school friends. To have both parents home all the time! The party potential was absolutely nil. But he never minded it. He was the darling of his family, close to both his hippie parents. His mom, with her waist-length hair and Birkenstocks, practiced yoga daily in a town where the other women played tennis, popped Elavils, and wore Pucci into the city for their husbands' business dinners. His father was totally cool, as parents went. When one of his patients, a fifteen-year-old girl, got pregnant in her sophomore year, he took her to Planned Parenthood himself, then sat with her when she told her parents so they wouldn't kill her. Which, incredibly, they didn't.

In the summers, Neil's dad worked as a doctor at a camp in upstate New York, and Neil spent many happy years there. He grew his hair, smoked pot, and was catnip to every girl who met him. He looked like Al Pacino in *Serpico*.

He met Sari in his junior year at Harvard. Her parents were on the faculty there and she had the same close relationship with them as he had with his own parents. When he went to their house, it felt as if he had never left home and he liked that. Sari was very pretty, with her own dark good looks, and possibly the smartest person Neil had ever met. His dad was crazy for her, and the feeling was mutual: It was because of his loving example, Sari always said, that she had become a pediatrician herself.

Though Neil had never planned on marrying young, he did, and he and Sari enrolled at Harvard Medical School together. It was in those years that one of Neil's sisters married a lawyer, a straitlaced type out of keeping with the rest of his Woodstock Nation family, but they all figured that was why she liked him.

After they'd been married for two years and still hadn't had a baby, the lawyer came home one day and announced he was getting a divorce. He said he was completely justified in doing so. The Bible, he claimed, said that if you marry a woman who proves to be barren, you have the right to find another wife.

Neil's sister was devastated; the entire family was. Neil went to the gynecology department to look at the latest research on fertility. It was 1982, and he was shocked at how little there was to learn. He decided then to make fertility his specialty, and in ten years he was at the forefront of the field. In ten more years the science had exploded and so had his career. The good news about his sister was that she had finally remarried and, with Neil's help, become the joyful mother of healthy twin boys, now ten years old. (Her former husband had also remarried and remained childless. His Bible, apparently, made no provisions for male infertility.)

Although Neil eventually found himself one of the hottest doctors in New York, Sari had gotten her own share of publicity, years earlier, even making the cover of *Manhattan* magazine when she opened her pioneering Brooklyn clinic. She and Neil had rehabilitated a brownstone in Park Slope—a neighborhood that was still a bit raffish at the time—and there was a photo of her holding one of their three children and looking up into the flue of a fireplace that Neil kept on his desk for years. My personal force of nature, he called her.

Being a force of nature left Sari little time to act as a wifely accessory to Neil's career, which he didn't care about one whit. Carnegie Hill Hospital was brilliantly endowed to do the kind of research he wanted to do, and having to periodically drink Château Lafite Rothschild at sprawling Park Avenue apartments didn't seem too high a price to pay. Lee Morris had taken a particular interest in him early on. The old man was a prickly sort, an autocrat who expected an entire emergency room to grind to a halt if he had so much as an ingrown toenail. After listening to a presentation of Neil's, Lee called up the young doctor and had him over for a drink. Lee saw the value of having a local miracle worker tucked into his back pocket. He could say to virtually anyone in New York: "Baby trouble? I've just the man for you."

He actually never pushed his privileges too far, and Neil, in turn, didn't mind showing up at the dinner parties thrown by Lee's stunning, much younger wife. The first time Neil came to the Sutton Place duplex, he found himself, champagne glass in hand, standing utterly alone on an expanse of marble floor. Everyone else seemed to know one another, and they were all gathered in clumps at what seemed like a very far distance. Neil amused himself by imagining the range of diseases he might be suffering to justify his quarantine.

"Dr. Grossman?"

The most beautiful woman in the world stood before him. Her blond hair seemed almost white in the light shining behind her, and her dark blue eyes seemed huge in her delicately heart-shaped face. Her lips were slightly parted, and she reached out her hand.

"Tuberculosis," he blurted.

She looked alarmed. "*What?*"

He blushed. "Oh, I, I'm sorry," he said. "I mean, no, I don't have tuberculosis, and neither do you, I'm sure. Though now of course I wish I did, because I would be far away in a sanatorium in the mountains and would never have to admit who I am or that I ever said it." He felt the prick of adrenaline under his armpits as his heartbeat galloped, and he wondered just how slippery the marble was underfoot.

The most beautiful woman in the world motioned to a waiter, who approached with a tray of drinks. Neil surrendered his empty glass as she helped herself to two flutes of champagne and handed him one. Her smile was warm.

"To your health, Dr. Grossman. And mine," she said, smiling. "I'm Ponce Morris."

He felt the blood flood his face. He hadn't been this lame in front of a girl since he was fourteen and had spent ten minutes at the final social in camp trying to unfasten Joan Schwarz's bra in the back before realizing that the clasp was up front.

"Mrs. Morris, to your health," he managed, before gulping the champagne. He pressed his lips together so he wouldn't burp. What the hell was wrong with him? He was a doctor and a married man, and in his day, abbreviated though it might have been, quite the ladies' man.

The bell rang for dinner, and he didn't see her again until it was time to leave. He had calmed down considerably since the cocktail hour, and had made impressive progress persuading a wealthy dowager intent on having grandchildren to fund an upcoming study.

"Mrs. Morris, thank you so much, it was a lovely evening," he said smoothly.

Ponce laughed. "No shortness of breath now? Are you sure?"

Neil stared. What did she mean? Had she seen that he'd been so light-headed when he met her that he thought he might fall?

She smiled. "Just checking on your tuberculosis," she said, shaking his hand. "I believe you're cured."

On his way home that night he convinced himself never to drink champagne again. It made him behave like a fool. With any luck, he assured himself, he wouldn't see that woman again for at least a year, and by that time she would have forgotten all about this.

To the contrary, by the time Ponce and Lee divorced four years later, Neil had seen her plenty. They were occasional dinner partners, either at her home or someone else's, and they met often on his hospital's cocktail-party circuit. Sari had managed to turn up a few times, and she and Ponce got along well. Although Neil had overcome his initial awkwardness with Ponce, that volcanic thrill of seeing her the first time had never quite left him. He sometimes found himself thinking of her during his workday, or over the weekend. Aimlessly. Recalling a word or a laugh.

When Ponce and Lee split, Neil had called her. Did she

need any help? He knew a great lawyer. Did she have a place to live? Did she want to grab a drink and have some company? He couldn't have been more solicitous.

Ponce was direct, as always. "Neil, you're sweet, but here's the situation. I am a lawyer, I'm still working at Corning Hilliard and I am surrounded by other lawyers. I've rented a studio apartment near Bloomingdale's, which is convenient to the office, and I'm actually involved with someone at the moment, so between that and work I am well fixed for drinks. I appreciate your kindness, but let me give you some advice. Lee is very, very angry with me right now. And he is nothing if not vindictive. If he were to hear that you were lending me a hand, doing anything—and I mean anything—for me, he could make your life miserable. You don't need that. So thank you for being decent and for being a pal. Give my best to Sari."

Their paths did not cross again for almost three years. He thought of her less and less, truth be told, especially after reading that she was having a very public affair with John St. John, the mystery writer. But one evening during rounds, after Lee had been diagnosed with cancer and installed in the finest room Carnegie Hill had to offer, Neil made it a point to stop in. He was shocked to find Ponce sitting there, in a chair by the bed, reading *The New York Times* as calmly as if she were on the bus.

Lee, who was sedated, lifted two fingers in greeting, then closed his eyes. He hated people seeing him at such a disadvantage. He had discovered that closing his eyes made them go away. Ponce took Neil's arm and led him out into the hall, shutting the door behind her.

"How *are* you?" she asked, as warmly and as full of light as he remembered. She did look a bit older. Too thin. Pinched around the gills. But she was obviously exhausted. She told him about taking a leave from the firm to nurse Lee. He started asking questions, but she just shook her head. "We can talk about it later," she said, gesturing toward the door. "It's just complicated, is all," she said. "He was very, very good to me for a very long time. I feel I need to do this now."

He took her hand and held it in his. "I admire you," he said. "And I think Lee must appreciate it very much."

When Lee died a few weeks later, Neil called and asked to see her. "This time you're going to say yes," he heard himself say. And she did. She met him at Lee's apartment with two of his lawyers and spent an hour talking about Lee's bequests for the hospital, making sure that Neil's department was provided for. Then, with the lawyers still there, she walked Neil to the door. "Thank you for coming," she said. "I'll call you."

Weeks went by. Neil was angry. Yes, he was behaving like an adolescent. But so what? He wanted her to pay attention to him. And why shouldn't she? He was a catch. Of course, he was also married and the father of three children. So why didn't he feel that way?

She called on a Monday. "I've left Corning for good," she said. "Packed my last box today. And I'm ready to celebrate."

His anger vanished. "Where? When?" He sounded too eager, he thought.

"Come over at six," she said. "I have a bottle of Cristal that's been waiting for an occasion." She heard him hesitate. "Oh, that's right. As I recall, champagne gives you tuberculosis. I have a full bar, too, Dr. Grossman. Don't worry."

At six he walked through the elevator door into her apartment. The Cristal was opened, a vodka was poured, and by six-thirty, they were in bed. At ten, he announced he was leaving Sari.

"I've never felt this way in my entire life," he declared, holding her close against his chest. "I've heard about this, I've read about this, but nothing I've ever experienced has been like this."

Ponce smiled gently. "Neil, I am not a home wrecker, and neither are you," she said quietly. "Now listen. I have no intention of getting married again. And tonight aside, you have no intention of destroying your family. So let's not discuss this again."

He looked hurt, but she wouldn't budge. "I mean it," she said, and by the time he got home and was pulling back the covers on the bed with Sari fast asleep in it, he knew that Ponce was right. Christ, what had he done? He studied his wife's peaceful face in the light from the hallway and felt terrible remorse. He looked away. The truth was, he simply couldn't help himself. It was like a fever. Not like insanity, because he knew just what he was doing as he was doing it, and he loved it. Every second of it. But Ponce was right. He did love his family. Hell, he even loved his wife. None of it made sense. Except that being with Ponce that night surpassed any other sexual moment of his life. He didn't know why. It just did.

He got up and took a pillow with him to sleep downstairs. Sari didn't deserve this. He was wrong. The whole thing was wrong.

Nevertheless, he called Ponce the minute he left the house the next morning. No answer. All day he kept calling, in between every appointment. No answer. Finally, at five o'clock, she picked up.

"I've got to see you." His voice was ragged.

"Well, okay. I'm home tonight."

Again he was there at six, and this time he stayed until midnight. This went on every night for the rest of the week. Late on Friday, Ponce smiled at him. "Bored yet?" she asked. "'Cause you have a weekend in Brooklyn ahead of you."

He sighed. He was in the throes of an addiction that he felt might consume him. *Wished* would consume him. Obliterate him. Make him never have to think about his family. His wife. Or his parents, who had lived together and worked together every single day for fifty-one years and couldn't stand the notion of being apart for even an hour. It's how he thought he would be with Sari. Of course, their situation was completely different. Neil's mom had worked with his dad — not alone, on her own career. And Neil was proud of Sari, he really was. She was a fine person, an excellent doctor, a loving mother. And wife.

How much did he really know about Ponce, anyway? She too seemed to be a fine person, one with a highly developed sense of justice. Well, not about sleeping with another woman's husband, certainly, but about everything else. She was a nice person with a good sense of fun. Was he in love with her? He didn't know. But he was obsessed with her. When he was away from her, he couldn't stop thinking about her. When he was with her, he couldn't stop touching her. He was gone. Just gone.

Ponce had gotten up to get him a drink and now sat beside him on the bed.

"I will see you whenever you like," she said. "Within reason, of course. But you go home tonight and pay attention to your family. Think about them. They are the focus of your life, Neil, not me. You only think I am."

She was right, of course. Within weeks, Neil found himself adapting. He worked out a way not to think about Ponce when he was at home, and he worked out a way not to think about Ponce when he was at work, and he spent the hours at her apartment feeling more vital and purely himself than he had since he was a teenager. Until the moment he had to leave, each moment burst with possibility. Then, like a junkie, he fought against wanting more, every second, until he got it.

For her part, Ponce was surprised by how much she liked Neil. Felt for him. Yes, she liked sleeping with him, but more than that she liked the way his mind worked. When he talked about his research, about his patients, she saw a perfect nexus of heart and brain that moved her. She admired his dedication and his curiosity and his devotion to knowing more. To trying to help. She looked forward to seeing him, and missed him when they were apart. Like the song said, it was almost like being in love. Or maybe it was love. After all, love had quite a reputation in some circles. People swore by it. In her own life, anytime she had come close to it, she'd felt as if a giant's hand were closing around her throat. She couldn't breathe, she couldn't see, the person who claimed to be loving her had her fixed in place, and wriggle though she might she could never break free.

As Ponce turned off the shower, she heard the doorbell ring and a muffled call of "Room service!"

"One minute," Neil called.

She put on a robe and combed out her hair, and as she walked back into the room Neil was opening the wine.

"Hey, beautiful," he said, smiling.

"Hey, yourself," she said, taking a glass. They stood in front of the large picture window and looked out at the lights spread beneath them. "Do you know, when I was in the shower, I couldn't remember what city we were in," she said. "And it didn't even matter, because I'm with you, so I know where I am." She looked up at him, serious. "I've never felt that about someone before," she said.

He put down his drink and pulled her close, cupping her

face in his hands, tracing her cheekbones with his thumbs. "I feel the same way," he said tenderly. "That's why we're so high up tonight, Poncie. It's our heaven."

From her very drafty room at the Drake Hotel in Chicago, Babette looked out at the large chunks of ice floating on Lake Michigan and tried to stop shivering. She was more nervous than anything else, she thought, glancing at her open notebook. Yes, it was late February, but still. She was just overreacting—and with good reason. She had been dumbfounded when Topher approved her coming here, though once she discovered it was Shawsie who'd convinced him, it all made sense.

The dragon lady fashion director, Camille LaCroix (known to her staff alternately as La Cross We All Must Bear and Chlamydia, the Dark Secret of the Fashion Closet), had never seemed to like Babette. Or anyone else, for that matter. The previous year, one of Camille's assistants had brought home a voodoo doll from Mardi Gras in New Orleans, and everyone in the fashion department had taken a turn stabbing it with antique hat pins they had bought especially for the occasion.

When Babette hand-delivered Camille the written pitch for the Carmen story, the older woman looked at her as if she were carrying typhus. Babette figured it was a lost cause, but what she couldn't have predicted was the squabble between Camille and Topher during the ideas meeting the following week. When it was Camille's turn to talk and she had started praising, yet again, a hot young Parisian designer, Topher interrupted her.

"Camille, you know what, doll, *Boothby's* is actually an American rag," he said, leaning back in his chair and lighting a cigarette in flagrant violation of the building code. "Are there no designers in *this* country who interest you?"

She blushed, just a bit. "Ah, Topher, but of course—"

He cut her off. "Not Donna or Calvin or Ralph. Sick. To. Death. *Comprenez?*"

The tension in the room escalated. Usually Topher was easygoing during these meetings. He had long ago assembled a top group of talent whom he trusted. This kind of display was rare indeed. But who knew what had gotten him going? It could have been an offhand remark from a rival editor at a cocktail party, or some pointed comment from a pretty waitress in Tribeca young enough to be his, um, niece. It was easy to tap into the encroaching terror they all felt as they got older that the magazine might not be cutting-edge anymore. Fashion was the first place that particular wrinkle showed.

Or perhaps Arnold Rubinstein, publisher from hell, had called Topher at five a.m. from his treadmill just to let him know that the last issue had struck him as a bit—how you say in English?—feh.

Camille recovered quickly. "There is much new talent here, *absolument*," she said. "We can look at the scene in Miami or Los Angeles."

He shook his head. "I'm tired of both. Where else?"

She took a deep breath. "Well, there is great activity of late in Chicago." That Camille LaCroix found herself speaking the word "Chicago" out loud was the height of absurdity, she knew, but she had been around long enough to recognize when bosses grew tired of her. She had worked at *Boothby's* almost four years now, longer than she had lasted at either *Vogue* or *Elle*. As early as the previous fall, though, she had begun to sense impatience from Topher. Maybe he thought the ad dollars looked flat. Maybe she really had pushed France too much at a time when it was just not popular. When he started making burqa jokes, saying that at least they'd be something different, she sat herself down and did some homework. She received the same press releases that Babette was pilfering from her staff, and she'd spent a few hours on the Internet after that. She knew she was going, but not without a fight.

"Chicago?" Topher seemed stunned into at least a moment of silence, so Camille went forward, talking about a crop of interesting designers there, both homegrown and immigrant talent. Young, she stressed. New.

Well, by the end of the meeting, she found herself headed for a shoot in Chicago. "Most of my people are not free for this, you know, with the fall collections coming up," she said, beginning to backtrack. Having saved her ass in the short term, she was now threatened with freezing it off somewhere in middle America, a dismal-sounding region where she had never set foot and had planned on keeping it that way.

Topher waved her off. "Pull one or two of your people away from the fall collections, for chrissakes. How many of you need to go look at the same clothes anyway?"

Shawsie, who had kept quiet in the wake of Topher's ill humor, piped up. "You know who you can take with you? Babette. Especially since you know she wants to go."

Camille's eyes opened wide.

"Yeah, she copied me *and* Topher on that pitch, actually," Shawsie said, as the color flooded Camille's face completely this time. "You know, one of the things we've always tried to do at *Boothby's*, Camille, is to let the assistants have the chance to learn something, not just fetch us lattes all day long. I believe your spirit of mentoring needs work."

Before she could respond, Topher said, "If Babette wants to do the Cuban chick, let her try. If it sucks, we can use it as a sidebar. And you can take full advantage of that gung-ho attitude of hers by having her arrange the studio time and the catering and all the other crap you can't spare your own precious staff for."

He thought he saw something then in Camille's expression, and he didn't like it. "No, babe, not even close," he said, lighting another cigarette. "Not my type, particularly. But here's a lesson for you: These kids are only twenty-five once. Who else would kill themselves to go to Chicago in February? And if she screws it up, fine. It's only Chicago. Right?"

Camille nodded vigorously. "*Oui*, right," she said, getting up to head back to her office. That she had lost Shawsie was a terrible blow.

All Babette knew at the time was that Camille summoned her a few days later.

"You copied your pitch to Shawsie *and* Topher?" was how she began.

Babette started to stammer. All the fashion assistants had told her to do it. Camille was a credit-grabbing bully, and it wasn't until one of the associate editors had started copying Shawsie on her ideas that any of them got through. That girl left soon after, to become the fashion director at *Harper's Bazaar*. But once she had gone over Camille's head, the whole department followed suit. Like any pack of wolves, they moved together, smelled weakness together. Camille was sitting on one shaky throne and now they all waited together.

"Well, yes," Babette finally managed. "Everyone in your department does it, and they told me to do it, too."

Camille's mouth tightened. She didn't like the sound of that at all. How had she managed to lose her grip on Topher? Was it that wretched girl who had gone to *Bazaar*? It seemed that the trouble surfaced then. Well, whatever it was, she knew she had to, what did these childish Americans say, start to "play ball"?

"We have decided to do a spread about the Chicago fashion scene as a whole," Camille went on. "You can do your story on Carmen, if there turns out to be a story, but you will be there to, how you say, make the trains run on time. You help my people book the studio, arrange the catering, *oui?*"

Babette was beside herself with excitement. The fashion kids all said that Topher was turning on Camille and she'd be out in a matter of months, if not weeks. Maybe if Babette did a good job she could move over there just as a nice new editor came in.

"Yes!" she exclaimed. "That is so fantastic! And I know the Carmen story will be great. Really."

Camille had already turned away, picking up the phone. Babette wasn't sure if she was dismissed, so she stood, waiting. Finally, Camille flicked her hand.

Babette was too exhilarated to care. She had virtually flown back to her own desk and immediately called the PR firm about arranging an interview with Carmen. She called her mother. She even called Robin and left a message on his cell.

Then she went down the hall to Shawsie's office. Babette waved at her through the glass wall, and Shawsie, in the middle of a call, motioned her to come inside.

"I can't thank you enough because I know that without you, Camille would never have said yes," Babette gushed when Shawsie hung up.

"It's nothing," Shawsie said. "We really do believe in letting assistants try to learn something here. In this business, there's something to be said for developing talent and keeping it in house. And your pitch fit perfectly. How did you know about Chicago fashion?"

"Well, I spent some time in the fashion department," Babette said, "and looked through the releases—the other assistants showed me some — but it's just so nice that you and Topher stuck up for me."

"How did you know we did?" Shawsie asked.

"One of the assistants said that Camille came out of that meeting spitting mad because you guys ganged up on her." Babette caught herself. "I mean, I'm sure you didn't—"

Shawsie laughed. "Sure we did. Well, that's fine. Just have a good trip, and write a good piece." She turned to pick up the phone again.

"Uh, Shawsie, can I ask you something?" Babette shifted from one foot to the other. "Did you ever ask Ponce about having a drink?"

"Oh!" Shawsie clapped her hand to her head. "You know, I did, Babette, I'm sorry, I've had so much on my mind, I forgot to mention it. It's just that Ponce has such a heavy court schedule now, she's swamped. And she has a close friend who lives out of town who's having a personal crisis that she's helping take care of, so yes, I did ask, but she's just so jammed, I think we might have to put it off for a while."

Babette was crestfallen, though she tried not to show it. "Oh, okay. Thanks for asking."

She fretted about that conversation for the next few days, the victory of her Chicago trip dimmed. She had been counting on that drink, convinced that with just one more meeting she and Ponce would click for real. But she knew better than to pressure Shawsie, who had already done her a good turn. In fact, Babette had resolved to return the favor. She was through sleeping with Robin. Shawsie had been nothing but nice to her from the beginning, and it was time for Babette to step up.

The following week, Babette spotted Rachel Lerner sitting in an empty office. She must be closing a piece, Babette thought. That was the only time she came in. There she was, grim and focused, her oversize glasses perched low on her nose, her hair pulled back in a knot with an unlit cigarette dangling from her mouth. Babette breathed deep and worked up the courage to approach.

"Hey," she said, standing in the doorway. Rachel was wearing a black cashmere twinset, gray pants, and pearl earrings. As an office wag had once characterized Rachel's dress code: ready to attend a funeral at a moment's notice.

Rachel looked up over the tops of her glasses as if somehow a barnyard animal had made its odoriferous way into her personal space.

"Excuse me?" she said, which immediately conjured images of Babette's grandmother in Georgia, who just hated when she said "Hey" instead of "Hello, how are you?"

"Oh, uh, hi, Rachel, how are you?" Babette stammered.

"Fine." Rachel waited.

"Well, uh . . ."

Rachel waited some more.

Babette stood immobilized at the door, picturing at least seven different pieces of jewelry the other woman could have added to soften that headmistress ensemble. She forced herself to focus on the business at hand.

"I'm going to do a profile on this hot new fashion designer in Chicago, and I sort of just wanted to get your advice because, you know, you're so great at writing profiles and everything."

"What do you want to know?"

"Well . . . maybe some help with the questions I should ask?"

Rachel didn't change expression. "Like?"

Babette opened her mouth, but nothing came out. She wondered how Rachel got anyone to tell her anything in those in-depth interviews she did. Maybe her subjects all wept because they were terrified.

"No, really," Rachel went on. "What's the story?"

Babette recited the facts from the press release.

"Well, past the clothes, which I assume you'll have to evaluate in some way, I would think the story is the relationship with the mother."

"It is?"

"It's a big part. Are you speaking with the mother?"

"Uh, I don't know. I don't think she speaks English."

"Then find someone who speaks Spanish and bring her with you. Don't depend on them to get a translator for her. You'll never know if they're telling the truth."

Babette waited.

"You don't know the real circumstances of how they escaped or how they got to Chicago or what's gone on since," Rachel continued. "For all you know, at least part of the family could be here illegally. But in any case, I would concentrate on the emotional connections: between Carmen and her mother, Carmen and Cuba, Carmen and her clothes. Right?"

Babette nodded. This had been a major mistake. She thought desperately of how to change the subject. "Uh, can I ask you something else?"

Rachel had already turned back to the computer screen, but again she stared at Babette over the tops of her glasses.

"You're good friends with Ponce Morris, right?"

Rachel nodded.

"Well, I was thinking that she would be a great profile subject for *Boothby's*. I thought if I do a good job on Carmen, maybe I could do a piece on Ponce."

Rachel raised her eyebrows. "*Boothby's* is a national magazine, and Ponce is only known locally," she said. "Who'd be interested?"

Babette dug in. "I think most people know who Lee Morris was, and the fact that she's running around New York with all these men whose wives never even say boo—"

Rachel shook her head disdainfully and cut Babette off. "What do you mean, running around?" she asked. "She just happens to be close friends with a number of couples—*both* people in a couple, including the wives. She's not sleeping with these men, if that's what you're implying."

"I'm not implying that at all. What I'm trying to say is, well, I heard that you once described Ponce as a spare wife, and I thought that was such a great way to put it, because she *is* as close to the woman in a couple as the man and because she isn't a lesbian, or a threat to anyone's marriage, so that's actually the angle."

Rachel narrowed her eyes. "How do you know I said that?" she asked, recalling her lunch with Ponce at the Four Seasons.

Babette felt her throat close. The way she knew, she realized too late, was that Robin had told her. Ponce had told Shawsie, and Robin said that Ponce had loved that phrase, as he did—wasn't Rachel clever!—but she knew she couldn't possibly tell that to Rachel.

"It was at Jacqueline Posner's party," she said, feeling her heart thump. "You must have said it to someone who repeated it. I, I can't really remember now. But that doesn't matter. It's such a great description! It would even make the perfect title for a piece about her, don't you think? I could put an asterisk next to it and make sure they print 'Courtesy of Rachel Lerner' at the bottom of the page." She smiled and hoped she wasn't sweating through her blouse.

Rachel didn't actually smile, but she shrugged and

Babette was fairly sure she accepted her story. "That's certainly not necessary, but if you can convince Ponce, then go for it," Rachel said, turning back to her computer screen with finality. "Gus says that Lee lived for publicity, and Ponce lives to avoid it. So good luck."

Babette retreated and immediately started worrying about Carmen's mother. Maybe Rachel was wrong. It was a fashion piece, not a profile, right? Shit! Why had she even bothered? But she was compulsive enough herself to call the public relations people and ask if Carmen's mother was available. They said they'd have to check. She secretly hoped they'd say no. Then it wouldn't be her fault.

She walked over to the thermostat, which insisted it was 70 degrees and picked up her list of questions one more time. A car was coming to take her to Carmen's showroom down in the Loop. The PR people had said that it would be up to Carmen whether Babette could speak to her mother, so she should ask her at the interview.

Babette looked at herself in the mirror. She had bought a red cashmere sweater, just so Carmen would know how much she liked color herself, and paired it with a bright pink cardigan tied over her shoulders. She so hoped Carmen would like her. If she did, the piece would write itself. She didn't want to do anything to make her subject uncomfortable. After all, what if someone was doing a piece on her and wanted to speak to *her* mother? She would rather die.

The phone rang. Her car was downstairs.

On the way downtown, she stared out the window at Michigan Avenue. Neiman Marcus. Saks Fifth Avenue. Burberry. She watched a line of people stretching out the door of a small popcorn shop. That looked like fun. Would she ever have fun again? Her fashion department scheme had seemed so promising. But for the three days she'd been here, setting things up for the shoot, it seemed she had done nothing but take endless shit from Camille, who, predictably, hated Chicago on sight. It was cold, it was provincial, there was nothing to eat except big ugly hunks of red meat. When Babette and the two other assistants wanted to visit the Art Institute on a lunch break, Camille refused. This was not a school trip, she had scolded. They were here to work.

The car stopped. Babette took a deep breath and didn't seem to take another until she had entered the anteroom and given her name to the receptionist. Soon enough she was led inside, where a small dark-haired women knelt next to a fitting model, pinning a hem. "Hello," she said, the pins still in her mouth, hurriedly finishing the job. She rose and extended her hand to Babette.

"I am Carmen," she said. "I am glad to meet you."

Babette smiled. "So am I. I mean, I'm glad to meet you, too."

The next hour passed as if in a dream, Babette thought later. Carmen was so lovely! She showed her all her designs and spoke eloquently about Cuba and the world she'd left behind. She talked about arriving in Chicago as a child and feeling that the cold wind was like a knife that could cut her in half. She recalled her faulty English and the hours she had spent in the public library with a kind librarian who had helped her. How cool was that, Babette enthused. *Her* mother was a librarian! She scribbled down notes but also kept her tape recorder going the whole hour. She didn't want to miss a word.

When it was time to leave, she thanked Carmen profusely.

"You know, you should come to Bloomingdale's tomorrow morning," Carmen said.

"What do you mean?" Babette asked uneasily. Tomorrow was the first day of the shoot, and she was scheduled to be in the studio from ten till six.

"I'm doing a personal appearance there at ten," Carmen said. "Not exactly prime time, but the new designers have to take what we can get. My mother is coming, so you could talk to her if you still want to. The PR people said you asked to meet her."

Damn. Babette had completely forgotten about the mother. If she didn't meet her, Rachel Lerner would tell everyone she was a bad reporter. But what about the shoot? She would have to throw herself on Camille's mercy.

"I'll be there," Babette said.

She practically floated back to the street. The interview had gone perfectly. Her questions must have been good, because the answers were great. She'd done it! But as soon as she got back into the waiting car, her elation evaporated into the fear of having to ask Camille about being late to the shoot. She gnawed at her fingernails the whole way back to the hotel, trying to think of what to say. When she was in her room, she called.

"*Oui?*"

"Uh, Camille, hi, it's Babette."

"Yes? The studio is booked, yes?"

"Yes, it is. Uh, but the only thing is, it turns out I have to go to Bloomingdale's tomorrow at ten for the Carmen piece. It's only for an hour, I'll be at the studio by eleven-thirty, but it's the only way for me to talk to Carmen's mother. And I'm worried that if I don't talk to her and Topher asks me why, I'll be in trouble."

Camille sighed but held her tongue. She knew better than to get in the middle of this one. "Yes, fine, eleven-thirty," she said, and hung up.

Babette was back to being elated. She knew she should sit down and type up her notes, transcribe her tape, and write a lead when it was all fresh in her mind—everyone said that was the way to do it, not just Rachel—but she was too happy to sit still. She called the two other assistants, who, exhausted as they were by doing extra reporting of their own, were thrilled for her. They agreed that a celebration was in order and, using their *Boothby's* credit card, took themselves to Morton's, where they ordered forty-eight-ounce porterhouse steaks, drank dirty martinis, and gorged on cottage fries and onion rings. They took the leftover steak back to the hotel in doggie bags, and after stopping into one of their rooms to get a plastic shoe-shine bag, filled it up with meat, and took the elevator to La Cross's suite. Trying not to laugh too loudly, they hung it on her doorknob.

"Trust me," one of the assistants gasped to Babette as they ran down the fire exit stairs back to their own rooms: "Paris was never this much fun."

Babette wasn't sleeping well. Too much booze, and too much steak. When she awoke around two to pee, she couldn't remember if they had really hung a bag of meat on Camille's door or if she had only dreamed it—but she did manage to remember that she hadn't prepared a single question for Rosa.

By nine she was showered, dressed, and filled with the same nervous energy that had plagued her for weeks about this piece. It turned out that Bloomingdale's was in a mall almost across the street from the Drake. As she made her way up the escalators, she noted an elevator marked "Four Seasons Hotel." She decided to get a table in its coffee shop and write down some questions for Rosa.

Once inside the Four Seasons, however, she was dismayed to discover that there was no coffee shop. There was a lounge, though, a concierge said, if she didn't want to sit in the dining room. She should just walk straight back through the lobby, past the gift shop.

She followed his directions and the soft plush carpeting and lavish floral arrangements combined to calm her down. She saw the gift shop and stopped to look inside. Montrose Merriweather had just sent her a gorgeous accordion-pleated Hermès scarf from Paris, and she figured it might be fun to send him a souvenir from Chicago.

She picked out a paperweight with a miniature Sears Tower inside and snow that swirled when you shook it. She paid the outrageous twenty-two dollars to the woman at the cash register and started out.

Oh. She stopped. There, toward the end of the lobby where she had been headed for coffee, stood Ponce Morris.

Could it be? Or was she still shamefully hungover?

No, it was Ponce, all right, in tan corduroy pants and a beige cashmere sweater, folding a newspaper under her arm. Excited—maybe they'd get their drink together after all—Babette started toward her to say hello, but what she saw next froze her in place. Neil Grossman stepped out from behind Ponce, pulling on his suit jacket. The two of them walked a few steps, then he leaned over and whispered something in her ear, which made her laugh. She turned her face up, and he kissed her, full on the mouth. He pulled her toward him with an ease that spoke not of new love but of something warm and familiar.

Babette stumbled back into the gift shop—there was no

place else to go without being seen — and kept her head down, digging inside her purse. She saw them stop near a bank of elevators where Neil kissed Ponce again. Then he kept on going, back out the way Babette came in. Ponce disappeared.

Babette bought a roll of Life Savers so that the woman behind the counter wouldn't think she was completely insane, then left the gift shop and headed toward the elevators. A security guard approached.

"Oh, I'm sorry, am I lost?" she asked.

The guard smiled. "Not if you're a guest here. But if you're not, these elevators aren't for you."

"No, I'm not." She walked out into the lobby past the concierge, pulled her cell phone from her bag, and called information.

"Thank you for calling the Four Seasons, how may I direct your call?"

"Ponce Morris, please."

A moment passed. "Is this a guest, ma'am?"

"Yes."

"I'm sorry, we don't have anyone registered by that name."

"Oh. Well, how about Dr. Neil Grossman?"

"Hold the line, please."

After four rings, the call went to voicemail. No answer.

Babette looked at her watch: 9:50. Damn!

She took the elevator to the wrong floor and had to reenter the mall from the street. Well, so much for Thom as a source, she thought, taking the escalator steps two at a time. Chad may have seen Ponce in Neil Grossman's office at all hours of the day and night, but she certainly wasn't there about a baby!

She arrived at Carmen's personal appearance right on time. She sat through a demonstration of the clothes and how to wear them, what tops went best with what bottoms. Babette knew she should be taking notes, but she couldn't concentrate. When everyone started to applaud, Babette snapped to, got up, and congratulated Carmen, who led her to a short, round woman who was wiping her eyes.

"Mama, this is the writer from *Boothby's Review,*" Carmen said.

"Ah, hello," her mother said.

"You must be so proud of your daughter," Babette said, as Rosa continued to dab at her tears. She nodded and let loose a string of Spanish. Babette looked to Carmen, who had already been pulled away by her admirers.

Another woman smiled at Babette. "I Rosa sister," she said. "Carmen aunt."

"Oh, hello," she said gratefully. "What's your name?"

"Isabella."

"Very nice to meet you. Uh, I have some questions?"

Fifteen minutes later, Babette had five paragraphs of boilerplate. This Isabella could work for the FBI, Babette thought. Then again, maybe Rachel had just made her paranoid. But when she looked at her notes, she saw that any question about the boat ride, or getting from Miami to Chicago, or how the rest of the family supported itself, was when the English failed. Proud of Carmen? Loud and clear. Historical details? All vague. Fucking Rachel.

Babette glanced at her watch. She'd be late to the studio. She ran out to the street entrance of the Four Seasons, eyes peeled for Ponce, who was nowhere in sight, and gave the doorman two dollars to get her a cab. She made it to the studio by 11:29. Camille, thankfully, was with the photographer.

Had she mentioned the meat, Babette asked her pals as soon as she arrived. Not a word, they assured her. She probably devoured it for breakfast.

When the crew broke for lunch, Babette offered to stay and work the phones. She settled herself behind the reception desk, trying to absorb what she had seen that morning. She ate a turkey sandwich and considered her options. All this time she had thought that the most important thing worth having in New York was access—to power, money, fame. What she hadn't realized until this morning was that you could have something even more valuable: information.

Especially when it was someone else's secret.

Chapter Six

It was nearing seven as Babette hurried from the subway to Robin's office, a studio apartment in the building where he lived with Shawsie. The Brodys' home and Robin's office were separated by at least ten floors, so Babette was reasonably sure she wouldn't run into her. She certainly never had the few times she and Robin had crashed there late at night.

Babette entered the lobby and ignored the doorman's wink. "Miss Steele is here," he announced on the house phone, and she turned her back on him while waiting for the elevator. She took off her gloves and tried rubbing some warmth back into her hands. Being this nervous didn't help matters. She had stuck to her resolution to stop seeing Robin for well over a month now, and she felt pretty good about it. But how could she know she would find herself in a situation like this?

"Hey." He opened the door and gave a halfhearted wave to welcome her in.

"Hey." She unwound her scarf and stuffed her gloves into

her coat pockets. She took her coat off, but when he didn't offer to hang it, she dropped it on a chair.

"Drink?" Robin asked, gesturing toward a few bottles of liquor grouped on an end table.

"Yeah, I'll have a cosmo."

"Shit, Babette, I don't have that kind of stuff here. What's in a cosmo? Vodka? You want that?"

"Never mind," she said, exasperated. "Can you manage a beer?"

He retrieved a bottle of Heineken from the refrigerator and gave it to her without a glass. She sat on the couch and watched him pour a scotch before he took the easy chair opposite her, never meeting her eye. When she phoned him the day before, she'd said they needed to talk, that it was urgent and he had to see her in private, immediately. No bars or restaurants. He agreed, feeling trapped and slightly nauseated. He knew what was coming next: He hadn't called, he hadn't bought her a Christmas present, she deserved to be treated better, blah blah. But what she didn't know was that he had been doing some thinking of his own.

"Listen," he began, reaching for his cigarettes. "I'm glad you called. I was just going to call you. Because here's the thing. This is really, really hard for me to say, but I've given it a lot of thought, and I think we have to stop seeing each other."

Babette held her beer and tried not to look surprised. "Go on," she said.

"I've been doing a lot of thinking, with the new year and everything. I know resolutions are bullshit, they never work, but in my life now, something has got to change. This baby thing has been killing me—and Shawsie. And I'm convinced that if I change, if I try to, you know, stay home more nights, spend some more time with Shawsie, maybe things'll work out better. I mean, I know it sounds crazy, but I almost feel like God's been punishing me."

She raised her eyebrows.

"No, I don't mean that about you! You are the furthest thing from a punishment a guy can have. You're gorgeous and sexy and smart—well, you know all that. It's not you, it's me. My behavior. It's rotten, really. I'm a married man, and I need to try to do better at that." He looked like he actually might cry. "Can you understand that at all?"

Babette stared at the floor for a long time. "I guess I can," she said finally. "I mean, it's hard to hear. But I get how you must feel. I think it's great you want to try and make your marriage work. It's the right thing to do. Shawsie's a great girl."

He nodded eagerly. "She is. And jeez, Babette, so are you. Thanks so much for understanding." He was so relieved, so happy, he looked like a kid at his own birthday party.

She took a sip of beer and put the bottle on the table. "Um, I'm sure you know all about this, since Shawsie's such good friends with Ponce, but I need you to tell me something, just for myself."

"Sure," he said brightly. "What?"

"How long has Ponce been fucking Neil Grossman?"

"*What?*"

She could see that he didn't know a thing about it.

"Are you insane? Neil Grossman is the most happily married man in America!"

As he got up to pour himself another drink, she began to tell him what she'd seen in Chicago. He poured too much— because his hand was unsteady or because he needed a triple, she couldn't tell.

"No shit," he said, heading back to his chair. "Wow."

Babette shrugged. "I guess Shawsie has some secrets of her own."

"She has no idea about this," Robin protested hotly, reaching for another cigarette.

"How do you know?"

He didn't answer. He just knew, that's all. Shawsie told him everything, always had. She didn't keep secrets from him. He felt his heart pinch. He was the one who did that.

"I've told you that I'm uncomfortable talking about Shawsie, and that hasn't changed," he said. "Leave her out of this." He smoked. "And by the way, why are you telling this to me?"

Babette finished her beer and held up the bottle. He went to the refrigerator and brought her another.

"Because I need your advice," she said. "From the minute I met Ponce at Jacqueline Posner's party, I was dying to get to know her better. I asked Shawsie to arrange a drink for the three of us, and she gave me some lame excuse about Ponce's court schedule so I knew Ponce must have said, 'Forget it, it's not worth my time.' Then I was thinking I might try to write a profile about her and get to spend time with her that way.

"But I've come to realize that Ponce Morris has decided she has enough friends in her life and I'm not going to be one of them," Babette went on. "I've had to make my peace with that. It was naïve of me to expect a total stranger to let me into her life just because I wanted her to. Ponce Morris doesn't owe me anything. And I don't owe her anything, either." She drained her second beer.

"What I saw in Chicago is news. No one knows this affair is happening except me—no one in the media, that is. In that respect, Ponce has actually given me something even better than her time. Because the one thing I know about New York publishing is that if you print a scoop like this, you are launched. So I've decided that I want to go back to my original idea of writing a piece about Ponce, but use her affair as the news peg. Do you think it's something Topher would run?"

Robin clutched his head in his hands and tried to keep up. "Do I think Topher is going to run a piece smearing Shawsie's best friend? No, I don't. Jesus, Babette."

He tried to focus. Seriously, there was no way Shawsie knew about this. Robin knew how hard she took his cheating, and he knew that she kept her feelings about it pretty close to the vest. He also knew that was easy to do with a friend like Ponce, who never forced an issue, ever.

But for Ponce not to tell Shawsie that she was cheating, too? With the most virtuously married doctor in New York? What a hypocrite. Shawsie would be furious. This idea emboldened him. Fuck Ponce! That morally superior cunt, always looking down on him because her great friend could have done so much better. *He* was a cheat? Well, what about her? What about Grossman? That guy was doing what comes naturally all over the fucking place. What a racket he had going!

"You know, Babette, I think the real story here is Grossman."

"What do you mean?"

"The guy is the top fertility doctor in the country right now, with three kids and this great marriage to a wife who's like the Jewish Mother Teresa with a medical degree, and he's sneaking around with this rich, spoiled divorcée who famously never even *wanted* children. He's the scoop you're looking for. Scandal and ambivalence. It's *Peyton Place* for Freudians."

"You think so?" Babette looked hopeful. "So if Topher wouldn't do it, then who?"

"*Manhattan* magazine, hands down. You need a weekly that'll get it done fast and play it up big. It's an incredible scandal."

Robin was starting to like this idea. All those years of Shawsie thinking Ponce was so much more reliable, so much more trustworthy, than he was, and Ponce never told her this? And how stupid could Ponce and Neil be, necking in a hotel lobby where anyone could see them? Hell, maybe Grossman even deserved to be exposed now. No, it wasn't exactly Neil's fault that Robin had to keep going in there to come into a cup, but the only solace the guy ever had to offer was this continual horseshit about the great strides of science. Well, fuck science. Neil was in for some old-fashioned human drama. Just like he and Shawsie had. All the fucking time.

"Well, if I write it," Babette said, "I want you to help me. You're a great writer. And I've never written a long piece before."

Robin felt queasy. "Listen, any editor at *Manhattan* magazine can take a reporter's notebook and turn it into a piece overnight if you've got the stuff. You don't need me."

"Of course I do!"

He lit another cigarette. "I'm the husband of Ponce Morris's best friend. Why would I get involved in this?"

Babette's eyes filled with tears. "Because you just told me you don't want to see me anymore so you can be a better husband. So not only are you dumping me completely out of the blue, but you're saying you won't even help me with my work? With something you're so good at? Jesus, Robin, I didn't think you were that mean. I thought we had some good times together, and I hoped we could stay friends. I thought I could count on you for at least some things." The tears spilled over.

"Oh, hey, no! Don't cry about it." He got up to search for a tissue and found only a cocktail napkin. "I'll definitely look at it, okay? Really. Jeez." He sat back down. He should have realized how upset she'd be about his breaking it off. That was stupid of him. Okay, so he would look at the piece, move around some commas. What would it cost him?

"Listen," he said authoritatively. "Here's my advice. Start by making a list of the people who know Ponce and Neil, and follow the trail back to whenever their relationship began. I mean, from how you describe them, this has been going on for years. So if they've kept it a secret this long, there's no huge rush on your end, you know? You can do it smartly. The only thing, though, is that you have to be right. I mean, I didn't see this kiss. You're sure it wasn't just 'Bye, pal, nice to see you in a city not New York, have a great day'?"

"No, it wasn't like that at all. It was romantic. Intimate."

"Fine. So first you make sure your facts line up, from a variety of sources. That's where you take your time, make sure to get it right. Because the piece won't make the splash you want if it's only your word against theirs. You have to have a foundation of facts. Right?"

"Sure. But you know how you said before that the scoop is Grossman? That may be, in terms of the gossip factor, but I also think that learning anything about Ponce is news because for all the pictures that have been taken of her through the years, she's never really been interviewed—not alone at least. I mean, Lee spoke to people all the time, and she was in some of those pieces. But I think she's a scoop, too. Annabelle's known her forever and says just terrible things about her. How dumb she was for leaving Lee in the first place, and then being a lawyer and never fighting for the money that was rightfully hers. How if she was really a good lawyer she'd still be at Corning but no one there wanted her. How except for her little handful of friends, she's such a bitch to other women and never goes to lunch or helps anyone with their charities."

"Well, I'm not sure that's a tragedy," Robin began, then

caught sight of the grim expression on Babette's face. "Hey, you know what? I think you're right. She's a controversial figure in New York because she doesn't play the game. And people who are rich enough to play the game and don't are about as entertaining a target as you can find. So go get her. By all means."

Babette smiled. "Okay."

"Okay." He smiled, too.

She glanced at her watch. "I guess I'd better go. 'Cause you're spending more time at home these nights, right?"

"Right." He stood and started toward the door. She got her coat and came up behind him.

"Bye, bunny." She grabbed playfully at his ass. "I'll miss you."

"Oh, hey—"

He reached for her, but she evaded his grasp. "Now, now," she said. "We need to think of Mrs. Brody, don't we?"

She stood in the doorway to his office, big and blond. In this light, he would swear she wasn't wearing a bra. He reached out to feel for himself, and she grabbed his hand and sucked his middle finger. He groaned and reached for her with his other hand, but she pulled his finger out of her mouth and backed out of his reach.

"'Night, Robin," she said, starting down the hallway. "Thanks for being my friend."

Chapter Seven

At her desk, Shawsie turned her chair away from the floor-to-ceiling window that gave her a full view of her two assistants and tried to hold her temper. One of them had buzzed her smack in the middle of her conversation with the manager of the Olsen twins, whom she had been trying to nail down all week. She continued pitching her cover story, and the buzzer sounded again.

She spun in her chair, red-faced even as she kept her tone measured, and was shocked to see both assistants standing outside, motioning her frantically to pick up the other line. Finally one of the girls scrawled something on a slip of paper, opened the door, and put it on the desk in front of her.

"Dr. Grossman!" it read.

Shawsie looked up, astonished. He never called her himself. It was always one of the nurses.

"I'm terribly sorry," she said to the Olsens' manager. "There's an urgent medical call I have to take. May I phone you back?"

She didn't wait for an answer.

She punched the button as the assistant closed the door behind her. "Neil? Is there something wrong?"

"No, not at all. I'm just calling to—"

"Because I meant what I said last time. I'm not adopting. I've really thought about it and—"

"Shawsie, that's fine. You don't have to adopt."

"That's good, because I won't. And I don't want you putting any thoughts in Robin's head about that either. He's—"

"Shawsie, stop! Did you hear what I said?"

"Yes, of course I heard. Wait a second."

She was hyperventilating. She put one hand down on the desk, took a deep breath, and forced herself to hold it for five seconds before exhaling. "Okay," she said. "I don't have to adopt. Why not?"

"Because your numbers have doubled right on schedule. By Thanksgiving, you're going to have something to be truly thankful for."

She gasped. "Are you sure?"

She heard the smile in his voice. "I'm sure. And because you're in shock right now, I want to say this loud and clear: You are pregnant. Write it down if you think you can't remember."

"What? Are you joking?"

"I'm not. Look how you just reacted. After people try for so long and fail, they protect themselves against hearing bad news. Then they can't hear good news either. I've told women they were pregnant, and they call back the next day as if we've never spoken. They won't let themselves hear me, because they're afraid it won't be true."

Shawsie wiped her tears with the heels of her hands. "Thank you," she said, trying not to break down entirely. "Thank you so much."

Neil laughed. "Are you kidding? This is the best part of my job, when I can do it. As I've told you and Robin, the science has made great strides, but we have a long way to go. There are still too many patients who don't get lucky."

"I know," she said, searching her bag for a tissue. That had been the fear that had jolted her awake every night for the last two years.

"I understand the toll this process can take on a marriage," Neil said. "It's a real accomplishment that you stuck with it so long and refused to quit. You can both be proud of that."

After he hung up, Shawsie held the phone in her hand. She needed time to pull herself together, and her assistants would pounce the moment she seemed to be free.

She looked at her watch. Robin had mentioned that morning what a packed night he had in store: covering a wine tasting for *Him*, grabbing dinner with his editor there to talk about future stories, then ending up at the Acorn for a late party celebrating some hip-hop star Shawsie had never heard of.

"You could always meet me there," Robin had said genially.

Shawsie tried to keep the irritation out of her voice. "Thanks, but Neil keeps saying I need to take it easy, so I probably shouldn't have a late night. Right?"

"Right," he answered with tense resignation. She had been "taking it easy" to no avail for so long neither of them knew what it meant anymore.

Shawsie dialed Robin's cell, which went directly to voice-mail. "Call me, honey, it's really, really important," she said, feeling the tears start again. Why hadn't she had the presence of mind to ask him where the tasting was, or the dinner? She knew the answer to that: She had stopped asking those questions long ago because Robin didn't want her to know the answers. Because it was never the "where" that was the problem. It was the "with whom."

This was absurd, she thought. Two years. Two years they had worked on this together! How could she not reach him?

She did what she usually did in this sort of situation. She dialed Ponce.

"Hello?" Her friend's tone was slightly querulous. That meant she was fighting with her hair, Shawsie knew, before leaving the apartment.

"Hello, there," she said. "Where are you off to?"

"Well, if you can believe it, I'm taking Gus and Rachel to Sir's tonight. At least I am if I can get my damn hair to find a position and stick with it."

Shawsie felt a stab of disappointment. She had so hoped Ponce would say, "I'm staying right here in bed watching the game, with a pizza on the way. Want to join me?"

"Sir's is an odd choice for those two, isn't it?" Shawsie asked, thinking of that restaurant's rich, staid, somewhat older social crowd.

"It is indeed, but Rachel insisted," Ponce said. "Neither she nor Gus have ever been there, and Rachel can't believe the entire décor is oil paintings of the owner's springer spaniel. She refuses to go anywhere else until she sees it. I'll tell you"—she paused, and Shawsie heard a whoosh of hairspray—"it must be awful to be a writer. To be so curious about everything. I think I would find it exhausting."

"I know what you mean." Even as she said it, Shawsie heard how false that statement rang. If she had been a little more curious through the years, she might have a better sense now of how to locate her own husband. But the truth was, whenever she had a question about where he was or whom he was with or—most plainly and dangerously—why he wasn't with her, she just put her head down and worked harder. She had never faced the reason why, but she forced herself to now. During their teenage years, she and Skip used to mock their mother, calling her "Helen Keller Live and In Person," because when it came to never seeing or hearing anything she didn't want to deal with, she was the expert. Well, Shawsie's famous efficiency aside, she had turned out exactly the same. Which was a hell of a revelation to digest minutes after discovering she was becoming a mother herself.

"Shawsie? Are you there?"

"Oh, sorry, Ponce. I've got a lot on my mind."

"Is something wrong?"

Shawsie squeezed her eyes shut and fought against telling her the truth. This was the moment she and Robin had been waiting for, after all. From now on, things would be different. The baby that was going to make them a family and make Robin stay home at night was really on the way. She kept imagining the look on Robin's face when she told him, his joy and relief. All the strain of the waiting and the failure, falling away. Things would change now. Neil said so himself. They were lucky.

"Everything's fine. I just can't find Robin at the moment, that's all." She struggled to keep her voice steady, an effort that was not lost on Ponce.

"Well, Mary Elizabeth, if you would like some dinner, why don't you join us? A little chicken hash might do you good." Sir's was the closest thing the Upper East Side had to a country club dining room, and as Shawsie had grown up eating at the club her parents belonged to, Ponce knew it was the kind of food she liked. Granted, the menu was the only thing comforting about Sir's. That restaurant was work. The same people who were sought after for dinner parties like the one Jacqueline Posner had thrown all clamored for the chance to see and be seen in neckties and pearls, eating corn fritters and deviled eggs with knives and forks in the dim glow of the dog's gilt frames.

"No, Poncie, that's okay. I'm just not up for the scene tonight. I think I'll go home and get into bed with a good book."

"Well, I envy you," Ponce said. "'Night."

After Ponce hung up, she wondered if she should call back. She knew that Shawsie regularly hit bad patches with Robin and would circle around them, seeming to weigh whether or not to break down and reveal her unhappiness. But she never did, and Ponce never forced her. Her own low opinion of Robin aside, Ponce knew it was impossible to see into the corners of someone else's marriage. All she could see from the outside was Shawsie's responsibility for such an untenable arrangement. She should have either left him or given him an ultimatum ages ago, and because she hadn't Ponce felt justified in slipping him some zingers of her own. That was wrong. In the past few months in particular, she had grown aware of Robin's increased sensitivity to the deadly aim of her potshots. So she'd decided to leave Shawsie's marriage to Shawsie and keep her mouth shut. And had.

Ponce was still congratulating herself on her judiciousness when she walked into Sir's and was in such a reverie as she sat down that she didn't notice the person waving at her from across the small back room.

"Jacqueline!" Ponce exclaimed, pushing out from the banquette of her corner table. The two women kissed, and Jacqueline gestured toward her empty table of four. "Sit with me a minute," she urged, signaling the waiter to bring Ponce a drink.

"Isn't it funny," Jacqueline said. "After all these years, you and I are still the first ones anywhere. Our husbands trained us well!"

"They did, indeed. Now tell me, how *are* you?"

Jacqueline chattered animatedly: She had no idea it would be this easy, really. She did her work, she saw her friends, her maisonette was coming along right on schedule, she'd almost certainly move in by Memorial Day—just in time to leave for Southampton, if she could. It depended, of course, on what Mike would do; that house was still his. But the best news was that she didn't miss him half as much as she'd thought she would. What an incredible relief, not to follow the market anymore!

Ponce thought it best not to mention the very beautiful Norwegian investment banker Mike had been dating, with whom he was reportedly smitten. "Has M moved in yet?" Ponce asked.

Jacqueline shook her head. "No, and I can't imagine what it's about. The marble in those bathrooms is Carrara, it's gorgeous, and it was custom-cut less than ten years ago. Replacing it is a spectacular waste of money and time. I think he's stalling. I think New York appeals to him in principle, but he doesn't want to leave what he has. And why should he? The man essentially lives in Tara, just with flat-screen TVs and central air-conditioning. I can see that he'd want a place to stay here on business. But to make a real home? Those Southern boys never come north for long."

"You mean, Babette Steele isn't enough of a reason?" Ponce asked, with a laugh.

Jacqueline didn't laugh with her. "You know they've been seeing each other, right?"

Ponce was surprised. "I knew no such thing. You just said he was avoiding New York."

"Avoiding living here. He's visited a few times since my party, and he's seen her during each trip. He told me so himself when I ran into them at the Four Seasons a few weeks ago. He seemed quite taken with her, actually. She was eating a chocolate soufflé and was all bubbly and excited about her job at *Boothby's*. She said she was going to call me about a piece she's writing about you."

"*Me?* She's writing a piece about me?"

Jacqueline shrugged. "That's what she said. I told her she must be planning on writing fiction, because in all the years I've known you, you've never given an interview to anyone. But she said you live such a glamorous New York life, and between that and your work for the city, you're a great story. I mean, obviously, the minute she calls me, I'll tell her I need your permission before I say a word."

"Of course. Though wouldn't it make sense to contact the subject first?"

Jacqueline squeezed her friend's arm. "I think you're supposed to feel flattered by this. Or at least amused. I mean, she's a kid. Who's obviously impressed by you."

"Mrs. Morris? Your guests have arrived." The maître d' stood by her side.

Ponce stood. "Well, I suppose I am more fascinating than I ever imagined," she said lightly.

The two women leaned toward each other in the representation of a kiss before Ponce walked back to her table. As the waiter pulled it out to let her onto the banquette, Gus and Rachel waved across the room to Jacqueline.

"You know, I thought you were exaggerating about this place," Rachel said, taking her seat. "I find it rather amazing that you weren't."

"You mean about the dogs? Well, if you ask me, they beat portraits of ancestors any day."

"I agree. And the guy actually calls the dog 'Sir'?"

"He actually does. And I can tell you that the twin burgers are his favorite thing on the menu."

"Well, I can tell you that those burgers wouldn't fill a cavity of mine." Rachel leaned over her menu, studying it intently. "Caviar, too! I guess comfort comes in all shapes and sizes."

"Gus, tell me the lead on the news tonight," Ponce said. "I left home early." Gus started talking, and Ponce watched him. He had always been a handsome man and still was; his liquid brown eyes were slightly hooded, which in his youth had given him a romantic aspect. These days, it could make him look tired. With his steel-gray hair and dark mustache he resembled Omar Sharif, a comparison Rachel made often and Gus, amused protestations aside, agreed with wholeheartedly.

They were deep into a discussion about the Iraq war and the disgraceful way—according to Ponce—the networks were covering it when Gus interjected, "You know, Walter Gluckman, television news legend, is actually giving a lunchtime speech to all the young staffers next week about Vietnam and what it used to mean to cover a war on television—like, at the minimum, asking tough questions. But of course the real purpose of the lunch is for him to criticize me in front of an audience. He wants everyone to know that if he's asked to even consider retiring and I take over his show, he will not settle for being the proverbial thorn in my side but will insist on being the literal knife in my back."

Gus smiled. "We've actually had two of these lunches in the past six months or so," he went on, "and Walter showed up to the last one with Annabelle as his cheering section. So, it occurs to me, Poncie, that with the precedence of an outsider attending, I could tell him you've just dropped by to say hello and that since you and he are such old, dear friends, I've insisted you come to lunch. I mean, it won't stop him. He's completely unhinged. But I could use the moral support."

Ponce was thrilled. "I would love to," she said. "That is a definite reason to get out of bed."

Gus turned to Rachel, suddenly concerned. "Is that something you want to go to, honey?" he asked.

Rachel took off her glasses and closed the menu. "Fuck Walter Gluckman," she said. "I'm having the hanger steak."

Ponce laughed. "Well, I'm certainly glad that's settled!"

Rachel looked around the room. The women all wore black with pearls—South Sea pearls, large as marbles—roped around their necks, and the men's navy blazers were identical. "I must say, I applaud the owner's appreciation for metaphor," she said. "Talk about obedience."

Once the caviar appetizer Ponce ordered for the table had been devoured and discussion of the war had waned, Rachel said to Ponce, "We haven't heard a thing about you tonight."

Ponce waved her hand. "Nothing to tell, really. Though I must say, I did have the strangest conversation with Jacqueline before you all got here." She recounted the story as she glanced at Jacqueline's table. She wasn't sure who her companions were, but as one woman spoke intently Ponce watched Jacqueline listen sympathetically, eyebrows straining toward each other with concern. In vain, it turned out. The Botox held them firmly in place.

"Jacqueline thinks I should be flattered by this," Ponce added. "She thinks that Babette's a kid who idolizes me and I should just take the compliment."

"Babette talked to me, too, about doing a story on you," Rachel said. "I told her good luck, 'cause you don't do interviews."

"What is this insistent fascination she has?" Ponce asked. "There's something creepy about it."

"I agree," Gus said. "And you never know with people like that. The flip side of adoration can be revenge."

His wife kicked him under the table when she saw worry flash on Ponce's face. "That's ridiculous," Rachel said. "Judging from the conversation I had with her, she's gaga about you. And don't forget, she's an assistant with two three-hundred-word pieces to her name. Well, three pieces now, I guess. She went to Chicago last month to do what'll probably end up a sidebar on some Cuban designer."

Ponce felt her stomach drop. "She was in Chicago?" she asked, forcing her voice not to escalate. "When, exactly?"

Rachel shrugged. "Who knows? It was for the fashion department. I mean, Chicago in February, what an event. Also, as I believe I pointed out at your party, she can't write. And even though I've had caviar tonight too"—she turned to Gus and kissed him—"I'm still not sufficiently transported to give her a free pass. Three hundred words seems to be her limit. She may want to write a piece on you. But that doesn't mean she can."

The waiter put the entrées on the table.

Ponce picked up her knife and fork. "I'm sure you're right," she said pleasantly. Rachel oohed and aahed over her food, Gus talked again about Iraq, and Ponce cut her burgers into ever tinier cubes. She tried retracing every step she had taken during those two days in Chicago with Neil. Where had she been that was public? The airport. The hotel dining room. She had seen no one. She chewed and swallowed, chewed and swallowed. That may be, she thought. But she couldn't help but think that someone may very well have seen her.

. . .

Babette walked into Bemelmans Bar at the Carlyle, and M waved from a corner booth. Before she even sat down, a waiter was tableside.

"I'll have a cosmo," she said, vaulting herself along the seat cushion as M held his martini protectively aloft.

Once she was settled, M looked out around the dark, half-empty room and tapped an unlit mentholated Benson & Hedges 100 on the table in a frustrated staccato. "Damnedest law I've ever heard of," he growled. "That pint-size mayor of yours should spend a little time in tobacco country, grow some shoulders. Then he might know what it means to need a smoke."

"Oh! I completely agree!" Babette felt it best not to mention that courtesy of the anchorman she'd dated, she had partied quite hearty with that pint-size mayor, and even though he didn't smoke, he could hold more alcohol than most men twice his size. And be at his desk by seven a.m.

"I'm so glad we could at least have a drink tonight," she trilled. M had come to town for one night only to attend a dinner that seemed to involve a number of Japanese bankers at a private club. He was leaving the next morning for Tokyo.

"You know," she went on, "one day, I'd love for you to explain your business to me. I'm not sure I understand it."

M's smile bordered on a smirk. "I'm not sure you want to, sugar. I think it best to focus on its just rewards."

Babette had encountered this kind of reaction from M before. While he was usually deeply charming, he sometimes showed a bitter condescension to her questions about his business—or anyone else's, for that matter. He seemed to consider curiosity about finances from a woman unseemly. Babette knew to let it pass, and she turned her head toward the pianist instead, applauding politely at the end of his number.

The waiter set down her drink as well as a fresh martini for M, who took a long, satisfied sip. "Tell me what's on your calendar this evening," he said. One drink down, he seemed more relaxed.

She gave him a high-wattage smile and leaned in, displaying some scant cleavage via a push-up bra. "Well, I'm working, too," she said cheerfully. "I've started my reporting on the Ponce Morris profile, and I'm meeting with one of my editors about it."

He tapped his cigarette again. "Oh? Then *Boothby's* is publishing it after all?"

"No, they're not." Her very full drink had spilled over its sides, and she wiped her fingers on a cocktail napkin. "This is a freelance editor, actually. Someone who agreed to help me structure it, 'cause you know I've never written a long piece before."

"Well, I hope Mrs. Morris is being generous with her time."

"Oh, I haven't spoken to her yet," Babette said, and she was chagrined to see M's face fall.

"What kind of profile is that?" M was no neophyte in this regard. He'd been on the covers of *Forbes* and *BusinessWeek* himself.

"It's the kind where you do your reporting first so you can ask your subject everything you found out about her later."

M looked down at the smooth white skin on Babette's inner arms, like a child's, and atop the almost preteen swell of her small breasts. He felt himself getting an erection and stopped listening to the long-winded explanation of her reporting methods.

"What time is your meeting?" he asked, cutting her off midsentence.

"Seven-thirty."

He slid quickly out of the booth, miming a check sign to the waiter, then pointed upstairs so that it would be charged to his room.

"I'll have my driver drop you," he said to Babette, grabbing one of her arms, hard, from the inside, and guiding her quickly out the door.

Robin walked out of the private dining room at Daniel and into the bar, where he snagged a table for two and congratulated himself on not falling into it headfirst. It was not quite eight o'clock, and he was supposed to have met Babette at seven-thirty, but he had been only midway through the Bandols by then and couldn't very well pick up and go. Aside from a woman with red lipstick laughing loudly at something the bartender had just said, the bar was empty. The parade of prosperous-looking men in their charcoal suits and women in their habitual black continued into the dining room without stopping in the bar. Could she possibly have stood him up? Too much to hope for.

When he saw her coming from the direction of the ladies' room, he ordered two glasses of champagne. At the table, as she leaned toward him, flushed and apologetic, to deliver a chaste kiss on the cheek, he smelled her toothpaste—and someone else's aftershave.

"Busy day?" he asked slyly as she took the chair opposite the banquette on which he sprawled.

"Half in the bag?" she parried. She reached into her purse for a mirror and put on more lipstick. She hadn't quite recovered from her cocktail hour with M. It wasn't the sex that had thrown her, it was his distance during the drink. Did he think she wasn't up to writing this piece? That she was just a secretary pretending to know what she was doing? When she had explained her reporting process, he hadn't seemed the least bit interested. Then again, he *was* on his way to close this enormous deal with the Japanese, or at least the first part of it, so maybe he wasn't at his best. He hadn't showered her with his usual barrage of compliments, and she worried that he was growing tired of her. That just couldn't be, she thought, picking up the flute of champagne and downing half of it. She needed more time.

"Well, cheers to you, too," Robin said sourly, holding up his full glass.

"Oh, sorry. What's the occasion, by the way?"

He shrugged. "I don't know. Glad to see you?"

She picked up a slip of paper from the table. "Yeah, ecstatic."

He grabbed it out of her hand. "Like you wouldn't do the same?" he asked, jamming the voucher for free champagne into his pocket. The French importers who had hosted the wine tasting had encouraged the attendees to stop into the bar and try it.

She reached into her bag while he signaled a waiter. "Could we get a bottle, please?" he asked, holding up his glass. When he turned back a manila folder was open on the table in front of him.

"It's a rough draft of my piece on Ponce." It was hard for Babette to keep the pride out of her voice.

Robin ran his hand through his already tilted hair. She had a *draft*? For chrissakes, he'd been trying to write one measly chapter for the last three years. It had been all of a month since she'd come to see him at his office.

He put on his glasses. "'The Spare Wife,'" he read out loud, stopping to look up. "Oh, Rachel's line. No honor among thieves, eh?"

"I'm not a thief," Babette protested hotly. "I told her I was going to use it when I wrote a piece about Ponce, and she acted like she couldn't care less."

He picked up the sheaf of papers and felt their weight. Shit. Shawsie had left him three messages on his cell, he had discovered while waiting for Babette. She sounded weepy and shrill, and Robin just knew it was going to be another failed IVF. He also knew that the right thing to do was to skip the Acorn and spend the rest of the night at home comforting her. The waiter arrived then with the bottle and fresh glasses, and Robin felt Babette's eyes on him like lasers. He would do this first.

Once the champagne was poured, Robin settled back to read. Babette sipped her drink and watched him expectantly. She had gotten some really good stuff, she thought, which had been especially difficult since she couldn't contact anyone too close to Ponce. That had eliminated Shawsie, Neil, Rachel, and Gus. Her plan instead, as Robin had suggested, was to get as much information as she could, then present it all to Ponce for her reaction. That way, he said, if Ponce decided not to cooperate, she could do the story anyway, because all her reporting would be in place. It made sense. She'd decided against calling Jacqueline Posner. Annabelle Gluckman said that Jacqueline and Ponce had a history of helping each other out, so Jacqueline would never say anything Ponce hadn't approved.

Of course, Annabelle had given Babette lots of juicy stuff, all off the record: dishy details on Ponce's parties—flowers, clothes, music, celebrities. And she had a great story about Ponce confronting Jerry Morton, Lee's business partner. It was one night right before she and Lee divorced, and everyone had had too much to drink. When it was time for dessert, Ponce instructed all the women to move their seats to switch partners and refresh the conversation. Well, as the story went, Ponce ended up with Jerry Morton, who made some sort of pass at her and put his hand probably on her thigh, though the crotch was the detail in the story, and Ponce had taken her dessert fork and speared it into the back of his hand.

"You can go now," she'd told him. "You're done." All the women, who loathed Jerry Morton because he had been grabbing at their crotches for years, had rallied round, and the next day, Annabelle said, Ponce received countless sets of dessert forks from Tiffany and Cartier along with thank-you notes for a night well spent.

Babette had also interviewed the maid of a friend of Annabelle's who once worked for Ponce. Granted, Babette didn't get much out of her—they met in a coffee shop on Third Avenue, where the woman cried most of the time, begging her not to call the INS—but she did recognize Dr. Grossman from the photo Babette showed her. He used to come every Wednesday evening to give Mrs. Morris B-12 shots, she said. Babette loved that.

But her best decision, she thought, had been calling in a private investigator. She knew better than anyone that her reporting skills weren't strong enough to do this on her own, especially not fast and in secret. Within weeks, she had pictures of Grossman entering Ponce's apartment building wearing a jacket and tie, then leaving it disheveled, hours later. Just that day, the PI had FedExed Babette some of Grossman's credit-card records, though Babette had been too nervous to examine them in the office. Meanwhile, her own credit card was in danger of getting maxed out paying this guy. But once she sold the piece, she knew she'd be set. Topher might even promote her to contributor, just to ensure that the next great piece she wrote would be for *Boothby's*.

The one gamble she had taken with an interview that

ended up working perfectly was Sari Grossman. Babette figured that even if Sari told her husband and he told Ponce, it wouldn't matter, because Babette had saved Sari for last. Ponce would either speak to her then or not.

Babette had gone to Brooklyn on her lunch hour one day when Topher was in London, which meant that much of the staff left for lunch and never came back. She'd waited in a room filled with coughing, sneezing children for more than an hour before being let into Sari's office.

"Go ahead and sit down," Sari called, poking her head in. "I have half a hummus wrap to finish while I return some calls, but I'll be there in five minutes, okay?"

Babette was happy to be left alone. There were numerous pictures of Sari with Neil and their children, everyone smiling. There was a shot of Sari with a baby on her shoulder, looking at a fireplace in what appeared to be a construction site. She really did seem as dull and dutiful as Annabelle always said she was.

"Thanks for waiting." Sari came in and sat behind her desk. Babette began with her usual introduction, that she was writing a personality profile of Ponce, then talked specifically about what big benefactors of Neil's Ponce and Lee had been at Carnegie Hill Hospital.

"Can you tell me when you met Ponce?" Babette asked.

Sari thought a minute. "I'm not sure I remember," she said. "You know, we're not close friends of Ponce's, by any means."

"I figured that," Babette said, "but I would think there are a lot of politics involved in handling the head of the hospital's board. Not just in meetings, but at all those legendary dinner parties Ponce used to throw."

Sari waved her hand. "Oh, I hardly ever went to those," she said. "That was Neil's responsibility. I had small children at home and the clinic to run, so it was the rare occasion when I would put on eye shadow and schlep to the Upper East Side." She smiled comfortably.

"Weren't you at all curious?" Babette pressed. "I mean, both of you establishing completely different careers must have been a tough thing to do. Did it ever bother you that your husband might be spending more time with Ponce than with you?" Babette's smile was brightly inquisitive.

"Neil spends more time with everyone than me," Sari said fliply, then realized that Babette didn't get the joke. "Obviously," she continued more soberly, "without Ponce being Neil's champion and making sure that Lee's estate underwrote his research, Neil would not have had the resources to become the doctor he is today. She's given him everything he's needed."

"Is that so?" Babette asked, wide-eyed. "I hadn't realized that."

Sari nodded. "My joke with Neil is that I'd give Ponce my firstborn as payback, but since she has no interest in children she wouldn't want him!" She laughed. Babette laughed too, flooded with exhilaration.

"It really is hard to repay a debt like that," she said. "I guess Neil could do just about anything for her and it would be all right with you."

Sari glanced at her watch. "He could peel grapes and feed them to her on his knees as far as I'm concerned," she said, standing. "Ponce Morris is a kind, generous woman, and on behalf of my family I can truly say I am indebted to her."

Babette smiled at the memory, as Robin continued to focus on her pages. She sipped more champagne and congratulated herself on a job well done.

Robin kept reading and tried to keep his face impassive. The writing was way better than he had expected. Rachel Lerner's snooty bitchiness aside, the girl had talent. But the reporting was still weak. She had to at least try to get Ponce and Neil themselves into the piece. He made some notes in the margins. She also needed more background on Neil; she had almost nothing there except what she had seen in the hotel lobby. He recalled Shawsie's plaintive messages from earlier in the evening and felt his usual pang of helplessness. How many other couples out there had Neil taken on this ride? Babette could certainly find a few. Give some perspective to the legend of his great success.

Some of the material on Ponce was good, but Babette needed more. Robin tried not to let himself get too distracted at the delicious vision of all those wives who had let their husbands out to play with Ponce. The imaginary friend's not-so-imaginary affair would be all the prompting any one of them would need to drop her like typhoid and play the damn golf or watch the damn football themselves.

He closed the folder and lifted his glass.

"To you, Ms. Steele," he said. "This looks like the beginning of a brilliant career."

"Yes!" She held her arms up in victory. "Awesome!"

"Well, hold on a minute. You're not done yet."

Her expression dimmed.

"You have much more reporting to do. The whole revelation of the piece is the affair, and you've done a decent job explaining who the woman in it is. But just because Neil has a big reputation doesn't mean we don't need to know more about him as a person. You haven't done any of that. And if you're still thinking of taking this someplace like *Manhattan* magazine, then you need more on who Ponce is now. The old stuff is good, but you also need the new. So I'd say that right now it's maybe a B. If you want to make it an A, here's what you need to do."

He dictated instructions while she took notes with a pained face.

"Hey, you know what? You don't have to do any of this," he concluded. "You can bring it somewhere now and take the chance they'll reject it, and then the scoop will end up as an item on Page Six, because the gossip is the only thing anyone really cares about. But that would be a shame, because the writing is truly good. If you just slow down and spend a little more time, you could turn this into something to build a career on."

She thought of her drink earlier in the evening with M and felt a twinge of regret—and panic. What had she done wrong, exactly? She wasn't sure, but it would seem that building a career remained a damn good idea.

Robin finished his champagne and regarded the empty bottle with sorrow, thinking fleetingly of the Acorn. He knew he couldn't go there, not with Shawsie miserable at home. Still, the prospect of all those weepy hours stretching till dawn gave him pause.

"You going to the Acorn?" Babette asked, digging for her coat check.

"No. Yeah. I don't know."

She laughed. "I like a man of conviction."

He stood slowly. "I've actually got to get home."

She looked at her watch. "Nine-thirty. Wow. It really is the end of an era."

"Jeez, Babette. Give me a break."

She gave him a naughty grin. "I would if I could, bunny."

"Come on," he said. "I'll get you a taxi."

. . .

Shawsie stopped pretending that she was reading her book and put it down on her nightstand. It was nine o'clock, right when the party for the hip-hop star was scheduled to start at the Acorn, and she got out of bed and put her clothes back on. She couldn't wait one more minute to see Robin's face. The elation, the excitement! She felt like a kid on Christmas morning. So what that she couldn't reach him before? She knew where he'd be now. That was what mattered.

Inside the Acorn at nine-thirty, nothing much was happening. A few people clung to the rim of the empty dance floor as music blared. Shawsie took a quick look before asking a bartender where Skip was.

"In the office," she said. "Want to go up?"

"Sure." She climbed the stairs and walked to the end of the hallway, where she knocked on a door with a sign that read KEEP OUT, much like the one he had posted on his bedroom door at home. She called her brother's name and heard him cursing as drawers closed shut.

Finally he opened the door. "Hey, Shawsie, what are you doing here?"

"Can't I come visit?" she said affably. She took off her coat, stepped into the office, and looked around. He was alone, and she smelled just-smoked pot. She made a beeline for the green leather couch he had taken from their childhood rec room and sat on the far end, his favorite seat when they were growing up, which she usually managed to usurp. She looked at him, triumphant. "Ha ha."

"Jesus, Shawsie." He shook his head and walked back around his desk. "What are you drinking?" he asked as he picked up the phone.

"Ginger ale," she said to his raised eyebrows. "Bad stomach."

"You sure?" he asked. "Whenever mine gets bad, one shot of whiskey and I'm back in business."

She shook her head and from an end table picked up a picture of her parents. So young. She should tell her mother her news, she thought guiltily. And Gammy. Well, she would. First things first.

"Do you mind, by the way?" Skip gestured toward his hastily abandoned project, pulling rolling papers and a Ziploc bag from his top drawer.

"Fine with me," she said, leaning back on the couch. "I suppose it's comforting how some things never change." He said nothing, engrossed by the task at hand. She watched him awhile. He was still such a great-looking guy, something like Keith Partridge, but dissipated enough to be sexy.

"You expecting Robin tonight?" she asked.

He shrugged, without looking up. "I always expect Robin."

"I guess it's hard to pass up a hip-hop party, the two of you being such gangstas."

He smiled. "Pays the bills, Shawsie."

He finished his task and was just locking his desk drawers when a soft knock sounded at the door. A waitress walked in with a bottle of Johnny Walker Black on a silver tray, two glasses, a bucket of ice, and a small bottle of ginger ale.

"Cheers," Shawsie said after he had poured their drinks.

"So," he said, after taking a slug, "what are you doing here, exactly?"

"Just wanted to see my baby brother. And my husband. He said he was coming, and I figure he'll stop up here first to drop his stuff and grab a drink." She smiled. "And if I wait here, I don't have to listen to the music downstairs."

"Cool," Skip said, pouring himself a refill.

"Have you spoken to Mom lately?" Shawsie asked.

He shook his head. "No. You?"

She shook her head. "No. I will, though."

"Brave," he said.

"Yeah." She looked into her glass for a moment, debating whether she should just tell him her news. After all, she had waited this long to tell Robin, and if she could hold out a few more minutes he would probably be here, too. But Skip was her brother, after all. Her family. And she so desperately wanted to tell someone.

"Skip?"

"Yeah?" He looked uneasy, like when Red used to sit him down with his report card.

"There actually is a reason why I came here tonight."

He belted his next scotch. "No shit, Shawsie. You're like the only person I know who's asleep by nine."

From the hallway came a low rumble that made Skip turn questioningly toward the door.

"Very funny," Shawsie said, oblivious to the noise. "You know how tired I've been with our trying forever to get pregnant, and—"

The rumble grew louder, then came the sound of running, and the slam of a body against a wall. Skip jumped out of his chair just as the door flew open and bags and coats were kicked inside. Following them were Babette and Robin, engaged in a kiss so deep it was difficult to see either of their faces. His hands were down inside her open pants, grabbing her ass, and his belt and fly were undone. Her shirt was already off, tossed onto the unruly heap that had preceded them, and she reached her hands behind her back to release her bra. As they moved farther into the room, he shifted his mouth to one of her bare breasts, perfectly in sync, without stopping.

"Robin! Fuck! For chrissakes, stop!" Skip's voice shook with horror as he crashed his chair into the desk and ran toward them, arms flailing.

Robin lifted his head and emptied his hands and swiped at his mouth, while Babette said "What?" and turned to follow his stricken glance behind her.

"Oh my God!" she exclaimed.

Shawsie was on the floor in front of the couch, crouched over a pool of vomit. "I want to go home," she said.

Chapter Eight

"Mr. Evans. Your usual, sir?"

Red nodded as he headed toward a chair near a corner window. "Thanks, Bob. You're well?"

The waiter placed a small bowl of cashews on the table beside him.

"Yes, sir. Nice to see you again."

Red glanced around the room, emptied of its traditional standing ashtrays, and stopped patting his pockets for Marlboros. Smoking laws or not, he kept forgetting he'd quit three months ago. He moved the cashews closer.

It was four o'clock on a Monday afternoon, and cocktail hour at the Yale Club wouldn't kick into high gear until six. Red watched the dust motes drift in the late-afternoon sun and looked down at his shoes. For heaven's sake, when was the last time he'd bought a pair? The brown leather was cracked and worn beige in spots, and dried mud caked the grooves of the rubber soles. He put both feet flat on the floor, then yanked at the arms of his navy blazer to hide his fraying shirt cuffs.

"Cackie would kill you!" he could hear Ponce say.

She'd be right, of course. Then again, he hadn't planned on being out in the world, back in the world, quite so abruptly as these last ten days. He'd thought that when he was ready to reemerge, he would take himself to Brooks Brothers, where he'd shopped since childhood, and spruce up a few details. Except for Cackie's funeral, he hadn't needed a suit in ages; for the two years before she died their only outings had been to the doctor's office or the hospital. Not that he'd ever been much for clothes. He could still feel his mother's grip on the back of his neck as she'd catch him and his brother, Tom, racing through the hulking racks of navy blazers in the middle of the boys' department, the folded shirts gathered like Easter eggs along the walls, pale blue, yellow, and pink. His mother would release her hold, knowing that her warning look held him just as firmly in place, and the tape would loop around his neck while the tailor measured him and beamed at his mother to tell her how much he had grown.

And once the tailor finished sticking the pins directly into their wrists while shortening their new jackets— he smiled when he did it at these *very* good boys—they headed back across the street to Grand Central Terminal where their mother would collapse at the counter of the Oyster Bar with an ice-cold martini. Hers had a lemon peel curved delicately in its triangle of liquid, and he and Tom slurped raw oysters from their shells and scooped up oyster crackers by the handful. His mother ordered the same thing each time, a pan roast, and when she put the spoon to her mouth her eyes closed with bliss and Red would hold his mouth open for a spoonful of his own and for years he never thought of the city without smelling oysters, Worcestershire, and cream.

By the time they were back on the train to Greenwich, Mother would just shake her head and say how she couldn't wait for tomorrow, when she'd take their sister, Mims, into the city to shop at Best & Co., then to Schrafft's for hot fudge sundaes. "I need a reward after you boys," she would say. But once the train was out of the tunnel and the late-summer sun made them shade their eyes against it, she would reach over to Red and smooth a cracker crumb from the corner of his mouth, pull him close, and whisper down into his ear so no one else could hear, "What a handsome boy you are." She would do the same with Tom, and they would each be pleased—and a little embarrassed—and then they'd sit quietly until the train returned them home.

Red sipped his own martini now and wondered about his mother. What had she really wanted in her life? The three children she had? The perfectly pleasant husband who never seemed to say more than "Good morning" or "Good night"? She was certainly a productive woman, sitting on the boards of the Junior League and the Garden Club, and running the Library Committee. She read every book in that library and made sure her children did, too. Well, maybe not Mims. Mims had always been a pill, Red thought. She didn't like books, and she didn't like school, and she didn't like church. She liked playing tennis at the club—she was great at it, the women's champion—and she liked to sail. She gave that up, of course, once her husband drowned, leaving her to raise Skip and Shawsie alone.

Shawsie was so much like her grandmother, Red thought. Organized and at the ready, though when he remembered the frequency of his mother's martinis and his father's business trips, he recognized the turmoil that churned beneath her efficient veneer. The day he had published his first news-paper story, his mother read it in front of him, and her pride was fierce. "*Damn* good job," she said, and there was something in the set of her jaw that made him wonder if that might have been a career she'd wanted herself, instead of waiting around for her sons to grow up and her husband to come home.

The way Shawsie had endured Robin's infidelity all these years, similarly uncomplaining, tacitly accepting, hinted at something familiar in her that he was sad to see. Of course she deserved better. Now that the events of the past week or so had come to a head, Red wasn't quite sure what would happen next.

"You've got to get down here." That was Ponce's greeting when he picked up the phone, past midnight, nowhere near sleep. She began filling him in on what had just happened at the Acorn, and he settled back to absorb the inevitable — he knew Shawsie would catch Robin red-handed one day. But once he learned that Shawsie was pregnant, the jolt of anger he felt mobilized him. He cut her off.

"I'll deal with Skip. I'll call you back."

Red knew how much Ponce and Skip detested each other. As unpleasant as it would be for Skip to hear from Red, hearing from Ponce would have been worse.

"Skipper."

Red heard the doom in his nephew's voice from the minute he picked up the phone with a faint "Hey," tempered not at all by relief to hear that it was his uncle ready to grill him and not his sister's ferocious best friend.

"Jesus, Red, I tried to stop it! It happened so fast you couldn't believe it, and—"

"Did you know this was going on between Robin and this girl?"

Skip dragged on his cigarette. "Shit, Red. This is a bar I'm running. People drink, they do crazy things. Occupational hazard. I'm not a cop."

"That means yes, then." Skip stayed silent. "Where's the girl now?"

"Crying in my bathroom. She says her life is ruined, blah blah. Man, you know the whole story without my telling you."

"And Robin?"

"I don't know. I took Shawsie down to get a cab, she was screaming and crying and trying to get Ponce on her phone — who else? — and after I got her into the backseat, Robin tried to get in with her and she kicked him right in the balls."

Red had smiled. "Go on."

"Well, you know, he keeled over and I sat with him on the curb for a while, and then he got his own cab and left."

"You know, Skipper, you've always had an incredible gift for being in the wrong place at the wrong time."

"All I did was go to work, Red. It's not my fault!"

"Okay, get the girl into a cab and out of there. And, Skip? Why don't you consider putting a lock on your door?"

"I've got one! But I unlocked it to let Shawsie in!"

Red held his temper. He had been having the same circular argument with this kid since he was ten years old. Nothing was ever his fault. Circumstances always conspired against him. The idea that his square big sister who was fast asleep by nine on weeknights had come looking for her husband right where he was most likely to show up drunk with a girl hadn't sounded a single alarm bell. He could see about one inch in front of his own dopey face at any given moment. Then, when disaster struck, it was someone else's responsibility to clean it up. Just like his mother.

"'Night, Skipper."

Red arrived at Shawsie's apartment early the next morning. Ponce was mercifully in charge, with coffee at the ready, but he went straight into the living room to find Shawsie on the couch, her back to him. She'd refused to get into the bed she shared with Robin, Ponce told him. He pulled up a chair.

"Hey, little girl," he said softly, and he heard her start to cry. "I'm here now, Shawsie. And I'm going to stay here. Okay? Poncie and I are going to take care of you. So you don't even have to say hi to me, if you don't want to. I won't mind."

She turned and looked at his face. "Oh, Red." She started to wail then, great heaving sounds. He moved onto the couch and pulled her toward him, and she hung on him and cried with a bottomless sorrow. He rocked her and murmured and shushed as she went on howling, and they stayed that way for the better part of an hour. Somewhere, in other rooms, the phone rang. Once or twice, the service door opened and closed. A television was turned on and off, then a radio. Eventually, Shawsie grew quiet, and Red kept his arms tight around her. She sniffled on his shoulder and, spent, slept.

When Ponce walked into the room she found them both asleep. Red's head was thrown back, his clean-shaven face slack with exhaustion, mouth open, still holding his niece, who slumped against him like a child, impervious, finally, to the hurts of the world.

Ponce turned off a lamp that had stayed on overnight and went through the apartment switching off light after light. It was such a full place, she thought, like one of those antiques stores you see in Maine. Mismatched lamps, rocking chairs, hook rugs, polished wooden treasure chests. Somehow, they all fit together.

Funny, Ponce thought. Not a thing of Robin's anywhere—

not that she could see, at least. It was like that when she had been married to Lee, just the other way around. The only rooms that were really her own were her bedroom and bath. The others had been done by the decorator—supposedly under her supervision, though Lee was really in charge. She felt as much a guest in them as the people she invited to dinner.

Shawsie's place was different—not formal or forbidding. Every seat beckoned, every cushion called out a welcome. But maybe Robin never felt that way there, Ponce thought. Maybe it was just crammed full of too much stuff, with no space left for him.

Around noon, Red walked into the kitchen, where Ponce was reading the paper. She poured him some coffee.

"Hell of a mess," he said.

"More than you know," she answered and told him about Chicago. Of course, Red knew about her affair with Neil. Red knew everything that happened in Ponce's life, because that was the way she liked it. Red was smart and had unerring judgment, but he never judged her. "You're an original," he would chuckle when she refused to go to a big-deal party because it was thrown by someone she hated, or when she turned down impossible-to-get theater tickets because O'Neill bored the bejesus out of her. When Cackie was still alive, she and Ponce would discuss her romances and then Cackie would fill Red in over dinner. But in the past year, with its endless nighttime hours stretching toward ever reluctant dawns, he was so eager to hear Ponce's voice on the other end of the phone that they talked about all that, too. It was as if Cackie were still there: Each heard her in the voice of the other, so it felt natural to them both.

"I don't know if Babette saw something herself in

Chicago, or someone else did, but she told Jacqueline Posner that she's writing a piece about me," Ponce told Red.

He patted his pockets for cigarettes and ended up running his hands through his gray-streaked hair instead. "This is some piece of work, this girl," he said. "She's completely fixated on you. She's sleeping with my niece's husband. And working at my niece's magazine."

"Well, correction on that," Ponce said, pouring more coffee. "I called Topher last night to tell him why he shouldn't expect Shawsie today, and he went ballistic. He said that first thing this morning, he was firing Babette."

Red raised his eyebrows. "Is that wise?"

Ponce shrugged. "He thinks it is," she said. "She's only worked there a few months, anyway."

Red looked troubled. "Losing a job can make a desperate person more desperate," he said. "Where's Robin, by the way? Has he called?"

"He has. He's downstairs in his office, begging to see Shawsie. He sounds like a wreck, but I'm not even the tiniest bit sorry for him."

Red drained his coffee. "Does he know about the baby?"

Ponce looked surprised. "You know, I don't think he does. I sort of forgot about him in all this."

Red shook his head. "Too convenient, kiddo. What's Topher's number?"

She reached over to the phone on the wall and pressed a speed-dial button marked TOPHER.

"Red here. You didn't go ahead and fire this girl, did you?" He listened. "Damn!" He listened some more to a litany of loyalty, a history of friendship. "No, no, I understand," he said finally. And hung up. There was a reason Topher and Skip had been friends for so long, Red thought. Topher was another one who couldn't see three inches in front of his own face.

"He told her not to come in today at all," Red said, "to wait until tomorrow to clean out her desk, when no one is there. Keep a low profile. She was in tears, naturally. Pleading. He wouldn't hear it." He leaned toward Ponce. "You have got to get to the bottom of this," he said. "Find out what this girl wants. And make her go away. Fast."

She threw up her hands. "How am I supposed to do that?"

"You might start by going downstairs and having a conversation with Robin," he said. She opened her mouth to speak, but he kept going. "I know you're in a rage on your friend's behalf, Mrs. Morris, but get past it. There's only one of us who really knows Babette Steele, and it's Robin. So be smart. For starters, you might think about Neil, and what he has to lose, eh?"

Ponce had called Neil that morning to tell him about Shawsie's trauma, to make sure she'd be okay physically, but she hadn't mentioned her conversation with Jacqueline.

"Do you think—?" she began anxiously, but Red cut her off.

"I don't know. But you've got to find out."

With Topher's help, Ponce had been issued a temporary visitor's pass into Rubinstein Publications, and by ten o'clock Saturday morning she was sitting at Babette's desk. The girl was neat, Ponce would say that much for her. Besides a small bowl of wilting roses, the desk was bare except for a cup full of pens and a half-empty bottle of Poland Spring water. Pinned on the fabric wall next to the desk were a few leftover Christmas cards, a strip of black-and-white pictures of Babette and an unknown young man from one of those dime-store booths, and a wooden plaque that read, "Good Girls Stay Home. Bad Girls Go Everywhere."

Ponce tried opening Babette's desk drawers and found them all locked. Then she tried the top drawer of the nearest file cabinet. Locked. The one below it slid right open. She flipped through a few thin files: "Chicago Fashion," "Carmen," "Project PM." Except for some clippings about the Jacqueline Posner party, that last was empty.

Ponce reached into the bottom drawer, so full it jammed, and started pulling out clothing—crumpled T-shirts, yoga pants, a sports bra. A small plastic jewelry bag with one rhinestone chandelier earring inside. And at the very bottom, a worn canvas envelope filled with papers.

This must be it, Ponce thought, what Robin had told her about.

As soon as Red said that Ponce needed to go to Robin's office and talk to him, Ponce knew he was right. Robin opened the door right away, wild-eyed from crying and drinking, and his hand shook when he poured her a Diet Coke.

"Listen, Ponce, I know you hate me and—"

"I don't hate you, Robin. Let's just say we've had our differences and set that aside for now. What happened between you and Babette is for you and Shawsie to work out. That's not my business. But I've got to ask you a few other things. Please. I think I might be in some trouble here myself."

He seemed uneasy. "What do you mean?"

"Do you know anything about Babette writing a piece about me?"

In the moment he hesitated she saw that he did. He sighed. "There's no point in lying about it, I guess. Yes, I do. She's writing it on spec for *Manhattan* magazine."

"And? That's it?"

He slumped forward and hugged his knees. "You know

what, Ponce, I'm fucked three ways from Sunday here, so what the hell? She saw you in Chicago with Neil. At the Four Seasons Hotel. In the lobby. Kissing."

Ponce gasped. "Oh! She did? Well, did you deny it? Did you try to stop her?"

Robin's eyes grew wide. "Did I deny it? How could I? I wasn't there. It didn't happen to me. For chrissakes, Ponce, why are you kissing someone you shouldn't be fucking in public?"

"Robin, I've got to protect Neil. This is a disaster."

"I know it. I mean, the thing is with Babette, I was trying to dump her, and then she turned up here and told me she saw what happened between you two and that it was a scoop—because Neil is so famous—and she needed to think about her career, especially since I was dumping her. So, you know, I had to say yes, I would help her! What else could I do? But I've been trying to stall her these last few weeks, slow her down and hope that maybe she'll lose interest in it."

"Is it written yet?"

He lit a cigarette. "Sort of. She showed me a draft. It's not ready to publish, though Page Six would kill to break that news."

Ponce grabbed one of his cigarettes from the coffee table, and he leaned in to light it. "I need to fix this, but how?" she asked, taking the first drag she'd had in ten years.

"I don't know," he said. "The worst part is that Topher already fired her. Phoned her first thing this morning and told her they're having budget problems, nothing personal. She tried calling him on it, saying she knew the real reason, but he played it cool. Said he could understand her being so upset, and why didn't she go in tomorrow to pack up her things? Make it easier for everyone. He knew she wouldn't have the nerve to go in and face him today. So now she's got no job and no money. She needs to publish this thing fast. She's called me three times already."

Ponce pulled open the canvas envelope. One piece of paper sat on top.

"THE SPARE WIFE"

by

Babette Steele

Ponce stopped. She'd heard that before. Where? She strained to remember. Rachel. She'd said it to her that day at lunch. Was she in on this too? Helping the new kid? No, she couldn't be. Rachel didn't even like Babette. Ponce knew that. She forced herself to calm down and keep reading:

> It seems somehow fitting that our story begins with an ending. It was, as *tout* New York remembers, Jacqueline Posner's poignant farewell to the Park Avenue home she had made so lovingly for Mike Posner. Jacqueline seemed fragile that night, her long face white against her cloud of dark hair. If not for Ponce Morris, whose cool blond beauty gave the evening its spine and her friend her courage, the guests would have left before dinner was even served. But Ponce, in her rhinestone pants and silver charmeuse top, sparkled as surely as the stars outside the windows in the inky velvet sky.

The rest of the page was empty. Ponce opened a manila folder of black-and-white photographs. Neil outside her apartment building, crisply attired in jacket and pants, then leaving it, no jacket, hair tousled. There were shots of Ponce leaving and entering her lobby, then two of her going into Neil's office at night, hair pulled back, two more of her coming out, hair loose, clothes disheveled. There were none of them together.

She tried catching her breath as her heart pounded in her ears and she sorted through the pile, back and forth, unseeing. There was a notebook, some pages stained with coffee, the handwriting practically illegible. "B-12" was all she could decipher, although that was enough—Ponce knew what that scrap of information meant. This girl had done her homework.

Finally she folded the single page titled "The Spare Wife" into a tiny square and slid it into her wallet. She returned everything else to the canvas envelope and buried it under the dirty gym clothes. It was eleven o'clock, and there was still no sign of Babette.

When she arrived, a little before two, Babette found Ponce Morris at her desk, sitting with her feet up, reading a copy of *Vogue*.

"Oh, I get it, you're Shawsie's farewell committee, right?" Babette's face was flushed red from the cold, and it grew even redder as she unwound a scarf from her neck.

"This has nothing to do with Shawsie, Babette." Ponce put her feet on the floor. "I think you and I need to talk."

"Are you going through my things?" Babette yanked at the locked desk drawers.

"Obviously not," Ponce said.

Babette pulled open the file cabinet. "Well, how about this?" she demanded.

Ponce looked confused. "Is that one yours?"

Babette ignored her, diving into the bottom drawer and pawing through the contents of the canvas envelope. She wheeled around. "Did you take anything from here? I'm calling security!"

Ponce shook her head. "For heaven's sake, here's my purse. Look for yourself."

Babette turned it upside down. Ponce's wallet, a pack of Parliaments, matches, keys, and a packet of Kleenex fell onto the desk.

"Okay? Now listen, Babette. We have got to talk. Why do you have this vendetta against me?"

Babette snorted. "*Me?* You and your best friend just got me fired! You're a fucking millionaire, and I'm on unemployment now. And it's my vendetta against *you?*"

Ponce stayed calm. "Jacqueline Posner says you're writing a story about me. But I find it strange that you've never asked to speak to me."

Babette crossed her arms. "I tried having drinks with you. You weren't interested. I'm not important enough. So I figured I'd do my own reporting and call you last. Not waste your precious time."

Ponce kept her eyes on Babette's face. "I understand you were in Chicago recently. How was your trip?"

Babette's mouth tightened. "Fucking Robin. He told you."

"You would ruin someone else's life—not mine, certainly, but Neil's—for this? You would destroy his family and hurt his career for the chance to write a story? You're so young, Babette. There are hundreds of other stories. Why do you have to write this one?" Ponce heard the note of pleading in her voice and felt ashamed.

Babette savored her moment. "Gee, Ponce, this is even better than the drink. We skip all the niceties and go straight to laying bare our souls. Awesome. Well, let's see. I'm not going to stop, so what are you going to do to try and make me? You could call Page Six and tell them yourself. Head me off at the pass and ruin my chances of getting published—though no magazine has reason to pass up an eyewitness account as a follow-up. So go ahead. I have all their home phone numbers. Lovely people, the folks at Page Six. Very accommodating. They'd be happy to hear from you, I'm sure."

They were both quiet for a while.

"What is it you want?" Ponce asked, at last.

"Well, how about my job back, for starters?"

Ponce shook her head. "You don't want this job back. You're going to come in here and see Shawsie every day? Report to her? And expect her to promote you on your merits, just like any other assistant? Come on, Babette. You've closed this door all by yourself. Even I can't open it back up for you."

Babette sighed. "I guess you're right," she said. "I guess that just leaves my article. So if you'd like to cooperate, that would be great."

Ponce snorted her derision.

"No? Well, other than that, I'm pretty well set, thank you."

"Is it money? Do you want enough money to not worry about finding another job? Because I can give that to you."

Babette seemed to consider. "No, I'm good," she said. "I've waitressed before. I can do it again."

The door of the freight elevator opened, and a uniformed man walked toward them with some boxes. "Here you go, Babette," he said. He looked at Ponce. "Who are you?"

"A friend who came to say goodbye," Babette said. "She was just leaving."

"Want a lift down?" the guard asked.

"Yes, thank you." Ponce stood.

"Thanks so much for stopping in," Babette said. "That was just so *nice* of you. Next time we must have that drink."

Ponce didn't answer.

When Babette heard the elevator door slide shut, she turned her back and started packing her boxes.

Shawsie stepped out of the shower and peered down at her stomach. She certainly didn't look pregnant. Was Neil right? Had she imagined the whole thing? It felt as if a year had passed since he'd called her on Thursday. She could have delivered by now.

She climbed into a pair of sweatpants, pulled on a T-shirt, and started running a comb through her hair, before tossing it aside. Who cared? She had already seen Robin and couldn't tell which one of them looked worse. He had come to the apartment late Saturday night, when Red was already asleep in the guest room. Ponce had left early that morning, Red said, though Shawsie hadn't woken up herself until almost four. She had never slept that long in her life, though once she remembered what happened, she wished she could have kept on sleeping. But Red forced her to eat some soup and half a turkey sandwich from the corner deli. He had also gone out and bought her a gallon of organic milk. "It's good for you," he insisted, and she thought it so sweet of him that she downed two glasses.

Robin had cried. Shawsie, still on the couch, joined him. He said that maybe he needed to stop drinking.

"I agree," she said, passing the tissue box. "I don't want my child to have a father who drinks."

Robin picked his head up. "What? Wait a minute. Really?"

She turned away, sobbing. "No!" she yelled. "It was not supposed to be like this!" She bawled into her pillow.

"Wait, babe, how long have you known?" Robin circled his arms around her, nuzzling his face near hers.

She pushed backward with all her might. "Get *off* me!" she screamed, and within seconds she heard Red start down the hallway. He stopped, then retreated. Robin had also backed away, and crouched in a nearby chair.

"If you want to live to see tomorrow, do not call me 'babe.'" Shawsie's voice was low, and her eyes blazed with anger. Robin held his trembling hands up in the air. Shawsie caught her breath. "Good. That's where you should be. Away from me. Stay there." She moved to the far end of the couch. "I found out Thursday night. I called you, you never answered. I had no idea where you were, but you told me that morning you were going to the Acorn for the hip-hop party. So I went. The only thing you forgot to mention was that you already had a date."

"No! I didn't. I mean, that was an accident."

Shawsie pulled at her hair. "Is that what they call that now? An accident? Get out."

"No." Robin found himself, suddenly. "No. I will not get out. Shawsie, we're having a baby. I mean, after all that time and worry and trying. It worked." He looked stunned. "It worked."

They sat awhile longer. "I'll do anything you want," he said. "I'll stop drinking. We can get couples therapy. Jeez, now that we don't have to keep running to Neil, we'll have nothing but time on our hands."

He saw her face soften.

"Would you do that with me?" he asked quietly. "Would you give me a chance?"

She kept her head down. "Yes," she said, finally meeting

his eye. "I've always known that you lied to me, and I've let you. I was wrong. So it's my fault, too." He seemed to brighten at that, and she threw the tissue box at him. "Don't get so excited," she choked out. "It's still more your fault."

They both laughed then, and Robin got up and succeeded in putting his arms around her, and he leaned his face against her shoulder and told her how much he loved her and how glad he was about the baby. "I can't tell you how sick it makes me, what happened—" he said, but she pushed him away again.

"I can't do that now," she said. "And I think you can't be here for a while. I can't sleep in the same bed with you, I can't trust you. I mean, I could never trust you, but this! I, I almost wish I wasn't having a baby, so I could throw you out for good." She sniffled. "Things happen for a reason. I just have to figure out what this reason is."

Robin moved toward her, but she held up her hand. That brief respite of laughter was over. She was angry again. He knew it was desperate, but he wanted her back on his side.

"I had a long talk with Ponce yesterday," he said casually. She frowned. "Why?"

"Well." He felt himself warm to the subject. "Ponce is having her own troubles."

"With?" Shawsie looked suspicious.

"Neil." Robin looked at her face. Nothing.

"What do you mean?"

"I just assumed you knew about this and didn't tell me. Which is fine. I understand your keeping a confidence."

Shawsie looked baffled.

"You know," he said slowly, "about their affair."

"Affair? They're not having an affair!"

So he told her. About Babette seeing them in Chicago. About the piece she'd started writing. About how he tried to

slow her down, throw her off track. To protect his wife's closest friend and her secret.

Shawsie stood up. "You've really got to go now," she said.
"I'm beginning to believe I'm losing my mind."

He murmured an apology. He repeated how much he
loved her, how glad he was about the baby, how sorry he was
about the other night. Afterward, she lay on the couch for
hours, awake, thinking about her husband, who lied to her,
and her best friend, who . . . lied to her? Could it be true?
Why wouldn't Ponce have told her? They told each other
everything. Without Ponce, Shawsie would feel she had no
family at all. And Ponce felt the same about her. At least that's
what she'd always said.

Shawsie wrapped a blanket around herself and moved to
an easy chair by the window, looking down on the empty
Chelsea block with its row of tidy townhouses. There were
lights on in two windows. Was someone else awake? What
were they doing? As a teenager in Greenwich she used to
walk through her neighborhood in the middle of the night
when she couldn't sleep. She would look into windows and
see people passed out in front of their televisions. Or people
like her, who couldn't sleep themselves, eating ice cream
over the sink. She remembered one woman—whose husband had recently left her—emptying all the kitchen cabi-
nets and washing the shelves one by one. She had gone up
and down a stepladder, back and forth. Shawsie must have
watched her for an hour.

She drew the blanket closer. Lost. She felt completely
lost. For maybe the millionth time, she thought about her
father. She had always sorted her life into two pieces—before
his death, then after—and became convinced that if he had
lived, she would have been happier, because she would have

been smarter. For all her adult industry, at her core she had remained a child. It was as if at the moment he died she had been frozen in place, never learning, never growing. She was so easy to fool, because she was still the child who could be counted on to do the right thing. She believed anything she was told, because she was a good girl. No matter what happened, Shawsie would fix it. Shawsie would forgive. She had to. Because something really bad could change your life. It could stop your life. But if you fixed it, your life could mend and you would be happy. Everyone else would be happy. The brighter the light grew at the window the angrier she felt.

At nine o'clock on Sunday morning she left a message on Ponce's machine asking her to call. It was important. She knew they wouldn't speak until early afternoon, when Ponce woke up. That was okay, she thought, hearing Red start the coffee out in the kitchen. She had waited this long. She could wait some more.

After Ponce left Babette at *Boothby's*, she spent the rest of the day trying to find Neil. He wasn't answering his cell, his service couldn't locate him, and no one picked up at home. Although they rarely spoke on weekends, she always knew his plans. But when all hell broke loose with Shawsie, she'd forgotten to ask.

She'd gone straight through the pack of Parliaments she'd bought that morning, then bought a carton. All that money on hypnosis, down the drain, along with Neil's reputation, she thought darkly, opening a second bottle of wine. He'd had nothing but success for so long; he was probably due to take some kind of hit. That's how it worked. But this one could impact on every level. Disgruntled patients, jealous peers, spurned wife, all having a field day. Sure, it would blow over. But while it lasted, it would hurt.

She drank another glass and shivered, suddenly freezing. She squeezed herself into a corner of the couch, wrapping her legs with a throw—it was actually an old mink coat she'd always loved, now bordered in satin—and lit another cigarette. On the other hand, she was assuming the worst, and who could say what would happen? Neil had had an affair. He hadn't murdered anyone. He hadn't hurt his patients. He had fallen in love with another woman while he was married, that's all. He wasn't the first man to do it, and he wouldn't be the last. Everyone makes a mistake. And everyone loves someone who admits making a mistake. In court, you could sway any jury with real remorse. It just had to be real, that's all.

But Neil's remorse would be. To Sari. Because he was in love with Ponce, she had known that from the beginning. Look how he'd pursued her, as if his life depended on it. And his reaction in Chicago when she'd told him how she felt about him (she'd almost died when she'd heard those words coming out of her mouth, so unlike her), how he assured her he felt the same. On their first night together he'd been ready to leave Sari, and she'd discouraged him. That was three years ago. Well, Ponce thought now, maybe it was time for her to let him leave Sari. He could find an apartment and still see his kids, and Ponce could put the separate pieces of her life together and live the way everyone else did: be in love and in the world, all at the same time. Stop getting slammed into walls at midnight under the guise of conference calls to Australia. She was too old for that. And it was hell on her evening clothes.

She was halfway through that second bottle of wine when,

around ten p.m., her phone rang. The sound of rock music on the other end was deafening.

"Jesus, Neil, where are you?"

"In Cambridge. Nephew's bar mitzvah. Is Shawsie okay? Did something go wrong?"

The music receded as he walked.

"No, Shawsie's fine. But we may have trouble."

"What does that mean?"

She told him. It was finally quiet on the other end. She heard a horn honk. He was outside. Breathing hard.

"Did you hear what I said?" she asked.

"No. I'm not sure I did. You'd better tell me again."

She repeated herself, then listened as he breathlessly repeated the word "fuck." She could practically see him pacing the parking lot. "I'm fucked," he finally concluded. "My marriage is over. My practice is over. My fucking life is over."

Ponce used her courtroom voice. "Neil, I know you're upset, but I think we can work through this thing. If we don't panic, we'll be fine. We need to make a plan, that's all."

His tone was frantic. "Dammit! I knew this would happen. I knew it! This was wrong from the beginning."

"*What?*" So much for the courtroom. "Don't you dare tell me that! You wanted to leave your wife for me! And you know what? I think you should. You're upset now, you're not thinking clearly. But I'm thinking quite clearly, and this is the time for you to do it. So we can stop sneaking around. You're hysterical, is all. When you calm down, you'll see I'm right."

She heard a child crying then, some muffled talking on the other end. Someone was leaving, and Neil was saying good night. She heard him say the word "emergency." Then he said to her, in official doctor mode, "I'll be in the office on Tuesday. We can follow up then." He hung up.

She felt her heart clench. His *life* was over? What was he

saying? Neil *loved* her. Surely he would recognize that once he collected himself. She reached for the wine bottle. It was empty. She paced and forced herself not to think about the potential mess of it all—having to duck her calls, not to mention the photographers outside the courthouse, Shawsie. Oh God. Shawsie. This was the only secret Ponce had ever kept from her. Well, hell. That was the least of her worries now. She took a hot shower and two pills and passed out.

It was almost two o'clock on Sunday afternoon when she awoke. Next to her bed was a large bouquet of flowers. Big and stiff, the kind you see in hospitals. Pink. In the middle one tulip drooped forward, its big head down. That's a mistake, Ponce thought drowsily. Bad florist. She closed her eyes, then opened them. There'd been no flowers there when she'd gone to sleep. Hell, had she overdosed? Was she actually in a hospital? She bolted upright. Shawsie sat in the recliner in the corner, arms folded, watching her.

"Oh! Shawsie! My God, you scared me half to death. What are you doing here?"

Shawsie's arms stayed folded. "You tell me, Ponce."

Ponce frowned. "I, I'm not sure. Did I forget something? I mean, I took a pill, two pills, last night and—" She stopped. Shawsie knew.

"Give me a minute." Ponce climbed out of bed and went into the bathroom, washed her face, brushed her teeth, and pulled on a pair of sweatpants. When she emerged she asked, "Okay, why the flowers?"

"Skip sent me those," Shawsie said. "The day after the Acorn. The card read, 'Sorry and congratulations,' which is some kind of poetry, don't you think? Anyway, you know how

I feel about getting flowers, Ponce. That's why I wanted you to have them."

It was Ponce's turn to fold her arms. Shawsie hated being sent flowers. They were insulting, she said. One swipe of a credit card and all is forgiven. Cheating husband, idiot brother, anyone who won't sit down face-to-face and have a real conversation, come clean. The peonies can do it instead.

"I do know how you feel about flowers," Ponce said. "But I still don't get it."

Shawsie glared. "Don't you? I don't care how much you drank last night. I think you do."

Ponce sat at the foot of her bed and faced her friend. "I'm sorry I didn't tell you about Neil," she said. "You have every right to be angry."

"And you didn't because?" Shawsie's face was set.

Ponce hesitated, but Shawsie didn't budge.

"First of all," Ponce said, trying to focus, "he's your doctor and that made me uncomfortable. I mean, he's all about having children and he has this exemplary family—which seemed like the kind of thing you'd need to aspire to when your own husband wasn't coming home nights."

Shawsie's face grew red and she clamped her mouth shut and held it there, as if it might be the one part of her body she could force into holding up the rest.

Ponce plowed on. "I thought if you knew he was having an affair, even if it was with me, it would make you feel you couldn't trust him. I thought that if you knew he was cheating—like Robin—you might not go back to him if you didn't get pregnant, even though he's clearly the best one out there. And then you'd be spiting yourself, because no one else would do as good a job."

Shawsie still said nothing.

"And," Ponce continued awkwardly, "there is my role in this. I mean, I've spent years disapproving of your cheating husband, and then I sort of did the same thing. Though, when you look at it, it's not really the same thing at all. Neil and I are actually in love—"

Shawsie snorted. "Sure you are. That's why he's still married."

"Neil is still married because I've wanted him to be. He wanted to leave Sari, and I wouldn't allow it."

"Really." Shawsie's tone turned mocking. "And why is that?"

"You know I hated being married. I don't want to be married to anyone."

Finally Shawsie's mouth unglued. "No, you don't. You prefer your emotions by appointment. Then the other person can disappear and leave you alone. No fuss, no mess." She stood. "You've never been in love with Neil, not for one day. He's like every other man in your life—someone to adore you, pine for you, compete for you. For your great beauty to shine upon. For the two minutes of attention you finally bestow, because when it comes down to it, that's all you're good for. Because your bottom line is that you don't want *anyone*. You don't care any more about Neil than you did about Lee. You don't want a man, really. Men are messes. You don't like messes. You're a middle-aged woman who'd still rather be on a date. Because it has a beginning, a middle, and an end. Not to mention the competition thing, which you love, mainly because you don't have any.

"No one is more beautiful than you, no one is thinner than you. You like knowing that. No, you love it. You're in love with it. You didn't try telling me that you were in love with Neil because you knew you weren't. Have you ever realized that *all* your affairs have been with married men? Which ensures your always being alone. Goal! Score! You win. It's ingenious, really. You manage to cheat the person who's cheating to be with you. Bravo, Ponce. But that's the part you should be ashamed of. Someone else put so much at stake, and you didn't give a damn!"

Ponce's face was white. "Not one word of that is true," she said, her voice hollow. "Neil isn't a game to me. This is a three-year relationship. A real relationship. I am in love with him." She burst into tears, which moved Shawsie not at all.

"I didn't plan it," Ponce sobbed. "It just happened. And I thought he felt the same way about me, but on the phone last night, he was so, so awful. He was furious when I told him about Babette. Furious at *me*. And it was no more my fault than his that that stupid girl happened to be in the same hotel lobby as we were at the exact same moment!"

She dropped her head, engulfed by despair. Her voice was so low that Shawsie could barely hear her. "This man is so dear to me," she said. "He's nothing like Lee. He is so loving. Genuinely loving." She groped for a tissue. "How could you say such hateful things to me? I've been a great friend to you. For years."

Shawsie held her gaze. "Yes, you have. You've been a great friend to a great many people for years. That's not the point. When you're being a friend, you're behaving like yourself, not a beauty queen. The beauty queen thing is for men only. It's calculated artifice, like a carnival game that's fixed so you always win. It's actually so fake, so outmoded, and so silly that it's the closest you get to ugly. And I've seen you do it with every man you've been with, including Lee. Because you've never figured out how to be yourself *and* be a woman at the same time. But that's okay, and you know why? You're forty-two. That flawless face of yours is officially on the endangered-species list. You'll have to figure out what to do next soon enough."

Ponce kept sobbing.

Shawsie threw a key threaded on a red ribbon onto the seat of the easy chair. "When I leave, by the way, please do not console yourself by thinking I'm jealous of you—because I'm not. Yes, my adolescence would have been a lot less painful if I looked like you, but you know what? I actually grew up. Not completely, not perfectly, but some. And as imperfect as I am, in every way, I have still *felt* more things— good, bad, high, low—than you ever have. And that's enough for me. Actually, it's everything."

Ponce didn't lift her head.

Shawsie pulled on her coat and caught her breath. "I know I just attacked you," she said. "And the truth is, if these last few days hadn't happened the way they did, I probably would never have said any of this. I'm not sure I'm sorry I said it, because it's true—yes, it is—and at some point you're going to have to deal with it. I know you're upset now about what's happening with Neil, and I sympathize. Normally, I'd stay and hug and cry and listen. But you know, at this particular moment, I'm all tapped out." Her voice was flat. "My husband, the father of my child, is a cheater. He drinks. He lies. And I've got to decide if I'm going forward with him or without him. You have been my best friend for twenty years. You're a cheater. You drink. You lie. I somehow can't find it in my heart to feel your pain at this very moment. I'm too busy feeling my own."

And she was gone.

Chapter Nine

Three days later, Ponce walked through the lobby of the Palace Hotel, feeling like a fool. She wore sunglasses and a baby-blue pashmina scarf wrapped around her hair and fully expected a movie director to yell "Cut!" as she strode across the long, carpeted hallway.

After she told Neil about the private investigator and the pictures, he refused to meet at her apartment. She could understand that. But to insist on a hotel room! It made the whole thing feel as tawdry as she had assured Shawsie it was not.

"You're still there. Why?" she wailed when he called her from Cambridge on Monday.

"It's spring break, that's why," he said, annoyed. As if she would know! "Sari's up here with the kids at her parents' all week. I'm leaving tomorrow."

He insisted they meet at the Palace on Wednesday afternoon, because a colleague from San Francisco was staying there. That way, he said, if anyone saw him, he would have a legitimate reason. But it had to be at three. Later than that, he could run into someone having cocktails. Earlier than that, he could run into someone having lunch. Ponce felt as if he had completely lost his mind.

Still, she went. She pulled the collar of her trench coat up around her jaw for good measure and called the operator from the house phone. When she was connected to Neil, he gave her his room number and she got into an elevator. If a photographer was following her, she thought, he would have to be invisible. She had looked every which way and seen no one.

Neil opened the door and stepped back quickly, away from the light in the hall. After he closed the door, she went to hug him, and he hesitated. Only for an instant, then, yes, he held her, but that instant had already seared itself. She smelled his shirt and felt his heart pounding against her cheek and knew that it was over.

He opened a bottle of Heineken from the minibar without asking what she wanted. She poured herself a Smirnoff, then sat in the chair in front of the desk. He stayed standing.

"Ponce."

She looked up and said nothing. She wasn't going to make it easy for him, that much she knew.

"I feel terrible about this," he said, in a tone that didn't feel terrible at all. That was a tone from the dentist's chair, of wanting to get up and out of there as soon as he possibly could.

"I know you're upset, and believe me, I am too," he said, pacing the short space between the foot of the bed and the desk. Ponce started to see herself from the outside. You'd think he'd have sprung for a suite, she thought snottily. He'd have more room.

"When this first started between us, I know I said some crazy things about leaving Sari and the kids," he said. "But

you were smarter than me. You said no, you said how important my family was. And you were right. I should have listened. I should have let it go, let *you* go, so you could be with
someone who's free. I mean, what kind of life is it for you to
play second fiddle all the time? I know it can't be easy that we
never see each other on weekends or holidays. You deserve so
much better. So much more."

She continued seeing herself from a distance. And Neil.
Honestly! She knew he worked too hard to be able to watch
daytime drama, but this stuff was as canned as it came. Was
his conversation always this inane? Of course not. What did
they usually talk about? The Knicks. Yankees. Giants. That
was fun. His patients. When he spoke about his patients, he
was always so connected. Solid. When he spoke about his
family, he was always, what, abashed. He was connected to
them, too. He just didn't want her to know it.

"Here's the thing," he said, stopping in front of her. "I
think the one point we have to be together on here is denying
that anything happened. If we do that, I think we'll be fine.
Because then it doesn't matter what this girl saw. Or thought
she saw. Yes, I was in Chicago, you were in Chicago. We had
breakfast. Big deal! Why can't two friends have breakfast
together? We kissed in the lobby? Well, sure we did. We
kissed goodbye as two friends will."

Ponce just stared. Had he forgotten about those pictures
from the private investigator? The reason they were in
this room now? He looked at her expectantly, eyes shining.
The door was open, and he was almost through it. She said
nothing.

"Babette called my office yesterday, twice," he went on. "I
didn't take the calls. She wants to come see me, interview me,
which is obviously out of the question. So you know what I
did? I hired Mort Diamond."

Ponce raised her eyebrows.

He headed back to the minibar and opened another beer. This level of ingenuity deserved a drink.

"I'd been meaning to do it anyway," Neil said. "I've had so many requests for publicity, TV appearances, things like that. And he's the best PR guy there is. This morning, he called her back for me, told her I wouldn't be available. Told her that you and I are old, old friends, from when you were married to Lee. Very professional, just like that. She kept saying, 'Well, I know what I saw,' and he kept saying, 'I'm sure you did. Of course they kissed each other. They've known each other forever. Ponce Morris is one of the great benefactors of Neil Grossman's career.'"

Abruptly, Ponce stood. She couldn't bear another minute and she couldn't tell what kind of expression she wore, but she watched the self-satisfied smile die on his face.

"I can't listen to this," she said. She picked up her vodka and drank it in a gulp. "Sit down, will you? Your pacing is making me seasick." Surprised, he perched uneasily on the side of the bed.

"I need to ask you something, and I need you to answer me truthfully," she said. He paled, but nodded. "I thought I knew how I felt about you," Ponce said, "which means I believed I loved you, was in love with you. I saw how you were with me, in the beginning, especially, and I believed you were in love with me. Let's say now, for the sake of argument, we were both mistaken."

He started to protest, but she shook her head. "Don't do that now. It cheapens it." He colored.

"What I want to know is this: What was it about me, about *this*, that so appealed to you?" She waved her hand. "Not that I'm nice or smart or pretty. None of that. What made you come back week after week, call me, think about me. What was it?"

He looked at her face, set and somber, and felt a real pang. He hated the way he'd been behaving today. He never thought of himself as a cad, he'd certainly never set out to be one. Ponce didn't deserve this. He felt the same shame he'd felt each time he thought about Sari. She didn't deserve this, either. He knew he had to answer Ponce's question directly.

"Well. You know what I think?" he said slowly. "I mean, I hadn't put it into words until now. I can barely think things through and keep things straight these last few days. But if I had to put my finger on the one thing that compelled me? Probably the fact that you never wanted anything from me."

Ponce struggled to stay expressionless. "Go on," she said.

Neil drained his beer. "First of all, you didn't want a baby. And trust me, that's no small thing to me. All day, every day, ten, twelve, twenty women, all with the same quivering smile, the same cold, damp fingers, the same wish, this terrible, powerful wish that I fix them. Make their lives complete. I mean, Christ. I'm a doctor. That's it. On my best day, I'm a good doctor. I can help people, a lot of people, *make* a baby. But that's where it ends. They want so much more. And I can't do anything about that.

"I have a wife who is a brilliant doctor herself. A loving mother. And like any wife and mother, she wants me, her husband, to do a thousand things a day. Get up with the baby. Review her grant applications. Help pick new wallpaper. And that's fine, that's life. I get it. But being with you was not life. It was escape. It was fantasy. I mean, no one I know looks like you. No one I know lives like you. You were in this cocoon of luxury entirely separate from the world. You know the way you felt about the medical meetings, when we went away? It was like that for me. Every week. You didn't want a baby. You didn't want a career. Hell, Ponce—to borrow a phrase—you didn't even want a sandwich. And that felt like heaven to me. Maybe that makes me a bad person. Or a weak person. But it felt too good to stop."

She fought against crying. "Okay," she said. "I never needed anything. I never wanted anything. But if I was that remote, didn't it bother you that I didn't *give* you anything, either?"

He started to answer and flushed a deep red.

"No, go on," she said. "Please do this for me. I mean it."

He swallowed. "It didn't matter that you didn't give me anything, because I didn't need anything," he said slowly. "I was married. I was actually happily married. If I needed something, I got it at home."

She reached her hand out to the desk to steady herself. Neil stood and held out his arms, but she turned her back and ran.

Gus Fisher headed across the newsroom to his corner fishbowl office and ducked his head in briefly. "One more thing and I'm all yours, Poncie, okay?" He kept going before she could answer. She could hardly believe that Gus had invited her to this Walter Gluckman lunch only last week. With everything else that had happened, it felt like last year.

She looked out at the sweeping views of the Manhattan skyline. This was the kind of thing she would have loved when she first came to the city to work for Ford, this master-of-the-universe panorama, looking down on it all in that first flush of aspiring adult arrogance, convinced it waited only for you. Her gaze fell on the Chrysler Building, and she noted how flat its silvery scallops looked in this overcast light. She sighed. When the Chrysler Building looked bad, you knew you were laid low.

She pulled a Parliament from her bag and saw one of Gus's assistants shake her head through the glass wall. She held up her hands in surrender and put it back. That was the second time today. She had practically been arrested in the court building that morning when she dared put an unlit cigarette in her mouth on her way outside to smoke it. Hell, she had gone on more than one date with this mayor in his single days. She should have kicked his ass when she had the chance. Another short control freak. Just like Lee. Though not technically her type, according to Shawsie. He was already divorced.

She hadn't heard from Shawsie since she'd left behind Ponce's emergency key. That was five days ago and they were perhaps the longest five days she could remember.

She threw down her bag and returned to the window where she bit the inside of her cheek to stop herself from crying. She couldn't remember the last time she had cried. Before last Sunday, that is, when Shawsie came. Since then, she had barely stopped.

"Poncie, you're a champ. Thanks for waiting." Gus was back, heading toward his desk chair where he had draped his suit jacket. "And now," he said, throwing it on, "time for lunch. The finest dreck a corporate dining room can provide. I think the Friday special is halibut, which unfortunately tastes like the Thursday special, which is meat loaf. Though I suppose that's better than the other way around."

"Okay." She forced a game tone.

"Hey! What's the matter?" Gus turned his back on his newsroom audience. Ponce was always thin, but she looked drawn, almost dehydrated, as if she'd been sick. She was wearing a ton of makeup—not like her—which hid nothing.

There were dark sockets under her eyes, and when she went to pick up her bag he could swear he saw her hand shake.

"It's nothing," she said. "Just insomnia. You know me." She stepped past the protective shield of his body. "I'm counting on them having rolls and butter up there, because I am starved. Shall we?"

He knew her well enough to know that something was terribly wrong but that she would never discuss it a moment before she wanted to, if ever. How long had they been friends now, twenty years? He and his first wife, Terry, weren't even married when he met Ponce and Lee at Walter Gluckman's house when Walter was still married to his first wife, Gerta. Gus and Ponce became fast friends, sharing the instant chemistry of Ponce's holy trinity—politics, sports, and movies. After he and Terry split, they had a brief fling before chucking it in favor of their friendship. Gus had manfully confessed all this to Rachel, who had only shrugged. "How can you be faithful to someone you haven't met yet?" she said, and that had been the end of it. Still, Gus knew that every eye in the newsroom was currently focused on his office as all assembled wondered who the blond babe was visiting the recently remarried boss. So he decided to let it go.

"Sure," he said, heading for the door. "Let's receive the word from on high as only broadcast legend Walter Gluckman can deliver it." As they walked to the elevator, Gus threw a chummy arm around Ponce's shoulders, which felt pointed and brittle under the jacket of her navy Chanel suit.

"I can hardly wait," she said, locating a note of gaiety. "I've been looking forward to it all week."

The corporate dining room was set for sixteen at a long rectangular table, and Ponce was surprised to find the table empty. Gus pulled out a chair for her toward the middle.

"Walter likes to sit at the end," he explained. "So we avoid Business school 101. Or was that my shrink?"

"Poncie! What the hell are you doing here?"

She dropped the roll she had already grabbed and stood. "Walter, how *are* you?" She went for the full pitcher of syrup. It worked.

"You look like a million bucks, kid," he said, kissing her on both cheeks, then holding her hands out in front of her. "Like a magazine ad or something."

"Why, Walter, thank you," she purred. "Gus told me about these lunches, how you all analyze the news, and you know what a junkie I am! I couldn't resist coming and hearing you in person. You don't mind, do you?"

He puffed up. "Nah, of course not," he said. "Never hurts having a beautiful broad around. Helps the digestion."

"Annabelle is well?"

"Oh yeah, great."

Ponce sat back down as the room began to fill. Walter walked to the far end of the table and settled across from one of the few women, one young enough to be his daughter. Figured.

"Gus, how ya doin'?" A small, intense-looking man pulled out the other seat next to Ponce and extended his hand. "Don Oliver," he said.

"Nice to meet you," Ponce said. Gus had told her about this guy: He was the number two to the president of the news department and the network-appointed pain in Walter Gluckman's behind, assigned to *Current Events* to make sure the show's stories stayed in line with the right advertising demographic, which meant viewers a quarter of Walter's age. Oliver was an up-and-comer who kept his eye on just about everyone's job at the network, Gus said. Including his.

"Watch your back," she'd advised him.

He only laughed. "I never set foot in the office without my bulletproof vest," he said.

The waiter served plates of fish covered in brown sauce. "See what I mean?" Gus said.

Ponce pushed hers away. "Pass me your roll, I'm not eating that." She turned to Don Oliver. "Tell me who everyone here is," she said. He went around the table identifying the cast of characters, sotto voce and quite indiscreetly, she thought, in his fervor to show off in front of Gus. But he made a crucial error, she thought. When pointing out his superior, the president of news, at the far end of the table, a mild-mannered man known to be on his last legs with management, Oliver rolled his eyes in blatant disgust. If he was really on top of his game, Ponce thought, he would never show that card to a stranger.

The plates were cleared—most of them still full—and coffee was served. Then someone hit a glass with a spoon. Gus leaned toward Ponce. "Here we go," he muttered.

The president of the news department stood and made a few innocuous remarks. "With the White House beating us up on a regular basis, I'm not sure we need to do it to ourselves," he concluded. "But I think there's some benefit to discussing our approach, and of course there's no one with a keener perspective or greater insight on this issue than Walter." If Walter heard his perfunctory tone, he didn't let on.

Gus half rose from his chair. "First, though, I'd like to say to anyone who hasn't met her, this is Ponce Morris, a dear friend of mine, who is also a longtime friend of Walter's and an inveterate news junkie. She tagged along today just to hear some inside baseball. It's completely off the record, so don't censor yourselves."

People smiled cordially at Ponce as Gus sat and Walter stood. "Well, if it's inside baseball you're looking for, you've come to the right place," he said importantly, oblivious to the stony game faces that had attached like masks around the table. Except, Ponce noticed, for that young woman, who wore an air of breathless anticipation. From everyone else you could almost hear the collective sigh of resignation.

After some pointed comments aimed at two men toward the far end of the table, Walter began to ramble—from Vietnam to Watergate to Iraq. Ponce watched as a few people traced invisible patterns on the tablecloths with forks or knives; the rest used their BlackBerries in their laps. But Walter's speech pulled her attention. It was wrong. He wasn't forming his words correctly. She peered sideways at Gus, who wore an expression of deep concentration, although when she got a good look at his eyes, fixed on her dessert plate, she saw they were as vacant as if he were sleeping.

She turned back to Walter. His complexion was off. Maybe it was the lights, but he looked gray, including his lips. Ponce sat straight up in her chair. She had known this man for twenty years. Something was wrong. She searched frantically around the table for confirmation. Not one person was looking at him. Or at her. She forced herself to listen to what Walter was saying, and he was making sense, actually, speaking quite specifically about a recent news broadcast and how the copy had been badly written. But his words were completely at odds with his delivery, which seemed to worsen by the second. She caught his eye and looked at him questioningly. He held her gaze and smiled for a moment. Then he looked confused and he sat down in his chair, hard, on his way to falling in it backward to the floor.

When it crashed, everyone moved at once. People ran, called for an ambulance. In a stunning reversal of concentration, Gus had leapt up in an instant; he was the one loosening Walter's tie.

"I know CPR," the young woman said, and Gus moved aside so she could straddle the unconscious man and push on his chest while covering his mouth with hers. Ponce felt cemented in place. She was still registering the grayness of Walter's face. His smile before he fell. Sweet. Like a child's. Within seconds, it seemed, people flooded the room with machines and electric paddles and surrounded Walter on the floor. The young woman stood off to the side, crying now.

"Again!" one of the technicians called, and Ponce could see only the bottom half of Walter's body, which jerked when the paddles were applied. "No! Again!" Another technician turned to the group. "Okay, everybody out," he instructed, and they all filed into the hallway—except for Gus, who insisted on staying.

Ponce cornered the younger woman, who had started to sob. Still in her twenties, she had sprayed blond anchor-woman hair and the heavily muscled calves of a runner that always look disturbing beneath the hem of a skirt. Her lipstick was smeared across her face from the CPR, and Ponce dug a tissue out of her bag so she could clean it off.

The woman kept crying and Ponce gave her more tissues, knowing like she knew her own name that this girl had been sleeping with Walter. The door to the dining room opened and Gus walked out, pale and shaken. "They couldn't save him. I'm sorry. Walter's gone," he said. Everyone gasped, and the girl cried louder, and Ponce peered through the open door to see the top of Walter's head and the technician sitting on the floor next to him, methodically wrapping wires and cables back around the paddles in what looked like slow motion. The door closed.

Don Oliver sprang into action. As he dialed his cell, he called instructions to the crowd standing in the hallway.

"Jack, get Walter's B-roll ready for the six," he said. "Marty, call the *Times* and the AP. Susan, get everyone back in on *Current Events*. The Sunday show will be on Walter." He disappeared down the hall.

"I'm going to my office to call Annabelle," Gus said to Ponce.

"I'll come with you," she said. She turned to the girl, still crying. "Is there anything I can do for you?" The girl shook her head, edging anxiously away from Gus. "No, thank you," she said, heading down the hall.

"Is that going to be a problem?" Ponce asked as she and Gus walked toward the elevator.

"Nah. Young anchor. Wanted more air time. Figured it couldn't hurt."

"So nothing for Annabelle to worry about."

"What Annabelle doesn't know won't hurt her. At least that's what Walter always said." Gus grimaced. "God, I never thought this was a conversation I would ever have to have with her. I mean, with anyone." His face had turned ashen.

Ponce stopped at Gus's assistant's desk. "Please get some coffee and sandwiches for Mr. Fisher immediately," she told the woman sitting there, who apparently knew what had happened since she was crying. "And where's the scotch?"

"Bottom drawer, side cabinet. Ice in the fridge next to it." The woman was already on the phone calling in the food. Ponce walked into Gus's office and closed the door behind them.

"I see what you mean about Don Oliver," she said. "What a lethal creature. Walter hadn't been dead a minute and he was giving orders."

Gus frowned. "There was nothing wrong with that," he said. "He's a newsman, Poncie. Walter would have done the same thing, only he would have done it thirty seconds sooner.

Walter Gluckman dying is very big news. Oliver was exactly right."

Ponce poured him a scotch. "Maybe I'd feel better if Walter living had gotten as good a reception as Walter dying. Christ, Gus. No one listened to a word he said, including you. Most of all, you. Yes he is, was, a total pain in the ass. But you know what? He did it. He was there, and none of you were. And you should have paid him the respect to listen to him."

Gus held out his hands. "Poncie, come on," he said. "You didn't have to deal with him day in and day out. The guy was no picnic."

Her face was closed. "None of us is a picnic, I think. That's not the point." And before she started to cry, she picked up her bag and left.

Babette walked out of the sanctuary of Temple Emanu-El the minute Walter's service ended, and still there were people ahead of her in the lobby waiting to sign the guest books. She got on one of the two lines and pulled her coat around her. She wasn't sure if anyone had seen her, and she wasn't sure if she should show up at the Cosmopolitan Club, where the reception was being held. She needed to pay her respects to Annabelle, but the last people she wanted to see were Shawsie and Ponce.

The line inched forward. Babette had been officially unemployed for a week now. After fruitless attempts to get Robin on the phone, she had taken matters into her own hands and called John Carraro, the senior editor at *Manhattan* magazine, who she knew was Robin's close friend. It was Carraro whom Robin had promised to call when she had finished.

"I have a rough draft of a piece about Ponce Morris," she'd

told him. "Robin Brody's been helping me, and I've uncov-
ered quite a scoop along the way."

"Which is?" Carraro seemed distracted.

"I'm not telling you!" Babette said, annoyed. "I'm going to
write it first, and when you see what it is, I'm betting you'll
want to get it into print right away."

"Okay," he said. "I'll be out of the office next week—"

"What? No! You can't be!"

He laughed. "Fine, you tell my kids that Daddy was only
kidding and we're not going to Disney World for spring break
after all."

Damn. She hadn't figured on something like that. She
thought she could spend a few days fleshing it out and then
they would run with it.

"I can look at it before I leave," Carraro offered, "if you
have enough to go on."

She tried thinking clearly. Robin had cautioned her
against moving too fast, warned her that the scoop could
escape for a life of its own before she had done enough reporting to anchor it. But on the other hand, fuck Robin! He
wasn't returning her calls. He obviously had no intention of
helping her now that Shawsie had seen them together. It was
silly of her to expect he would. No. She was on her own.
Topher had paid her for the last week she worked, and that
was it. Her Visa bill with the private investigator's fee on it was
already overdue. If she didn't get moving, she was going to
have to call that bistro in the meatpacking district she had
seen advertising for waitstaff.

"I can bring it to you now," she said.

"Great," he said. "Come on up."

See? Access. In this city, that's what it all boiled down to.
Carraro was Robin's great friend, and because Robin had
helped her, so would he. As soon as she arrived in his office,

he sat down and read the piece, taking notes. He was especially jazzed about the Neil angle.

"Okay, here's what you do," he said, outlining how to enhance the portrait of Ponce as a younger woman. "We need to know more about her marriage to Lee, since that's where the money and power came from. And what about her friendships now? Who loves her? Who hates her?" She took notes, irritated to hear the same questions Robin had posed. She thought she had answered them. But Carraro encouraged her to keep moving forward. "You're almost there," he said. "Really."

She felt a surge of relief. She hadn't needed Robin after all! What an idiot she was to think she had. Like it was so hard to sell a scoop? Robin had really played her for a fool. She and Carraro agreed that she'd get right to work and have something to show him by the time he was back from vacation.

Babette was only a few people away from signing the guest book now. The two women behind her started to talk. "So which one are you going to?" one asked.

"Well, we have to go to both, don't we?"

Big sigh. "I guess you're right. What a bore."

"I hear Gerta is only having people over tonight, but Annabelle is having them tonight and tomorrow," the other said. "She says *she's* the widow, not Gerta. It seems to have escaped her notice that Gerta's only doing it for her children and grandchildren, because none of them have a relationship with Annabelle, but they still need a shiva of their own." A low laugh. "At least *they're* Jewish."

"Don't you think Annabelle's overplaying her hand, adding a second night?"

"Well, doesn't she always? I heard that when Annabelle

suggested the Cos Club, Gerta refused to even go. She said the kids could receive at her apartment in the evening, after the burial, and that Annabelle was welcome to join them. But Annabelle threw a fit because she wouldn't be in charge. She called one of the kids and cried and carried on until they all agreed to go to the club. And I hear there are two receiving lines, because Annabelle insists on having her own."

It was Babette's turn to sign the book. She wrote her name and address neatly on the dotted line, then turned and walked purposefully out the front doors. She would go to the club to pay her respects to Annabelle and tell her she was leaving town for the next few days. Annabelle didn't know she had been fired; she would think she was still at *Boothby's*, making a business trip. Going to Annabelle's home would be folly. The apartment would be packed, and Babette could just see herself coming face-to-face with Shawsie or Ponce. No. She put on a pair of sunglasses and walked fast, trying to beat the crowd, many of whom were still climbing into limousines to drive the few blocks to the club. This was the better way.

Red glanced at his watch. Ponce was meeting him here at the Yale Club at five to give him the lowdown on Walter's funeral. At least that's what they said they were doing, catching up in person for the first time since they'd converged for triage at Shawsie's two weekends before. That Red had a different agenda was known only to him. He drained the martini he'd been clever enough to stretch for the last hour and noted that the shaft of sunlight that had mercilessly exposed the shabbiness of his neglected wardrobe had finally faded. These early April afternoons carried a chill, and although it was still light at the window, you could feel the cold seeping in around it. This room was always drafty. He suspected the club kept it that way to encourage the purchase of warming cocktails. So who was he to argue? He held up his hand to the waiter and motioned for another. He patted his pockets for his cigarettes and shook his head, bemused. This was what he did now instead of smoking.

At five, Red headed downstairs to get Ponce past the guards. She looked fragile, Red thought. They had spoken by phone every day since she had walked out on Neil last Wednesday at the Palace. Five nights without sleeping, he calculated, five days without eating. She had also filled him in about her blowup with Shawsie. Well, when it rained it poured. She walked with him across the Main Lounge in her black slacks and white cashmere sweater, ramrod-straight. Still a model. A diamond on a thin chain sparkled at the base of her throat. In the sparsely populated room, every male eye was on her.

She took the chair nearest his. The waiter placed Red's martini on the table between them. "Pinot Grigio, thank you," she said. "Please don't wait," she told Red, motioning toward his drink.

"Thanks, I won't," he said, sipping. "So tell me."

"Well, the service was lovely, really. Actually dignifed," she said. "Gus spoke, beautifully! I mean, if I ever did anything in my life that was worth talking about, I would want him to be the one to do it for me. Then Walter's children spoke. Two of them, anyway. That son who ran away in the sixties showed up, but he just sat in the front row wearing the same ponytail and biting his fingernails. After that, there were some prayers and someone from the opera sang—that was Annabelle trying to impress the Mike Posners of the world, Walter had no use for the opera—and that was it.

"The Cos Club, on the other hand, was a zoo. There was

an incredibly long line for Gerta and the kids, stretching out into the hallway, and there was Annabelle standing all alone on the other side, calling out to people as they were leaving. It was pitiful! When I finally made it through Gerta's line and went over to Annabelle, one of Walter's sons came with me and asked her to stand with them, but she refused. So he goes back to tell Gerta, who belts down a shot of something. Then she comes over and tells Annabelle she has a choice: She could join their line that minute so they had a chance in hell of getting to the cemetery before sundown, or they were all going to walk out and leave her there."

Red laughed. "Gerta Gluckman always was the ballsiest girl on the block," he said admiringly. "It's a shame Walter never appreciated her."

Ponce nodded. "Annabelle acted all injured, but I think she was secretly relieved. She put herself first, of course, but once she did, the line moved right along. Now, tonight there are the dueling shivas." She pronounced it "sheevas." "Is that right, by the way?" she asked.

Red shrugged. "Christ Church, Greenwich, Connecticut. What do I know?"

"Anyway," she went on, "I heard most people say they were dropping into both places tonight just to be done with it. So tomorrow, Annabelle will have a tiny turnout and be insulted. The woman has no sense at all."

The waiter brought Ponce's wine.

"Excellent reporting on all counts," Red said, leaning toward her. "Now, how are you doing otherwise?" She sighed, and her face slid from animation to dismay.

"He called yesterday, completely apologetic, full of remorse. But not so full that he couldn't remind me that I'd never agreed to deny what Babette saw. I told him that of course I would. And that was it. He never mentioned the private-investigator photos, and neither did I. But I'm sure that's what will sink us."

Red set down his drink. "I don't know about that, Poncie. There are none of you together. He looks disheveled in front of your apartment building, but so what? Proves nothing. You came out of his office disheveled? Well, maybe you wanted to get pregnant and found out you couldn't. You were overcome with despair. Listen, the guys who work in your building are a big factor here, and they adore you. They're loyal to you. It's the tenants who don't tip, and don't give away their Yankee box seats when they're busy, whom they'd rat out in a minute."

He reached over to her lap and took her ice-cold hands in his. She pulled away. "If you are going to be nice to me," she said stiffly, "I am going to break down and cry in public and embarrass you. It's been—"

"Red! Dammit, Red! Great to see you!" A wide man in corduroy and tweed barreled across the floor, and Red stood to receive his bear hug. When he broke off, he turned toward Ponce. "Jimmy Maguire, Ponce Morris." Ponce remembered his name. He'd been the hotshot political editor at *The Washington Post* when Red had worked there.

Maguire nodded at her and turned back to Red. "Great to see you, fellow, even for an hour. What are we drinking?"

Red turned toward Ponce. "Actually, Jimmy and I have some catching up to do. We'll be in the room next door."

Ponce tried to contain her surprise. "Oh, well, I guess I'll be going then," she said, confused.

"No, no, that's not it at all," Red said. "You're going to stay right here and drink with the young lady Jimmy brought with him." He gestured toward the door, and she turned.

Shawsie was looking at her, concerned, and Ponce suddenly realized she looked as awful she felt.

"I'll see you girls soon," Red said, waving down the waiter.

"My tab, please," he said, pointing to them. "We'll be in the Main Bar." And though it didn't seem physically possible, he hefted an arm around Maguire and they were gone. Ponce walked over to where Shawsie waited.

"Red told me what bad shape you were in," Shawsie said tentatively. "And I know how much you hate making a scene, so I figured if I came here you wouldn't insult him by storming out."

"I know you're furious with me," Ponce said, her tone wobbly, "and I don't blame you."

Shawsie held out her arms, and Ponce burst into tears. Shawsie pulled her down onto a leather couch nearby and let her cry, muffling the noise with her oversize sweater. But Ponce's outburst didn't last long. She straightened up and grabbed her bag. "For someone who hates making a scene, I'm doing quite a job," she muttered, blowing her nose.

Shawsie held up her hand for the waiter. "One mineral water and another Pinot Grigio," she said.

Ponce wiped her eyes. "You're condoning my drinking now?"

Shawsie shrugged.

"Because I want to say something to you," Ponce went on, pulling herself forward on the couch. "I know we've been friends forever and that there are things about me you don't like—which I now know about in vivid detail—and I am genuinely sorry about lying to you, Mary Elizabeth. But leaving your husband out of this, I have to say on some level, this is it. This wretched creature before you may not be the friend you signed up for, but it is the friend you have. Yes, I drink. I drink because I like it, and I have no intention of stopping."

Shawsie's eyebrows flew up.

"No, I do not. Also, you're right, I'm thin. Every woman I have ever known has hated me for it, starting with my mother.

Well, too bad for all of you. I can't eat when I'm not hungry, and I'm tired of having to apologize for it.

"I cheat, you said. Well, when I sleep with married men, I suppose I do. But you were dead right about all that. I have affairs with married men because I *like* them being married to someone else. I don't want a mess. I've had plenty. I prefer being alone and always have. Thank you, Mother.

"The only problem with the equation this time," she went on, "is that I fell in love. Now I'm the mess." Her eyes filled again, and when she reached for her glass, her hand shook. "It is pathetic to think I could fall so hard just because a man treated me well without trying to control me. At least, I think that's why I did. Though I've always liked Neil so well. He has a kindness about him—a generosity, I guess. When I was with him, I felt so protected and cherished, really. That's a corny word but a true one. I had never been with a married man I missed so much when I didn't see him. I mean, I could never expect that he'd leave Sari, not with three small children. But when all this happened, I really thought he would." Her tears spilled over.

"This last trip when we were in Chicago," she said, "I thought I'd died and gone to heaven. We had the most wonderful night together. Everything else just melted away. And when we were in the lobby that morning with the prospect of a whole other night ahead and he kissed me, it was like a dream for me, to finally be so connected to someone. To feel what that is. At least what it is for me, which I suppose isn't much. But still. To have that one purely open moment of my paltry emotional life be pillaged by *Babette*. Someone so hateful. I could hardly even believe it. I can almost imagine it was my mother who sent her there, for spite."

She blew her nose. Shawsie looked at her and felt vaguely ashamed.

"You know what's the worst," Ponce said. "That night in Chicago, that first night, before Babette saw us, I told Neil I didn't even remember what town we were in but it didn't matter because I was with him. That had never happened to me before, that you could feel a person is a place, where you belong. And he said he felt the same thing about me. But what I meant was that he was a place in the world, to live in, together. What he meant was that I was a place outside the world, to escape to. Just like every other married man who's ever had an affair in the history of civilization. So I wasn't cheating the cheater after all. He was getting just what he wanted from me while I was busy being sweet sixteen, falling in love. God, I'm an asshole."

Shawsie lifted her water. "Welcome to the human race," she said.

Ponce drank her wine. "I guess I didn't tell you because, on some level, maybe I knew that I felt one way and he felt another. I'm not sure." She sighed. "It seems I've been disappointing people my whole life," she said. "I suppose it was only a matter of time before I got around to you. I think it's true, what you said about me being myself versus me being a woman. Maybe because I fought my mother so long, I refused to learn how to be one. For real, I mean. If I were a better woman, then maybe my feelings wouldn't shame me and I would be easier telling my secrets. I know that not telling you mine while you were trusting me with yours was dirty pool between girlfriends. It didn't feel that way to me, but I know it did to you." Her smile trembled. "I guess I didn't get to be a forty-two-year-old widowed divorcée with intimacy issues for nothing."

Shawsie didn't smile back. The waiter delivered more drinks. Ponce traded him for her empty glass.

"I appreciate what you're saying," Shawsie said slowly,

shredding a cocktail napkin, "but it's still not okay with me, just like that." She threw up her hands, abracadabra. Bits of paper floated to the carpet.

Ponce met her eye. "All right," she said.

Shawsie kept shredding. "Maybe because everything is wrong now. I mean, I'm pregnant, thank God, so that's right, but nothing else is where it should be. Not my marriage. Or you, really. The two things I count on most."

Ponce waited.

"I know I took a lot out on you, at your place, and I'm sorry to have been so tough," Shawsie said. "It was a cheap way out, but I needed one. I know the drinking thing wounded you. I mean, the way you drink, not that I love it, but at least you're not having sex in front of other people in bars. And as far as I know anyway, you've never missed an early-morning court date."

Ponce pursed her lips, offended.

"And you're not sitting in front of the television all day making your fourteen-year-old daughter run the house and pay the bills while your son needs to be sent to reform school and you can't manage to get to your shrink's office, even by three in the afternoon." She sighed again. "That would only be my mother."

"It would."

"But after all these years, you suddenly cut me out of your life and don't tell me something so important. Which I had to find out from *Robin*." Shawsie dropped the napkin and yanked her hair back, as if the absurdity overwhelmed her. "All I'm trying to figure out now is how to move forward. I've always counted on you, and all of a sudden I have to think about it. I may very well not have a husband to help me raise this child, and if I don't have you, what do I have?

"You know," Shawsie went on, studying the inside of her

glass. "I'm not all that different from you, which is probably why we've been friends for so long. In spite of what my life looks like at this moment, I don't like mess, either. My entire job at *Boothby's* is to avoid it by actively creating order. I wish that worked at home, but it doesn't. So I've looked the other way there." It was her turn to tear up. "I really love Robin," she said, wiping her nose with the back of her hand as Ponce handed her a tissue. "I know you think I shouldn't, but I do. He is so warm, so smart and dear, really.

"Don't make that face at me! I mean, after everything that's happened these last ten days, I know you think I'm deluded to say this, but I'm not. The one way I'm not like you is I'm not drop-dead gorgeous, if you haven't noticed. And as long as Oreos exist on the face of this earth, I will never be thin. When you have a problem, you skate through it so easily—not that you don't suffer, but in the long run, someone always comes along to fix it for you." She sighed. "Obviously, I lied when I said I wasn't jealous. I'm plenty jealous." Her smile was wry.

"I mean, I know this thing with Neil is bad, and I'm sorry you've been hurting. But it's hard for me to take it seriously, because I know that a year from now, or less, whenever, you'll be just fine. Some other wonderful man will be panting for the chance to make you happy. And good for you. Really. But no one is lining up to fix things for me, I can tell you that. I mean, I wish my father hadn't died. I just know that if he hadn't, I would never be so fucked up about men."

Now it was her turn to sob. Ponce put her arms around her, and Shawsie let her, but a minute later she pulled away, laughing. "You have the boniest shoulders I have ever felt," she said. Before Ponce could respond, Shawsie yelped. "Oh no! I got mascara all over your white cashmere sweater!"

Ponce peered down at it sideways and shrugged. "It was from Lee," she said. "More than time to get rid of it."

"Are you sure?" Shawsie regarded it blurrily.

"Of course," Ponce said. Shawsie leaned back on the couch, and Ponce hooked her arm through hers. "If it makes you feel any better," she said, "I always try to imagine my life had Mother died."

Shawsie's laugh was sharp. "Why am I not surprised?"

"Well, no, it's about more than her just being my torment. I loved my father, but he learned early on how to tune out my mother—and he did it to the rest of us, too. I so often think, What if Mother had just died? Got hit by a truck in the parking lot of the Blue Bird?"

They both smiled then.

"I mean, if she wasn't hovering over my father and me, always asking, 'What are y'all talking about *now*?,' maybe I could have had some real conversations with him. Not about sports, but about what I was thinking or feeling, about the things I might have wanted to do in my life. Or what he might have wanted to do in his." She picked up her wine. "But I'll tell you, Shawsie. That kind of thinking is a big circle. It didn't happen. It should have, but it didn't. And that needs to be the end of it. Don't you think my father regretted marrying my mother? He had to! I don't know enough about your parents' marriage to know whether your father got on that boat that day because he was trying to get away from your mother or because he just didn't listen to the weather report. But the older I get, the more I see there are these crevices in life where things fall in and you just can't reach them to pull them back out. So you can sit next to them and weep or you can get up and move forward. Now, you are *finally* having a child. You have got to stop worrying about who's not here and start worrying about who is."

Shawsie blew her nose. "I know that," she said. "And I know that I have to change things with Robin. Even he knows it. He's going to stop drinking, even if you're not. And he's agreed to go to counseling with me. I wasn't the only one who wanted a child, you know."

Ponce nodded. "That sounds like a good start."

Shawsie looked away. "It is, but I'm still not sure what's happening. You were in love, but you couldn't bring yourself to tell me. Robin is out doing God knows what, and he can't bring himself to tell me. I mean, why are the two people closest to me not talking to me?"

Ponce shrugged. "Maybe because neither one of us is as honorable as you, and we're both hoping you won't find out."

"Ladies!" Red stood before them, flushed and jolly, his arm continuing to defy the topography of Jimmy Maguire's back. "Mr. Maguire is leaving us now, and he wanted to say good night." Maguire shook hands with them both and gave Red a final parting hug. Red collapsed into the large chair next to the couch and motioned for the waiter.

"I'll have another, and so will she," he said, pointing toward Ponce's glass.

Shawsie frowned. "What is that, your third martini?"

Red frowned back. "Actually, Mary Elizabeth, it will be my fourth. Thank you for counting." He gestured toward Ponce. "One of the things I have always liked about Mrs. Morris here is that she has never counted my drinks. A trait, I might add, she shares with my dearly departed wife."

Shawsie flushed. "I'm sorry, Red. I guess I'm not myself these days."

He considered a moment. "Okay, kiddo. Apology accepted. But one word of advice: Becoming a mother does not require you becoming a bore." He peered at Ponce's sweater. "What the hell is that?"

Shawsie pulled the cocktail napkin from underneath Ponce's glass and dunked it in her water. "It's my fault," she said. "I cried on it and wrecked it with my mascara." She tried to dab at it, but Ponce waved her away.

"Crying? Have we had crying in my absence?" Red asked mockingly.

Ponce kicked him. "Cut it out."

Red patted his pockets, then sighed. "You two must forgive me," he said. "Seeing Jimmy Maguire reminded me I was alive once. For some reason, that particular fact seems to have slipped my mind."

Shawsie looked at her watch. "I should go," she said. "I thought I might stop at Annabelle's tonight, get it over with."

Ponce nodded and grabbed her bag. "I'll go with you," she said. "Tonight will be better than tomorrow."

Red placed a restraining hand on Ponce's arm. "Mary Elizabeth, you go anywhere you choose," he said, "but Mrs. Morris and I need to discuss the next steps of how she intends to handle the Babette Steele piece."

Shawsie cringed and sat back down. "Ponce, I'm sorry. I've been so caught up . . . Well."

The waiter brought the drinks, and Red looked at Shawsie. "Have you heard anything about this from Robin? Or about anything else, for that matter?"

"No," she said, evading his glance. "He's called me. A lot. But I'm not talking to him yet. I mean, I am, but—"

"I know you're not talking about yourselves at the moment, but have you talked about Ponce? Do you know if he's been speaking to Babette? Continuing to help her?" Red's gaze was intent.

Shawsie flushed, looking at the floor. "I, no. I don't know," she said.

"Well, I do," Ponce said. "Of course he's continuing to

help her. This whole thing began because Robin was fed up with me and fed up with Neil because of the IVFs, and manipulating this little tart was not only fun for an unemployed writer with time on his hands but sweet revenge. And it does occur to me, Mary Elizabeth, that if he's desperate to talk to you and feeling more and more isolated because you refuse, well, why shouldn't he spend more time fielding the editorial inquiries of his prize pupil? Especially if he can use them to screw me. He must well imagine that after what happened at the Acorn, I'm counseling you to divorce him immediately. Which if I was any kind of friend, I would."

Red sighed. "Shawsie, I apologize. We seem to have gotten off track here."

Shawsie, who had started to cry, kept her head down.

"Okay," Red went on, "why don't we leave Robin out of it for the time being and see what we might accomplish ourselves? Because a good offense is our best defense. Right?"

They both looked at him dully and he shook his head. "Now listen to me. I know there's trouble in paradise everywhere these days—including between the two of you—but I also know it'll blow over like the measles, so quit your bawling and pay attention here. I want both you girls to start making lists of people to call about Babette. We need to do our own reporting, and time is of the essence: Who knows her, who can find an Achilles' heel before the hourglass runs out. Yes?"

Their expressions stayed blank, and Red got annoyed. "Ponce! Concentrate! You have that trainer you've told me about, right? Well, didn't you say that Babette goes to him, too? Find out what she's been telling him."

Ponce looked as if she was beginning to understand.

"Yes, finally! There we are." Red turned to Shawsie. "Babette worked at your magazine for six months. Who were her friends? What was she up to? Are you getting me here?

Unless we all pitch in and find some facts of our own to discredit this creature, we risk her beating the odds and getting this article published. Because if *Manhattan* won't do it, the *New York Spectator* will, and I don't think they even have fact checkers at that rag, so let's pay attention."

Red was more alert than he'd been in ages, Ponce noticed. And in this light, at least, he actually resembled the dashing Red of yore. She felt the same flush of gratitude she had whenever she unsuspectingly spotted her younger self in the mirror. He was still in there.

"Will you do that?" he asked Shawsie, who nodded tearfully, looking at Ponce. "Absolutely. First thing tomorrow."

"Glad to hear it."

Shawsie stood, and Ponce did, too. But Red grabbed Ponce's hand and pulled her back down. "Mrs. Morris, I am an infrequent visitor to this lovely city of yours, and I was hoping you might have dinner with me," he said.

"Oh, Red, of course! I didn't know you'd want to."

"I do indeed. Now, Shawsie." He got up and hugged his niece hard and then, with both hands, brought her face close to his, nose to nose. She tried a smile. He used to do that when she was a little girl.

"Red, I'm sorry," she started, but he pretended to cuff her on the chin, as he also had when she was younger. "Stop being such a tough guy, Shawsie, eh?" he said softly. "Everyone here is on your side. And so is the father of your child, by the way. Remember that. Better late than never, okay?"

Her eyes filled again. "Okay."

Ponce looked up at her.

"We'll talk," Shawsie said quickly, then left.

Red and Ponce sat silently for a while, finishing their drinks.

"You knew I was right before," Ponce said. "About Robin. Under all that hair gel lives a bona fide snake."

Red patted his pockets. "Maybe so, Poncie. But maybe not. That boy's had a real scare, that much is certain. In his whole life, Shawsie is the only person he could ever call home, and to lose her would ruin him. I think he might realize that now."

"And you think he's really good enough for her?"

Red smiled gently. "She does, my dear. That's what counts." He glanced at his watch. "As I recall, Mrs. Morris, we have some unfinished business between us. So I would appreciate your joining me for that hamburger."

"Oh, Red, not tonight! I'm happy to sit with you, but I couldn't eat a bite."

He leaned over and grabbed her wrist. "If Cackie saw what you looked like, she would kill you," he drawled.

She started to laugh. "The problem with writers is that they never forget," she said. "Okay then. She would kill me, and she'd be right. I will do my best. Marshall's?"

"Where else?"

They started walking out, but she pulled him back. "Red, listen. About all this tonight. Thank you." She choked up. "Thank you for trying to take care of me."

"Hell, Poncie." His voice was gruff. "Do you think we made it this far to let some *child* beat us down? We're going to fix this thing. But first we're going to eat a hamburger with the works." He patted his stomach. "My friend the supermarket cashier would be chagrined," he said. "I suspect that Dr. Atkins would not approve."

"Dr. Atkins is dead," Ponce said.

Red laughed. "Then the hell with him," he said, and they walked outside together and hailed a cab.

Chapter Ten

The day after Walter died, Ponce called Annabelle and spoke to her for more than an hour. She described the lunch in detail—omitting the girl with the overblown calves—and told Annabelle repeatedly how much Walter had talked about her before the meal began. That was a lie, she knew, but Annabelle didn't have to.

Seeing Walter die had shaken Ponce. They had never been close, but he'd been part of her life with Lee from the beginning. She'd lived through Gerta and Annabelle, and through Lee's crazy obsession that his career was never as important as Walter's. Witnessing the extent to which such an accomplished man was ignored in his last moments had frightened her. What did it mean? If you weren't universally beloved, people felt justified in dismissing you?

To be fair, Walter had always been difficult. But still. Such a big career, such a big life. And to watch it sputter, disappear, within seconds. The sight of him lying on that dining room floor haunted her. So out of context. Out of order.

The notice in the *Times* said that Annabelle would be receiving from six until eight, so on Tuesday night Ponce arrived at seven-fifteen. Time enough. She rang the bell and, hearing the eager trot of high heels across the marble floor, felt immediately queasy. The unmistakable sound of an empty apartment.

"Oh. Hello." Annabelle gave Ponce the cursory hug of someone forced into a bond she never wanted in the first place.

"Annabelle?"

Shawsie walked into the hallway.

"It's only Ponce," Annabelle said, subdued. As Ponce stepped inside and shut the door, she got a face full of the widow's boozy breath.

Shawsie shot Ponce a look of doom, and they each took an arm and led Annabelle back into the living room, where she tipped toward the couch before they lowered her onto it. Ponce marveled at her outfit, a bright pink linen suit, perfect for Easter lunch. A torn black ribbon, the Jewish sign of mourning, was pinned to the lapel. Did she think it was like a broach, Ponce wondered, a decoration visitors might miss on something darker?

A waiter entered.

"White wine," Ponce said, and he quickly brought her a too-full glass. She sipped and peered into the dining room. Just what she'd feared. She and Shawsie were the only people there.

"Mike Posner's coming," Annabelle slurred, noting Ponce's survey. "His secretary said he would try to make it."

"That's great," Ponce said, trying to estimate the cost of the myriad platters of thick sandwiches and elaborate pastries set on tables decked with flowers. Annabelle didn't understand what this event was for, Ponce realized. Even though she still wasn't sure how to pronounce it, she'd been to enough of these gatherings to know that they were rituals, not feeding frenzies. You say you're sorry, you sit, reminisce, weep or hug if you're so inclined, have a drink, maybe a bite. You realize you're still alive, thank God, and go out to dinner. This wasn't a bridal shower or a wedding, a celebration based on the gorging of a joyful bounty. It was death, for chrissakes.

Annabelle slumped against the cushions, and Ponce told her again about the network lunch. Shawsie hadn't heard the story herself, but Ponce could see her sift through to the truth in an instant. She kept close to Annabelle and made all the right noises.

The clock in the front hallway chimed eight times. The waiter returned. "Mrs. Gluckman? Would you like me to clear?"

"What?" She looked at him blearily. "Clear? Why?"

"It's eight o'clock, ma'am. Receiving ends at eight."

"It does? Does that mean no one else is coming?" She burst into tears.

Shawsie reached over and took Annabelle's hand as Ponce stood. "Yes, please do clear," she told the waiter. "Wrap up everything and put the sandwiches in the refrigerator. Bring Mrs. Gluckman a mug of coffee and leave the percolator behind. It can be picked up in the morning. And for heaven's sake, put the liquor away."

He nodded, glad for direction. "Yes, ma'am. And would you happen to know where Mrs. Gluckman wants the boxes that were delivered from the network? They've been in the kitchen all day, and there isn't much room, and every time I ask where to put them, well . . ."

Ponce thought for a moment. "Bring them in here, if you don't mind," she said. "And open them up for her. She shouldn't be handling sharp objects."

Two other waiters carried in the large cartons, while a third set the coffee and a plate of sandwiches in front of Annabelle.

"Eat something now," Ponce suggested. "It's been a long day for you."

Annabelle did as she was told, and slowly some of the color returned to her face. Still, Ponce thought, she looked empty, old, the loose skin on her neck collapsed in rings against the collar of her suit.

When the last sandwich was eaten, Ponce stood.

"Annabelle, we will see each other soon. I'm so glad we could visit together tonight."

Annabelle looked confused. "Why are you going?"

"Well, I've got to be in court in the morning, and Shawsie has to be in the office."

Annabelle quickly grew teary.

"Look over here, Annabelle," Ponce said cajolingly, "at what the network sent today. "You'll have *hours* of pleasure going through Walter's things. What a comfort that will be."

Annabelle walked unsteadily toward the boxes. As she did, Shawsie and Ponce skirted around her.

"Look at this one!" Annabelle called loudly.

Shawsie turned. "What's that?" she asked, forcing an upbeat tone. Ponce could hear how exhausted she was.

Annabelle clutched a videotape. "I don't have my glasses. What does this one say?" she asked eagerly.

Shawsie held it up to the light. "'E. R. Murrow, 1952,'" she read.

"How wonderful!" Ponce exclaimed, sidling into the front hallway.

"That was Walter's very first job in television," Annabelle said, turning the tape over in her hands. She reached into another box and pulled out a few more. "Would you stay and watch with me?" Her tone was pleading.

Shawsie looked at Ponce and nodded. "Of course we will," she said kindly. "What a treat."

Ponce was trapped and she knew it. "Yes, of course," she said.

They followed Annabelle down the hall to a guest bedroom. It was too bad she and Shawsie were still sort of fighting, Ponce thought. If she reached over and pinched her now, she couldn't guarantee she'd take it the right way.

"There's a VCR in here," Annabelle said. "There's only a DVD player in our bedroom, and I still don't know how to work it." That brought a fresh round of tears, and she went off in search of Kleenex.

"I thought you were doing this last night," Ponce whispered.

Shawsie sighed. "Robin called right when I left the Yale Club and said he was going, so that was it for me. I went home and fell asleep. The only thing I seem to do well lately is sleep. Which, given the circumstances, is actually incredible."

"Okay, here we go! I took one of Walter's handkerchiefs instead." Annabelle opened it with a flourish. WAG, read the monogram. She settled into a rocking chair; Shawsie lay down on the bed, and Ponce sat beside her. Annabelle switched off the light and there was Edward R. Murrow. No sign of Walter, certainly. He was probably the errand boy at that point, Ponce thought, exasperated.

Honestly! How had she allowed herself to get swept up in this? Guilt, partly. Annabelle was friendless under the best of circumstances, and Ponce had been upset enough herself to empathize. After the lunch—once people heard that Ponce had been there—her phone had rung constantly. She was so rattled, so in need of company, that she gladly told what happened, but no one wanted to hear more than three sentences. Once they discovered that Walter hadn't had any famous last words—"Just collapsed, was that it?"—they'd churn past her description: "So sad. But what an extraordinary life. Will we see you at the Kofi Annan dinner next week?" Ponce finally turned off the ringer and let the machine pick up.

There were two Murrow shows on the tape. Shawsie slept soundly from the start as Annabelle wept and Ponce shifted her position on the soft bed between them. She had lied about having to be in court the next morning. Still, she couldn't wait to leave. Her thoughts drifted back to Neil, and she got the same sick feeling in the pit of her stomach she'd been getting for two weeks now. It was over. Hah. It was over if she was lucky. If she wasn't, it would be cocktail-party chatter until she dropped dead herself. But never at lunch, certainly.

When the tape ended, Ponce stepped into her shoes and nudged Shawsie. "Oh, Annabelle, wasn't that interesting! But it's so late now, we really have to go!" Ponce started for the door.

"No! It's not even eleven yet!"

Shawsie sat up on the bed. Annabelle sounded frightened, she thought drowsily. She didn't want to be alone.

"One more." Annabelle was begging now. "Here, look! I brought in a few of them. This is from a different box. Maybe it's an early *Current Events*. That would be something special, wouldn't it? At least it would be in color. Please?"

"Okay, Annabelle," Shawsie said warmly and Ponce couldn't believe she was sitting back down, but she was. It occurred to her that Shawsie kept agreeing to stay for the sole purpose of irritating her. Ponce leaned over, pretending to fix her shoe. "Stay awake this time, and right after the first show, we're gone, okay?"

Shawsie nodded without meeting her eye.

"Let's see, what does this label say?" Annabelle squinted. "Oh, never mind, we'll just start it. If anyone is wearing bell-bottoms, we'll know it's the sixties!"

She switched off the lamp and settled back into her chair. They waited for the lead on the tape to give way to a picture, but it just kept on going.

"Maybe this one is blank," Ponce said. "Do you want me to—"

Suddenly there was a grainy shot of Walter's office. Walter sitting at his desk, talking. The camera didn't move, and it was hard to hear what he was saying. After a few minutes, Ponce stifled a yawn. Probably some bright idea that had never panned out of having him introduce segments on *Current Events*.

Walter's phone rang, and he answered it. Ah, the working-journalist pose, Ponce thought. How contrived. Who would want to watch this? She saw Shawsie's head drop forward. She could just kill her. And Annabelle too. The half-life of Ponce's empathy had officially expired.

Walter was standing now, gesturing, "Come in." A young woman appeared and shook his hand awkwardly. He pulled her toward him. She pulled away and laughed. He pushed her down into a chair in front of his desk and stood in front of her, in profile.

"Well, you're right," she said, giggling. "One kiss wouldn't hurt." She reached toward his fly.

And at the exact same moment that Ponce realized she was watching Babette Steele give Walter Gluckman a blow job, Annabelle screamed.

. . .

Babette paced the Fifth Avenue block where Ponce lived. She couldn't believe it that morning when she'd picked up her phone to find Ponce on the line, dripping honeysuckle.

"I've been thinking about this profile you're writing about me and wondering if I've made a mistake not talking to you," Ponce said. "I mean, I'm sure you'd rather not paint a one-sided portrait of me that would be unfair in any way. Isn't that right?"

"Well, sure it is, Ponce," Babette answered. "You and I both know what a keenly developed sense of fairness you have. I can only follow your fine example."

"I was thinking you might like to come by this evening, for cocktails," Ponce said smoothly. "Say, six-thirty?"

Babette flushed with satisfaction. "Ah, the long-awaited cocktails," she gloated. "But you know, to be *fair*, why don't I save you some time? I saw you and Neil Grossman kissing in the lobby of the Four Seasons in Chicago, and no matter how much money he's paying Mort Diamond to say otherwise, I know what I saw. And I know what it meant."

Ponce's laugh tinkled. "Now, doesn't journalism mean that I get to tell *my* side of this story, too?"

Babette felt a twinge. Sound effects aside, that question bore the stamp of a lawyer.

"Of course," she amended quickly. "Of course you do. I'll see you at six-thirty."

Babette hung up and tried organizing her thoughts. It was Wednesday. She was seeing John Carraro at the *Manhattan* offices on Monday morning, his first appointment back from Disney World, and she had almost finished a draft. But whatever she would get from Ponce—a boatload of bullshit, no doubt—she'd have to do the whole thing over. And M was coming back from Japan the following night. He called to say he had planned the most wonderful weekend. She sighed. The anxiety she'd felt the last time she saw him, when he was so condescending about her reporting, had completely disappeared. He should stick to his business, whatever the hell it was, she thought smugly. She was doing just fine with her own.

Actually, the more she thought about it, the more she'd decided that M was getting to be a bit of a trial. He did have this insistence whenever he was in town that she drop everything to cater to his every whim. And with his taste for Viagra, his whims were continuous. The only good news there was that they didn't last more than an hour per pill.

But getting this piece in shape was her first priority. She knew that once it ran, she'd be besieged with other assignments, not to mention booked on television talk shows. She thought disdainfully of her Carmen sidebar running in the new issue of *Boothby's*. Such small potatoes. Who cared about fashion writing? She was on the fast track with this story. It actually turned out great that Topher had fired her. Really! She could have spent years there opening the mail, bowing down. And for what? She was rising up, and she couldn't be more ready.

She walked over to the foot of her bed—her makeshift desk—and reviewed her notes. Good stuff. Sari Grossman was still the best, though in the last few days Jacqueline Posner had also come through. Jacqueline told all sorts of wicked stories about Lee which gave the piece real spice and—to Babette, at least—raised real doubts about the backbone of his fourth bride. A cautionary tale, Babette thought. Marry a rich old man who's used to having his way, and you don't stand a chance. Well, she would not be making that mistake. This story came first. Then, if time allowed, the fabulous weekend with M would be the icing on the cake.

Six twenty-five. She'd been out here cooling her heels long enough, Babette thought. Had it been a real drink, a social drink, she'd never think to arrive early. But rudeness is as rudeness does. She went into the lobby and announced herself to the doorman. An elevator attendant took her up, and Babette was surprised when the doors opened directly onto Ponce's apartment. Talk about money.

Ponce was right there, waiting for her.

"Thank you, Mike," she said to the elevator man, who tipped his hat. "Babette, so nice to see you. Won't you come in?"

Babette walked into the tiny foyer and through the doorway. The first thing she noted was the sweep of the front hall. And this place was only the divorcée consolation prize. Well, touché. Maybe Mrs. Morris's backbone was intact after all.

"I hope white wine will do," Ponce was saying, leading Babette toward the study. "I don't keep much of a bar."

"Oh, sure. Fine."

Babette walked toward the window and peered out onto the stretch of Fifth Avenue she'd been pacing a few minutes earlier. It sure looked better from here.

"Sit where you like." Ponce gestured around the room, and Babette chose a leather chair near one end of the couch. Ponce sat in its twin, opposite her. Babette noted the distance and dug around in her bag for her notebook.

"So," she started, but the elevator scraped to a halt again in the outside hall. "Yes, thank you," she heard someone say, and she felt a stab of anger. Shawsie.

"What kind of setup is this?" Babette asked, standing as Shawsie entered the room.

"Oh, Babette, please don't get up on my account," Shawsie said. "I think I've seen enough of you standing for a lifetime. Though I do prefer you with your clothes on."

Ponce got up and poured orange juice into a wineglass and motioned toward Babette's seat. "Please sit down," she said. "We need to talk."

Babette stayed standing and crossed her arms. "You're obviously ganging up on me for a reason. So what is it? I don't have all night."

"Oh," Ponce said, "I thought you wanted to ask me some questions for your piece. No? Well, have it your way." She walked over to the television set and turned it on. Walter and Babette played out their scene.

"Shit!" Babette clasped her throat with both hands. "He *taped* it?" She bolted toward the set, but Shawsie and Ponce stood in front of it, side by side.

"Even if you want to attack a pregnant woman," Shawsie said, "there are two copies of this tape sitting in a vault at Corning Hilliard. So do your best."

"You're pregnant? Christ."

"I believe the standard response is 'Congratulations.'"

Babette waved toward the set. "Where did you get this?"

"It was among Walter's things," Ponce said. "And Annabelle's seen it already, so you can kiss that friendship goodbye."

Babette tried desperately to think of what to do or say next. This was awful. After everything that had happened these last two weeks, Annabelle was one of the only people in New York still talking to her. She sank down in her leather chair and gulped her wine.

Ponce and Shawsie looked at each other, satisfied, then Shawsie glanced at the screen, where the scene continued to play. She started to giggle. "You know, Babette, I've seen your tits twice now in two weeks, and I don't even know your middle name," she said. Ponce laughed, too, and Shawsie could hear her relief.

Babette looked down at her hands, knotted together, and said nothing.

"Well, we thought you'd see it our way," Ponce said with an air of finality.

Babette lifted her head. "What do you mean?" she asked slowly.

"That you agree not to go ahead with the piece."

"Why would I do that?" Babette looked incredulous.

"*Why?*" Ponce's face flooded red. "Because the minute Montrose Merriweather gets to town I will make sure that he views this tape. Do you think he's going to want to date, much less marry, some cheap tramp who gives out blow jobs for job applications?"

Babette drained her wine.

"I mean, really," Ponce said. "Did you think giving Walter a blow job meant he'd hire you?"

Babette shrugged. "Yeah, maybe. Old guys are fixated on blow jobs. Though I guess I don't have to tell you that."

Ponce flushed redder.

"At that point I hadn't been hired by *Boothby's* yet," Babette went on. "I was short on cash and had a friend who needed some help, and when I asked Walter for a loan a few weeks later, he just gave me the money and said to call it a gift. I mean, it was a fucking blow job. Is that such a major event in your pathetic little worlds?"

"No," Ponce said quietly. "The major event in my pathetic little world is that you saw me kissing a friend and are turning that into my beheading."

Babette walked to the bar and refilled her own glass. "Yes, thanks, I'd love some." She turned to Ponce. "Don't pretend you're not having an affair with Neil Grossman. He's been seen here regularly, and you've been seen going in and out of his office at all hours by people who live in that neighborhood.

I have proof. Look at you now, I can see your palms sweating from here." Ponce clenched her hands and tried not to look guilty. "So the moral of this story, Ponce, is there's not too much difference between giving a blow job for money and doing what you've done your whole life. None, actually."

Babette drained her wine. "There's also no reason for me to pull this piece. I've done the reporting, I have the scoop, and there's no way you can stop me."

"I can show this tape to Gus Fisher," Ponce said. "And Rachel. And Topher. Let some people in the media see what you're really about."

Babette laughed then, a genuinely amused laugh.

"Um, hello? Have you ever heard of Paris Hilton? Do you have any idea how cool it is now to have a sex video out there? I mean, even if it is with an old guy, people still see how hot you are. And this is with a famous old dead guy. Think of the nostalgia factor. Combine that with this incredible article with its incredible scoop for *Manhattan* magazine, and I am in demand. And what are the two of you? The sob sisters clucking in the corner. One causes the downfall of the hottest doctor in New York City, and the other, so sadly, has no choice but to raise her child alone."

Babette put down her wineglass and gathered her things to go. "You know, this drink wasn't half as much fun as I'd hoped," she said. "Some things are better left to the imagination."

Later that night, Neil phoned Ponce while he was out walk-ing the dog. They had kept in limited touch over the past week in a series of brief calls. Sharing information, they were both cordial and to the point, though Ponce could periodi-cally hear the fear seep into his voice. He was like a child, she thought. He'd done something wrong—that's all it was to him now—and he was steeling himself against the biblical punishment that awaited. It made her feel alone in a way that was foreign and unwelcome.

"Something bad happened today," he said without saying hello. "Page Six called Mort."

"And said what?" She worked to keep her tone steady.

"That Babette Steele has been running all over town telling everyone she's doing a piece on you for *Manhattan* magazine because we're having an affair and I'm leaving Sari. She says it's running next week."

"Next week?"

"Yeah. But Mort says that can't be true. That by this late in the week, someone would have called to check facts. And no one has."

Ponce told him everything that had happened in the last few days.

"And she doesn't care that it's on *tape*? Good God," Neil said. "What world are we living in?"

"Don't I know it. I really thought I had her, too. Shawsie and I were convinced. I thought I could call you and tell you it was behind us, that there was nothing to worry about now."

It sounded to her like he might be crying.

"It's not me I care about," he whimpered. "It's Sari."

"Of course you do," she said. "And I—"

He hung up.

She put down the phone. Something clicked in her brain. Enough. It was time to take care of herself.

At noon the next day, Red, Rachel, and Shawsie were gathered in Ponce's study. Gus, away at a mandatory orientation day with Terry and the twins at Dogwood, where they would enroll in the fall, had spoken with Ponce for an hour that morning. "Walter did the tape thing all the time," he told her. "After a few drinks, he liked showing them to the guys on staff. I somehow missed the one with Babette."

"That is despicable," Ponce protested, but Gus only laughed. "Listen," he said. "The guy loved television. He just couldn't stand that he wasn't on it himself."

When Ponce had told Gus about the call from Page Six regarding *Manhattan* magazine, he'd put her on hold and called a friend there. Half a minute later he was back to Ponce. "Not you," he assured her. "And if it's any consolation, he's never even heard of Babette."

Ponce told the assembled all of this, bringing them up to date.

"Has Page Six called you yet?" Rachel asked, and Ponce shook her head. Rachel shook hers, too. "I can see it now: 'Top Fertility Doc Bad Seed.'"

Everyone glared.

"Sorry," she said. "Look, maybe you can call one of them over there and offer to buy him a pony if he'll look the other way. It's worked before."

The house phone rang. Red went into the kitchen to answer it, and when he came back Robin was with him.

Red held up his hand, preempting a response from Ponce or Shawsie. "Robin and I had a long talk last night, and I felt it was important he come here today. He has a lot of information we can stand to hear right now. So start listening."

Robin pushed at his hair. "Well, first I want to say that, obviously, I'm truly sorry about helping Babette. I guess I thought it was harmless, and like so much else in my life, I seem to have guessed wrong."

No one spoke.

"Um, and since that thing at the Acorn"—he winced—"I haven't taken any of her calls. I counted on the fact that she would go ahead and call John Carraro to sell him the piece, and that's exactly what she's done. So he and I worked out a plan. He told her he was going to Disney World with his kids, but he wasn't. He's been here the whole time. So she lost this whole week and doesn't realize it. I don't know how to prevent this piece from happening, but I did buy some time to strategize."

Ponce lit a Parliament. "It's Friday," she said curtly. "Time's up."

Robin dug out his Dunhills. "When they met, Carraro gave Babette a list of people to call," he said. "That list came from me, and I called everyone on it first to tell them Babette was up to no good. I said they could either stonewall her and not call back, or talk only about Ponce's past. I also told them all to tell at least two lies, so when the fact checkers started calling and discovering discrepancies, the magazine might either delay the piece or consider it a big enough mess to kill it. Of course, there was always the chance that Babette would call people who were not on that list. But my hunch was that she wouldn't bother.

"You all know that Carraro's boss, the editor in chief of *Manhattan*, is Victoria Stone," Robin went on. "I'm sure you've read that she's had one baby courtesy of Neil Grossman and has spent the last two years trying to have another. Carraro's not sure if she hates Neil's guts or she's convinced herself he's the only doctor in America who can ever get her pregnant again, because he says Victoria is so crazy on the subject that her opinion of him changes by the day. So until John sees a more finished version of the piece, he won't even mention it to her. She could either refuse to run a word remotely critical of Neil or be so incensed with him that she'd run Babette's first draft. He said the hormone thing has driven everyone there nuts for years."

Shawsie flushed and said nothing.

"Great work, Robin," Red said heartily. "Really first-rate. The only thing we can get at this point is time, until we figure out what else to do."

"Yes," Ponce said to Robin, forcing a smile. "Thank you for helping me. You certainly have no reason to, but I do appreciate it."

"You're welcome," he said, then looked at Shawsie. "But I have every reason to."

Shawsie reached for her tissues.

Red patted his pockets as he watched Ponce stub out her cigarette. He looked frustrated. "I just wish I could see the story myself," he said. "I'd know in a second if it has a chance to be published or not. Robin, you've seen some of it, haven't you?"

He sighed. "I'm sorry to say it was actually pretty good."

Rachel frowned. "It was? Had someone edited it already?"

Robin shook his head. "No, I was the only one she showed it to."

Rachel reached into her bag and pulled out the new issue of *Boothby's*. She put on her glasses and thumbed through the pages. "Okay, listen to this. New Faces: Carmen by Babette Steele.

"'It takes a real talent to make you forget how the cold wind of a Chicago winter can cut you like a knife, but Carmen, the twenty-eight-year-old design sensation, might be the one to do it,'" she read. "'Ever since she fled her native Cuba when she was only eleven, her flair for color has brightened her world.'"

Shawsie groaned. "How the hell did that happen?" she said. "Camille has *got* to go."

"She does indeed," Rachel said, turning to Robin. "But my point is, that is an edited paragraph. Which means it was even worse before someone else got their hands on it. Was the writing you saw like this?"

Robin poked at his hair. "No. It wasn't. It was good. Different."

"I don't suppose you kept any of it," Rachel said. "Scrap paper? Sentiment?" She glanced at Shawsie. "Sorry."

He shook his head. "I didn't."

"Oh!" Ponce hit her head with both hands. "I am such an asshole," she proclaimed and ran out of the room, returning with her purse. She opened her wallet and started emptying it, dumping credit cards and business cards onto the coffee table. An old fortune from a cookie fluttered down. "Don't even think about it," she said to Red, who had reached his hand out.

She unfolded a small square of white paper. "I took this from Babette's drawer at *Boothby's* the day I confronted her there and completely forgot about it." She picked it up and read: "'The Spare Wife.'"

Rachel turned red and reached for one of Ponce's Parliaments. Ponce lit another cigarette herself and straightened the paper in her hand.

"'It seems somehow fitting that our story begins with an ending,'" she read. "'It was, as *tout* New York remembers, Jacqueline Posner's poignant farewell to the Park Avenue home she had made so lovingly for Mike Posner. Jacqueline seemed fragile that night, her long face white against her cloud of dark hair. If not for Ponce Morris, whose cool blond beauty gave the evening its spine and her friend her courage, the guests would have left before the dinner was even served.

But Ponce, in her rhinestone pants and silver charmeuse top, sparkled as surely as the stars outside the windows in the inky velvet sky.'"

Rachel yelped with indignation. "What the hell is that?" She turned to Robin. "This is a twenty-five-year-old kid who's written beauty captions for *Self*, but I don't think that even a mascara has a name as putrid as Inky Velvet Sky. And '*tout* New York'? It's like drinking tea with your pinkie in the air. Low *and* dated. No one under forty would write like that. Or even think it. The thing is overwritten and underwritten at the same time. Anyone knows that Jacqueline Posner has dark hair, and anyone could assume she'd be pale if she were upset. It's not specific enough. And what does it mean that Ponce's beauty gave the evening its spine? It makes no sense. The whole thing is off. It has an 'as told to' quality."

She looked around. "You all see what I'm saying, don't you? I mean, you can tell by the way Babette speaks that the Carmen piece is written in her voice. The only thing missing is 'Isn't it hilarious?' But this." She looked disdainfully at Robin. "You couldn't tell she didn't write this?"

He looked miserable. "No. I mean, it never occurred to me she hadn't."

Red spoke up. "Okay, Rachel, let's say you're right on this. Say one of us tells *Manhattan* magazine that the piece was written by someone not its author. How do we prove it?"

"Hell if I know. But I know enough about writing to know that that girl did not write this paragraph."

The intercom rang. Puzzled, Ponce walked to the kitchen to pick it up.

"What? Oh, damn!"

She came back in and sorted through the pile on the coffee table, picking up her calendar. "The car's downstairs to take me to my workout with Thom. I completely forgot to cancel."

Rachel looked excited. "No! Don't you dare cancel. Thom knows Babette better than any of us. You've got to go. You can ask him what writers she knows, who else she's friends with. Someone wrote this for her—it's just a matter of finding out who, that's all."

Ponce shook her head. "I am in no shape to go over there and do even one sit-up, I can assure you. And I never gossip with Thom. I've made that a point through the years. I can't start asking questions about Babette now. He'd know something was off."

Rachel was already up and walking toward the door. "Fine," she said. "While we're letting our hair down today, I'll tell you that of the ten sessions with him you bought me, I've only used two. I can't stand him, and I can't stand the sit-ups. So I'll take your appointment instead and try to find out what's going on. Wish me luck!"

Once she was gone, Ponce looked at the group. "Do you all think she's right?" she asked. Robin looked ashamed, but nodded. So did Red. Shawsie reached for Ponce's shaking hands and rubbed them in hers to warm them. "I hope so," she said.

"Does that mean 'Yes, but good luck finding out who'?"

Shawsie sighed. "I guess."

Robin picked up his jacket and walked toward the hallway.

"Where are you going?" Red asked.

"My office," he said. "I'm going to start with the A's and keep going. Maybe someone I know needed to make some extra dough."

Chapter Eleven

Thom leaned up against the wall and stretched his Achilles tendons. With the warm weather coming he looked forward to Rollerblading the distance from Chad's new house in Water Mill to the beach in East Hampton. Chad, of course, would drive. In their duo, Thom remained the sculpted figure of wonder. "It's textbook, sweetie," Chad liked to say. "With a trainer for a beau, I don't have to work out. You're beautiful for both of us. My very own trophy wife. Who never gets menopause."

When Thom turned away from the wall, he saw none other than Rachel Lerner walking toward him. What was that hag doing here during Ponce's session? He forced himself to smile. She was, after all, bought and paid for.

"Rachel, hey! How's it going?"

"Great, Thom." She seemed more pleasant than she had before, but so would a cobra. "I know you were expecting Ponce," Rachel went on, "but we were having lunch today and she wasn't feeling well but was too guilty to cancel. And I'm even guiltier about not seeing you, after she paid for it and everything. So I said I'd go instead."

He tried not to sigh. "Well, then," he said. "Let's get to it!"

She did the sit-ups without a single snarl. He gave her a few pointers on form. "Yes, thanks" was the only reply. Her obedience lasted through the lunges, then she rolled her eyes pleadingly. "I know it's early, but can I get a break?" she asked. Her tone so resembled a human being's that he agreed.

They sat on the mat. "Work's been a bitch lately," Rachel said. "We've been sort of short-staffed. Did you hear they let Babette go?"

Thom's eyes widened. "They did? No, I hadn't heard that. I only see her once a month."

Rachel nodded, looking sympathetic. "It must be awful for her to be out of work, just like that. But I guess she was the last one hired, so first one fired, you know how that goes."

He knew enough to know that that's how it went at factories in bad economies, not at Rubinstein magazines. Shawsie must have discovered the affair with Robin.

"Yeah, that must be it," he said, aping Rachel's expression of sympathy. "Has she found another job?"

She shrugged. "I don't know. But I heard she was freelancing, maybe doing a piece for *Manhattan* magazine. She probably has lots of friends who are writers who can help her. Don't you think?"

Thom shrugged back. "She doesn't talk about work much." He felt himself closing off instinctively, always wary about getting into gossip he couldn't get out of.

"Shall we go on?" He stood, and she had no choice but to follow. She moved dutifully through the weight machine circuit, though by the time he had her bending her elbows into

Gumby positions for her triceps, she looked ready to explode. He followed her glance as she abruptly let go of the handles and let the weights slam the armrests back.

A breaking news bulletin flashed on the bottom of a TV screen. When Thom saw that it was a friendly-fire incident in Iraq that had killed five soldiers, he lost interest. But Rachel seemed genuinely upset.

"Do you know someone there?" he asked respectfully.

She shook her head. "No, but my husband's the executive producer of *Real Time*, and he's got a crew over there," she said.

"Oh." Rachel had been such a supreme pill from the moment she arrived after New Year's that he had completely forgotten she was married to Gus Fisher, wunderkind news producer and, since Walter Gluckman died, candidate to either take over *Current Events* or go straight to the top as president of the news division. At least that's what Thom had read in the tabloids. He needed to revise his M.O., and fast.

"Is it a big crew?" he asked, concerned.

She rubbed an elbow. "It is, but it's not just that. He'll hate not knowing the minute it happened. He's spending the whole damn day at Dogwood with his five-year-old twins and his ex-wife on some tedious orientation for the class entering kindergarten next fall."

Thom saw his chance. "Well, as a future Dogwood parent, you must have heard about the whole grade-inflation flap?" Rachel shook her head as he launched into the tale of Seamus Ferguson, defender of English, or Irish, civilization in the face of cold Upper East Side cash, during which Rachel made a valiant effort to keep her eyelids from closing.

"I guess we didn't hear about it because it was in the high school," she said finally.

Thom nodded, and his tone was oh so casual. "I thought

you might have heard about it because Seamus Ferguson lives with Babette Steele's mother," he said.

Rachel's neck nearly snapped, she turned her head so fast.

"No kidding," she said, her tone as casual as his, though she proceeded to toss off questions like gunfire. By the end of her push-ups, she'd learned that Seamus Ferguson was a pill freak who taught English; that he was known to hate all high school athletes, probably because his own Olympic dreams were dashed in the accident that had turned him into a pill freak; that the class in which the boys' grades were questioned was Contemporary Irish Literature; and that his Creative Writing elective was, at least according to Babette, sought after by every nonathletic senior at the school. He was a published novelist, after all.

Rachel also learned that after his firing, Seamus Ferguson had wanted to sue Dogwood and Babette tried to raise money to help him with legal fees. Though he'd never pursued it, Thom said.

"So he's just been living in Riverdale, looking for a job?" Rachel asked.

Thom shrugged. "I guess. When Babette was here last month, she said he'd done some freelance editing and she got him some rewrite work because he wasn't picky and had plenty of time on his hands. She said you could tell him any story and he could tell it back to you even better."

Rachel smiled wide. "This has been great," she said, going to fetch her bag. "I really will make another appointment soon."

"But we haven't done our cool-down yet," he protested.

She was already out the door.

· · ·

Babette sat on a corner banquette in the back room of Sir's and in blatant disregard of the oil paintings surrounding her, practically purred, she was so happy. Granted, she wasn't entirely comfortable. She did need to keep shifting position—an insistent branch of forsythia kept stabbing the side of her head—and she felt rather hemmed in by this puny patch of table that was considered prime real estate here. But overall, things could not be better. She watched the maître d' pour a bottle of Dom Pérignon into crystal flutes and smiled prettily at M.

She could barely wait to bound out of her bed the following morning and into the office of John Carraro, article in hand. After her "drink" with Ponce and Shawsie the previous Thursday, she had made the executive decision to pretend it never happened and to tell Carraro instead that Ponce refused to cooperate. Babette had gone ahead that Friday and assembled her file carefully for Monday's meeting. It held not only her draft and her notes but all the pictures from the private investigator, along with a copy he'd gotten her of Neil's Chicago hotel bill, which included massages for two. In the room. She sipped her champagne. Friends, indeed.

She had even set out her clothes for Monday morning on her bed; she knew she would spend tonight with M. Tomorrow, she would wake up early, go home, shower, and dress. She had always laughed at that drippy poster her mother hung on the wall in her office at the library: "Today is the first day of the rest of your life." Well, she wasn't laughing now. Tomorrow was the first day of hers.

As for M, well, tomorrow was also the first day of the rest of her life without him. Not that the weekend wasn't successful. It had been glorious. The suite at the Carlyle, dinner at the Four Seasons, a cocktail party at the Knickerbocker Club. And a trip to Hermès, where Babette picked out an elegant pleated scarf, different in pattern from the one M had already sent her though somewhat similar to the one she saw now at a table across the room where an old-line socialite held court. The woman was a famous smoker, and her oxygen tank was wrapped jauntily for the evening in shades of pink and gold, as stylishly turned out as its owner.

Babette drank more champagne. The scarf had clinched it for her. Had M taken her some place like Tiffany for the purchase of a more meaningful memento, her choice about continuing their relationship might have been difficult. But if his intentions were mired in the category of "scarf," well, all bets were off. In any case, he was going to his plantation tomorrow and to Dallas after that, and did she really know what he was doing when he wasn't with her? Maybe he had a girl stowed in every city, waiting for her own trip to Tiffany. And why not, she thought magnanimously. What she knew was that her world was about to change. Drastically. So, time to move on. To even think of how her life would be different by tomorrow night, once Carraro had read her piece! Her fingertips tingled with excitement.

The waiter set down a bowl of caviar. Babette reached for a toast point and heard an unmistakable voice.

"Why, M! How wonderful to see you!"

For chrissakes, what the hell was Ponce doing here? Everyone knew that Sunday was socialites' night out at Sir's. Back from a weekend in the country, it was a chance to tuck into a little chicken hash while you reclaimed your rightful territory among the city's brightest lights. Something like Sir peeing on a hydrant. Or an heirloom rosebush. But why would Ponce, who made a fetish of proclaiming her lack of interest in all of the above, even bother to make an appearance?

"This is Rachel Lerner," Ponce went on, introducing her companion. Rachel extended her hand.

Double Christ! From bad to worse, Babette thought. How did *she* get in here? She hadn't had a distemper shot in years.

"Mrs. Morris, it is a delight to see you again," M said, having risen to full height before stooping down to kiss both Ponce's cheeks. "And of course I remember you, Rachel. Babette's fellow traveler at *Boothby's*."

In that moment it became clear to all three women that M had no idea of Babette's current job status. In her tight corner, Babette scrambled to her feet, banging the table. Her flute tipped, spilling a frothy pool onto the cloth.

"Oh, Babette, for heaven's sakes, don't get up," Ponce said, amused. "You have such trouble with that."

The maître d' appeared tableside with a napkin, eager to preserve two hundred dollars' worth of caviar.

"Marco, when you're through, go into the kitchen and get a shears from the chef," Ponce said. "Miss Steele is fighting a losing battle with that forsythia. François never should have opened without checking it first."

"Yes, madame," Marco said as Babette turned scarlet. That damn thing had been torturing her all night, and she had been afraid to say a word about it. She thought M would find her graceless, or demanding. Or both.

"Careful," Marco said, perhaps to himself, as he lifted the flute, finding it had broken on one side, leaving a long, curved V-shaped shard of glass on the table. When he picked it up, it flashed in the light.

"Oh, look at that, your karma's changing," Rachel said to Babette, whose expression was blank. "When you break a glass, it signals a change in your life's energy," Rachel went on. "Which is sometimes a great notion."

M picked up his flute. "I quite like Miss Steele's karma,"

he said smoothly. "It's like everything else about her. Just right."

Babette blushed but said nothing. She was furious and embarrassed and terrified all at once. She didn't know why. But something wasn't right. She could feel it.

A waiter returned with the shears and made a single snip.

"Perfection," Ponce said, turning to go. "Well, nice to see you both."

M made a slight bow as Marco returned with a fresh flute. "My apologies, miss," he said to Babette. It took her a minute to realize that he was talking about the forsythia, not the arrival of the recent company.

"Rachel Lerner seems quite the New York customer," M said, sitting down. "Do you have to work with her?"

"No." Babette tried not to chug her champagne. "She only works with one editor, and she's almost never there. Not that anyone misses her."

Babette watched Ponce and Rachel sit side by side on a banquette in the opposite corner of the room and noted the two empty chairs in front of them. Damn. Gus and who? She could already hear the repeat requisite greeting to M. Well, not this time. She was not getting up. Not for anything.

"Caviar?" M held out a toast point, arranged with a sprinkling of egg and onion. She felt herself relax, just a little.

"Yes, thanks." It was delicious. She had another and felt even better. What had that crazy moment been about? Everything was fine. The piece was written, her meeting was set, the weekend was almost over. Nothing had changed. But what was that nonsense about her karma?

Across the room, the waiter opened a bottle of Pinot Grigio and poured some for Ponce and Rachel, stowing it in a bucket while they studied their menus. Maybe no one else was coming. Maybe they were alone, after all.

"M! How nice to see you!"

Was it some rule of nature that anywhere Ponce Morris went, Shawsie just had to follow?

Again, M stood and shook hands—like an animatronic figure in a theme park, Babette thought derisively. True to her word, she stayed seated. Riveted to the wall, more like it. As she felt her pulse bang in the center of her skull, Babette realized that she couldn't have gotten up even if she'd wanted to. Because standing in front of her, staring back at her as if he had seen the very same ghost she had, was Seamus Ferguson.

"So nice to meet you," M was drawling, shaking his hand, too.

Shawsie turned to Babette. "Well, hello," she said. "Seamus was kind enough to meet me for a drink this evening, and he's agreed to pitch me some pieces for *Boothby's.* I told him I hadn't realized his talent before I spent this weekend reading him."

Babette clamped her mouth shut as she felt the champagne bubble its way back up her throat and she turned her stupefied gaze to Seamus, who she couldn't help notice looked guilty as sin. She wondered if he had kept a copy of her story. How else could Shawsie have seen it? Did she break into her apartment? No, that was ridiculous. Then again, maybe her idiot roommates had just opened the door and let Shawsie waltz right in.

Having successfully swallowed the wayward champagne, Babette tried taking a breath. Okay, so Seamus helped her write the piece. So what? Was she really supposed to have done all that reporting and writing herself so quickly when she'd never done anything like it before? And who knew she was going to get fired and be so stuck for money? Even more than that, who knew she'd be so stuck so suddenly to keep her reputation intact, not be the hotshot assistant who fizzled—the suburbs were littered with them—and come through with her future secure.

Because if she'd been dating, say, some bond trader when this all happened, then fine. She'd have gone to Short Hills quietly. But her stakes were higher. She had fucked up big-time with Robin and Shawsie, and she needed to save herself big-time. M was not exactly a junior executive with a hankering for two kids and a McMansion. And quite frankly, she would rather die than engage in anything called Mommy and Me anytime soon. She thought about her file, neat on her bed next to her outfit, all the photographs and the papers from the detective. She held on to the edge of the tiny table and tried not to shudder.

"Sweetheart," Babette heard from a great distance. "Are you all right?"

She wanted to answer but she was too busy watching the smirk on Shawsie's face, the glee on the faces on the opposite side of the room, as they clinked their glasses of Pinot Grigio. Her debasement was complete. Or so she thought until she watched Shawsie reach into her oversize black bag and pull out a book. When M realized she wasn't leaving anytime soon, he sat back down.

"This is such a classic, I'm sure you've read it," Babette heard her say. She was holding up *Coals to Newcastle*, Seamus's first and only novel. "It's an overlooked masterpiece," Shawsie went on. "Don't you think?"

Babette was aware then that M was grasping for her hand, looking concerned, but she was finally beginning to breathe again because she realized that Shawsie meant she had read his *book*, not her piece. For heaven's sake! She felt herself snap back to consciousness. "Yes, I have read it," she said, remembering to squeeze M's hand reassuringly, though his smile was somewhat unconvinced. "It's wonderful."

Seamus, who had wrapped his arms awkwardly in front of himself—not crossing them, but wrapping them as if in an invisible straitjacket—let go and grinned. "Thanks, love," he said, familiarly enough to make M look askance. "I always knew you liked it."

Shawsie leafed through the pages until she found the one she was looking for. "You know, this passage is so great, I can't stop myself," she said, holding the book high. "He had finished his long run right near home, as promised," she read in a lulling tone. "He drew in the wet spring air, thick with the threat of storm, and as he gradually found his breath and staggered unevenly toward the lit house, its windows golden with the rosy glow of the dancing fire, he gazed upward once more, drinking in the inky velvet sky."

Babette felt as if she had been punched. She watched Rachel laugh uproariously, M look at her questioningly, and Seamus, as puffed up as a parish priest, hold out his hands in modest surrender to the art of his own genius.

Shawsie closed the book and put it back into her bag. "Pretty amazing," she said happily. "*Tout* New York should read it, don't you think? Well, we've got to sit down to dinner now. Nice seeing you."

M half rose, but they had already gone. The waiter appeared with their twin burgers.

"This will do you good, sugar," M murmured. "I think that champagne has gone straight to your head."

Babette nodded numbly and picked at her french fries, forgetting to wonder if she was supposed to eat them with a knife and fork. She knew she had better eat something or she was going to pass right out. Because she was finished. If

Shawsie and Rachel knew about Seamus Ferguson, there was no question that John Carraro would too, if he didn't already. She pretended to listen to whatever M was saying. Her publishing career was over. Ruined. If she tried to go anywhere now, that tape would make its way to a new employer and so would her piece. Well, Seamus's piece. She couldn't figure out how they found it, but they had.

Across the room, Seamus hoisted a gimlet and Babette watched a caviar presentation, identical to the one she and M had, be served at their table.

"It is so nice to *meet* you," Ponce enthused to Seamus, who, at Shawsie's urging, had loosened his woollen tie and unbuttoned the top button of his polyester-blend shirt. When he removed his tweed jacket—yes, it was warm, wasn't it—the underarms of his shirt were drenched.

"Seamus, would you like some caviar?" Ponce asked properly, as if Prince Charles himself was sitting at her table.

He grinned, showing a full mouth of oversize yellowed teeth. "I don't mind if I do," he said. He took the toast point she offered, loaded with beluga, and as he chewed he rolled his eyes with delight.

"Lovely," he said. And reached for more.

One Year Later

Jacqueline Posner stood at the edge of the dining room and aimed a blow-dryer at the center of a pale peach rose.

"It is so amazing that you know how to do that!" Babette enthused, fluttering from table to table, lighting candles. "Your attention to detail is just so cool!"

"Babette, no! Don't light them yet. Let the waiters do it right before the guests arrive, okay?"

"Oh." She retraced her steps, blowing out the few she'd lit. The smell of sulfur swirled into the air with the thin bands of smoke. "Sorry." She stood still, unsure of what to do next.

"Why don't you go inside and check the bar?" Jacqueline suggested. "Lord knows this crowd likes to drink."

Babette loped obligingly toward the library, and Jacqueline unplugged the dryer. How had she let herself be party to this charade? M, that's how. Forever M. He had been spectacularly good to her, sending her three commissions this past year, and now that he was selling the plantation and buying the famous McMartin estate in Bel Air, she had that assignment, too. So how could she say no to this evening of foolishness? Babette was now a fact of her life and her livelihood.

"Uh, it looks great," Babette said.

Jacqueline looked up. "What?"

"The bar. The bar looks great."

"Is there ice?"

Babette's face was blank, and Jacqueline struggled to keep her voice even. "Check the ice. There's never enough. And did you remember to do a head count on the waiters? They should all be here by now."

The girl nodded dumbly and went into the kitchen. Jacqueline had already managed that last task herself, starting with a call to the agency. She did not want the unnecessary drama of finding her pal from two Christmases ago back for more action. The Jacuzzi was still there, but that master bathroom was no longer hers. She sniffed. Now that she'd seen the new marble, shot through with lurid pink veins, she mourned the loss of her own impeccable white even more.

She wound the cord around the dryer, uncertain where to put it. She wasn't sure Babette would know, even if she asked. M had moved in only six weeks ago—more than a year after he'd bought the place. He'd been so focused on the damn marble, he'd refused to move in until the bathrooms were pristine. Only then did he announce his engagement to Babette. When Jacqueline had sold M the apartment, she told him she couldn't possibly work on it for him. She'd lived there too long, and it had meant too much to her. He understood completely, of course, and true to his word, he'd never bothered her. The woman he hired instead appeared to have moved as slowly as he had, and there were gaps now on every wall and in every room. Jacqueline would never have been as sloppy.

Babette reentered from the kitchen. "The waiters are all

there," she reported. She reached around an artfully arranged swoop of peach and white roses and orchids on the nearest table and picked up the silver-framed engagement announcement that was the centerpiece of each table. She removed an invisible speck of dust from its glass. "It's so pretty, isn't it?" she said, half to herself, then blushed and put it back down. "I can't believe what a romantic M is, wanting to throw this dinner right here where we met and invite all the same people. It's such a time warp."

Jacqueline smiled. "It certainly is. I'm going to go upstairs and get dressed now, okay? Be back in a jiffy."

She walked down the grand hallway, inhaling the new paint. The windows should have been open all day, April showers or not. She stopped herself. This was no longer her home.

In her favorite guest room, she closed the door and threw herself across the bed. She had an hour. Somehow, for someone else's party, she'd managed to get everything done in record time. She pulled out her cell and dialed.

"Just remember," she announced, "you gave me your word that you were coming and you can't back out now."

"Hell, Jacqueline. I have never broken a promise to you, ever. You don't have to remind me."

"Okay, Ponce. But you don't have to sound so happy about it."

"It's not this silly party that's bothering me. At this very moment, I am looking at my aged face, and do you know what? It looks like a ruined soufflé, only it's collapsing from the bottom instead of the top. I swear, the first thing I think of every morning when I stand in front of the mirror is that Mrs. Ford is going to kill me. As if I have anything to do with it."

"Well, be of good cheer. Dr. Bain is coming this evening. Why don't you ask him to take a look?"

Ponce snorted. "How did they manage to rope him into this?"

"You know he was at my farewell party. It's the same list."

"I guess I forgot how you always manage to look younger than springtime. But what I meant was, what's his charity?"

"Something with harelips. But you swore to me that you weren't going to mention that."

"Why not? Half the people coming tonight wouldn't be caught dead in a room with Babette Steele, starting with me. It's bribery, pure and simple, and you know it. So do we all."

Jacqueline sighed. Why was she defending this? Because of M, certainly, not because of Babette. Never had one girl brought so much grief to so many. When the invitations went out, perhaps no one was surprised—disgusted, certainly, but not surprised—to find the accompanying letter from M, generously offering to make a contribution on each guest's behalf to the "philanthropic endeavor dearest to their hearts." They were to consider it a token of goodwill from their new neighbor that the party would celebrate the engagement of two people in love and also "benefit a wide and vibrant variety of not only those in need but those institutions that make this city great."

"It's sort of ingenious," Jacqueline said weakly.

"It's sort of blackmail that he basically knew everyone's pet charity in advance and made sure to call each one to notify them that they would lose a 'significant contribution' if the invited guest didn't show. I mean, the woman I work for at Home Again almost fell out of her chair at the notion that all I had to do was turn up at a Park Avenue apartment for dinner and *I'm* not the one who donates ten thousand dollars, *he* is. Of course, when I told her I would pay ten thousand dollars not to go, she refused to hear of it." She sighed. "And she's right. He'll have a stake now to keep on giving."

"See? It's not all bad," Jacqueline said.

"It's smart, I'll give him that much. Everyone wants to give him the benefit of the doubt because of his money. So it's perfume on a pig. Or a pig's fiancé." Jacqueline heard Ponce close a drawer. "Well, that's done. One more zipper and I'm good to go."

"Oh, yippee, so soon?"

"Not one second before eight. Bye."

Jacqueline squirmed into her dress, slipped on her shoes, powdered her nose, and ran downstairs. It was later than she'd thought.

M stood in the center hallway, hands clasped behind his back, studying the Vermeer on the wall.

"Is it too dark here?" he asked as she approached.

"I think so," she said quickly, walking past him into the library to check the bar. "You need more ice. Please get it now," she said to the bartender. Then she went into the dining room. Empty.

She called out Babette's name, got no response, and ran back up the stairs toward the master bedroom suite. She pushed open the bathroom door. Bingo. Babette sat on the edge of the tub, in tears.

"This is the worst idea, ever," she gasped in between sobs. "No one wanted to come tonight. This is all about M's money. I should have said no, but he was insistent and did it anyway, and I can see years and years of things like this happening." She hiccupped tearfully.

Jacqueline closed the door. "Years and years is if you're lucky," she said, gathering up tissues and sitting down beside her. "Look, Babette. You made a lot of mistakes. You hurt people. You made enemies. And you did it very, very quickly.

People either have very long memories in this town or very short ones. A night like this can go a long way toward making them shorter. Do you understand what I'm saying?"

She nodded, miserable. Jacqueline reached over and raised her chin. "Keep this face from dripping onto that beautiful dress, okay?" she said, pulling a towel from the warming rack and draping it barber-style around Babette's neck. At least Jacqueline assumed it was a dress. The top part looked almost like a bathing suit, it was so bare, despite its champagne-colored ruffle, with a dramatically plunging back. But Babette looked fabulous in it. She obviously spent a lot of time working out.

They could hear the doorbell ring.

"Okay, the first guest! Now listen to me. This is your chance to make things right. You may not be able to do it all in one night, but this is the freshest second chance anyone could have. So do right by it. Do right by M. You can have a long and happy life together, Babette. But a lot of that is up to you. Now fix your face and think lovely thoughts, and if anyone says anything awful to you, you just smile and float right by them on your way up to heaven. Okay?"

Babette giggled and got up. "Okay," she said. "I will. Thank you."

Jacqueline headed back downstairs, and wished that she still smoked. M was in the center hallway talking to Annabelle Gluckman.

"Jacqueline! Darling!"

The women bobbed their heads in simulation of a kiss.

"How are you, Annabelle?"

"Not too bad, actually. Solange offered me a buyout last month, and I've decided to take it. I hated being confined to an office, and it's time for a change. So I'm off to England for the summer. See some good friends, catch up."

Jacqueline knew from a good friend of her own in London that Annabelle had set her sights on a creepy old duke whose very rich wife had died at Christmas. The sport that summer would be managing to bump into him purely by coincidence at all the right house parties. Jacqueline had no doubt that Annabelle could pull it off. After all, Walter had been her fourth husband.

"And what are you doing this summer?" Annabelle asked.

"The Crandalls' house," Jacqueline said.

Annabelle's eyes widened. "What do you mean? They redid it two years ago."

"They did. But they're moving to a new one. Still in Southampton. Just away from the beach. Bitsy said she's tired of hearing the ocean."

There was a noise behind them, a thudding sound, and the two women turned to see Babette catching herself on the banister after tripping on her dress. Her face looked no worse for wear, Jacqueline could see, though her eyes were a bit glassy. Jacqueline took a white wine off a waiter's tray and handed it to her. "Cheers," she said, and moved on.

"Hello, Babette," Annabelle said, a bit primly.

"It's great of you to come," Babette said awkwardly. "I mean, I know you've had a really hard year."

"It would seem we both have," Annabelle said sharply. Babette blushed. She had made it a point to prostrate herself before Annabelle following the incident with the tape. She wailed her heart out and begged for forgiveness. Youthful indiscretion and all that. Little by little, Annabelle had given in. She had long experience in the wisdom of keeping one's options open and in these last few weeks, certainly, was very glad she had done so. In the last year, no one in publishing would touch Babette; word of her seamy enterprises, both on screen and off, had spread like wildfire, and no one would even consider hiring, what, a plagiarist? More of a contractor, perhaps. Either way, no one was biting.

Babette had never taken the waitress job, though she did move back in with her mother, who was herself in need of a roommate. Once Seamus Ferguson was discovered and did indeed write one piece for *Boothby's*—about the man who'd taken his place on the Olympic running team and ended up drinking himself to an early death—he wasted no time getting himself on the book-party circuit. Sipping a gimlet at a chic Madison Avenue restaurant, he recognized a woman whose son had been his student at Dogwood. They chatted about the son's bright future, the woman's acrimonious divorce, and Seamus's upcoming article for *Boothby's*. She took him home with her that night, and he never left.

"Hello, Babette."

The icy voice with its Southern drawl practically gave Babette goose pimples. She turned around and extended her hand, but Ponce didn't seem to see it as she reached toward a tray for a glass of white wine. Ponce then waved at Jacqueline, who had both hands on Fred Engel's shoulders, guiding him into the guest bathroom. Finally, she turned back to her hostess.

"Babette, let me ask you something," she said, stepping closer. "Did you ever come right out and tell M about everything that happened? Or does he still not know?"

Babette exchanged her empty wineglass for a full one. "I decided that honesty was the best policy," she said. "I figured if I didn't tell him, someone else would, so what would be the point of hiding it?"

"How did he take it?"

"Not so bad, really." She flushed, and Ponce could only imagine how the two of them had gotten to this point. The arrival of Robin Brody caught Ponce's eye, and she watched

M approach him. Babette went to greet him as well, and he reached out his hand to her in an expansive let-bygones-be-bygones pantomime. He leaned over and brushed her cheek.

"Sir, nice to see you again," Robin said formally to M, shaking his hand.

"No 'sir' necessary," M said briskly. "Glad to have you." He turned and walked away. Ponce saw that it was Babette's dalliance with the younger man that had rankled him. The dead and buried Walter Gluckman was clearly the lesser of his concerns. She also saw, just coming through the front door, Shawsie. Her friend had never looked better than in these past few months, but talk about a one-track mind. She hadn't come three feet into the place and already she was pulling out pictures of Linda. Healthy, bouncing, redheaded Linda, whom Shawsie had named after Katharine Hepburn's character in *Holiday*. "A beautiful, independent spirit who ends up with Cary Grant," she said. "What more can you want for your daughter?"

Ponce walked toward Shawsie, but Babette got there first.

Shawsie immediately put her pictures away. Babette looked toward them questioningly, but Shawsie shook her head. "Couldn't possibly interest you," she said. With Ponce by her side, Shawsie made an exaggerated display of examining Babette's outfit before declaring, "Surf's up!"

Babette flushed as the two of them walked arm in arm into the library. Fly up to heaven, she thought to herself. Fly up to heaven.

The door opened. Neil Grossman. This was the moment Babette had dreaded most. Neil had refused to come tonight, even after M called the chairman of the board of Carnegie Hill Hospital. When M finally agreed to increase the donation from ten thousand to a hundred thousand, cooler heads prevailed and Neil accepted the invitation. M had offered the same amount to Sari, who got on the phone herself to tell him he could make it a million dollars for her clinic, she'd still never come and he should still go to hell and take Babette Steele with him. He didn't fight her. There was no denying the hit both Neil and Sari had taken courtesy of Babette.

Although the *Manhattan* article had never run—Babette called John Carraro first thing that Monday morning to say that her scoop had fallen through, and he'd played it completely straight, so, so disappointed—Neil had blinked. Terrified that Page Six was going to call Sari, miserable that he had cheated—because that's what it was, not love but cheating— he had broken down that Sunday night and told his wife the truth, every detail about his affair with Ponce: how long it had lasted, how often he'd seen her, what lies he had told, which medical conventions she had traveled to with him. After an initial bout of hysteria, Sari stayed stoic and heard him out. When he awoke the next morning, oddly refreshed, he discovered that she had taken the kids and gone.

Granted, it was only to her parents' and only for a week, but when she came home she was clear. She could no longer trust him and she wanted a divorce. He begged and pleaded for another chance and she refused, right up until the moment, a few days later, that she agreed. They had three young children, after all. It was the right thing to do. Neil was elated. She would not be sorry. His mistake had been grievous. He would do everything in his power to make amends.

Their life resumed. His practice was safe. On Christmas Eve they put the kids to bed, poured some brandy, and sat together in front of the fire. Sari took Neil's hands in hers and told him that the previous day, she had filed for divorce. She had fallen in love. It was a prominent pediatrician, on the board of her clinic. She hadn't realized how lonely she'd been, for so long, she said. The Ponce thing had been the wake-up call she'd needed. She wanted him to pack his things and be out by New Year's Day. He had had his chance. Now she wanted hers.

"Uh, hi, Neil. Thanks for coming," Babette said, extending her hand.

He did not extend his. "I don't believe we've ever met," he said stiffly. "I'm Dr. Grossman. And I would like to thank Mr. Merriweather for his generous contribution to Carnegie Hill."

Babette dropped her hand. "He's in the library," she said. He was already walking past her.

"Hey, was this a pool party and no one told me?"

Babette squared her shoulders and turned toward the door. "Hello, Rachel," she said.

"Wow, what a dress! Is that from the Barbie Dream House collection?"

Gus Fisher stepped in front of his wife and extended his hand. "Babette, thank you for having us," he said, pinching Rachel's arm as he walked past her.

Unperturbed, Rachel continued. "So, pretty incredible that, what, a year ago, there you were, an invitation-stealing assistant at *Boothby's*, and now, this brief time later, the chatelaine of the grand household. Some digs, eh?"

Babette held her head high. "Ten bedrooms, eight baths. Not bad at all."

Rachel put on her fascinated interview face and egged her on. "And what would you say you like best about it so far?"

Babette fell for it. "Well, it is pretty amazing having your own bidet. I mean, it's not like it's even a hotel or anything. I wake up every morning and use Jacqueline Posner's bidet. Every day!"

Rachel stifled a laugh. "It's good to have a goal in life, Babette. I'm so glad you've attained yours. And at such a tender age."

Gus circled back and was unamused to find Rachel still standing there. Last fall he had been appointed president of TCB News, the enormous promotion everyone had predicted. The job was going swimmingly. His only management challenge was Rachel. "I think we should grab a drink, don't you?" he said, giving her no time to answer while practically lifting her into the library.

Babette grabbed another drink of her own. Heaven felt a long way away.

M appeared at her side. "Darlin', this house is filled with all sorts of people tonight. I don't believe you've greeted half your guests." He led her down the grand hallway and she was soon engulfed in delighted hellos, admiring comments about M's spectacular generosity, and best wishes for the future. She liked it much better at this end.

In the library, Ponce, Shawsie, Robin, Rachel, and Gus stood together. "No one at *Boothby's* could believe it when I told them I was coming here tonight," Rachel said. "Most of them had forgotten about Babette, but now that they're up-to-date on her adventures, they're dying for every detail." She shrugged. "Marry a rich guy and disappear. It's every fraud's dream."

"Oh, but she hasn't disappeared at all," Robin said. "Babette Steele has a new job." Everyone looked shocked. "*Boulevard* magazine hired her."

Boulevard was a glossy magazine that decorated all the doctors' offices on the Upper East Side. "It's a shopping column," he went on. "I mean, talk about not missing a trick. The week she got engaged, Babette called up the editor in chief and told her she would be traveling all over the world, so she'd be in a unique position to write a first-person account of the state of international shopping. But here's the best part: The editor told her to write two sample columns, which she did. And do you know what she's calling them? 'Mine!'"

"How delightful," Rachel said. "But here's my question. Does M know that his little minx was reduced to spending six months winding watches at Tourneau on Madison Avenue? Remember when Gus went in there and she almost broke her face trying to dive behind the counter? Tick, tick, tick. Gather ye rosebuds. But never mind the existential concerns. Coordination has never been this girl's strong suit."

"Speak of the devil," Robin said under his breath as he turned toward the bar. Babette entered the library without M.

"Hey, Babette," Rachel called. Babette came over quickly, so Rachel would lower her voice.

"Robin was just telling us about 'Mine!' It's so great to see you haven't lost that signature get-up-and-go. But don't you think it stereotypes you as the wife of an old rich guy?"

Babette bristled. "No, I don't," she said. "When you travel around the world, a lot of what you buy are gifts. So it's relevant for everyone."

Rachel frowned. "If it's about gifts, shouldn't it be called 'Yours!'?"

Babette looked confused as the bell rang for dinner.

Ponce turned her back. "The hell with that," she said, walking toward the window. "I'm not done drinking." Jacqueline came in to shoo them inside. "Did you see Annabelle's knees in that getup?" Ponce asked her. "They're as big as babies' heads."

Jacqueline shook her head. "Stop that now, and go inside so we can get this thing over and done with, will you?" she said, turning to go. But Ponce walked toward the bar. When the front door opened a moment later, she faced it with a martini in hand.

"Red!" she called. "In here!" He followed gratefully.

"Better late than never," she said, handing it over. "When you asked me the last possible moment you could arrive before dinner, I didn't think you'd take it so literally."

Red turned toward Shawsie and Robin. "You probably don't remember this, but I was on the original guest list," he said. "I think I canceled the day of. Probably when I realized it was four in the afternoon, I hadn't showered for a week, and I couldn't get out of bed."

Shawsie kissed Red, and Robin gave him half a hug. An awkward silence ensued. Despite Red's cheerleading for them to stay together, Shawsie decided a few weeks after the incident at the Acorn that they would not. Actually, she decided a month into couples therapy, after Robin inadvertently confessed to falling off the wagon after attending his third AA meeting and bedding the girl in charge of the coffee.

That was it for her. She wanted a divorce, and she wanted to raise the baby herself. Robin threatened to take her to court. Shawsie laughed in his face, and so did his own lawyer.

As her due date drew nearer—and as she heard of his next involvement, a twenty-three-year-old publicist with family money and breast implants—Shawsie finally agreed to a visitation schedule that still gave her sole custody. Robin pleaded, but she was adamant. "Earn it," she said. "If this really means something to you, show up on time, take exquisite care of her, and maybe when she's thirty I'll reconsider." But Shawsie's tough talk aside, the separation had been brutal for her. "When it comes to protecting someone else, I can be so fierce," she told Ponce. "The worst part is that if there wasn't a baby at stake, I would have probably taken him back again."

When Ponce supported Shawsie's decision, it caused a rift in her relationship with Red, who was adamant in his belief that Robin and Shawsie could work it out if they stayed together. He was furious that Shawsie decided otherwise.

"Hell, Red," Ponce said at the time. "I understand you raised three great kids, but be honest. Cackie did most of it. You were always working. You can't expect a tomcat to turn into a pussycat just because he says he wants to."

"Don't give me those Southern-fried clichés," he protested hotly. "Look, Ponce. You know how much Shawsie always wanted a family. How much she missed having one. She could have one now. All the elements are there."

"They most certainly are not! Just because you share the same address with someone doesn't mean he comes home at night. Look, I think it's noble and grand that you're such a defender of family values. But think about what that man did to your niece. Do you really want to trust him with a three-year-old? Who knows what that child might wake up in the morning and find?"

They didn't speak for two weeks after that—the longest they'd ever gone even when Cackie was sick. Then one day Ponce came back from court to find Red sitting in her lobby. "Wanna walk?" he asked. She changed her clothes and they did just that, all the way down Fifth Avenue, through the Village, and into Tribeca, where they collapsed at a bar. Red argued his side again. Ponce argued hers. He allowed how he might be a little stubborn on this one. His kids didn't have a mother anymore, and that was a real sorrow in his life. She said she understood. She still didn't think it meant giving a womanizing drunk free rein to mess up two other people's lives. If more women in the world had the sense to behave like Shawsie, she said, she'd be spending less time in court each week. He finally allowed that she might be right.

They each ate a hamburger — not half as good as at Marshall's, they agreed — and as they walked out onto the street, he grabbed her and hugged her. "You're the greatest, Poncie," he said hoarsely. "A hell of a pal. To Shawsie. And me."

She laid her hand on his unshaved cheek and was surprised to find herself so overcome by emotion she couldn't find words to speak. He led her to a cab, and they rode uptown silently. She dropped him off at the Yale Club and went home. The next day he called and they talked as they always did. Neither mentioned the previous day.

But ever since New Year's, Red had seemed restless. He put the Connecticut house on the market. "You'll regret this," Ponce warned. "Cackie loved that house."

"I'm past regret," he growled.

"Where are you going to live?"

"Not sure."

"Washington?"

"Not sure."

The bell for dinner rang again, and this time they had no choice but to go in. Ponce headed straight for Jacqueline. There was one important factor in this setup tonight that she couldn't figure out. What exactly was in this for M? With all his money, all his connections, why would he choose to marry a small-time operator like Babette? He hadn't been divorced a year.

But Jacqueline saw Ponce coming and spied something on a waiter's tray that needed tending to as he disappeared into the kitchen and she followed. She knew just what Ponce wanted to know, and she couldn't tell her. Not even Babette knew. If there hadn't been a termite infestation on the covered veranda of the plantation's main house that necessitated laying new planks, she wouldn't have been down there to discover the answer herself.

Because when M had proposed, he told Babette he was madly in love with her, pined for her when they were apart. He listened carefully to her litany of confessed misdeeds and proclaimed that they would start a new chapter together. They would repair things in New York first, then move on to California, beacon for new beginnings. He would sell the plantation. It was time to learn, time to grow. But while the need for Babette to begin anew was clear, he skillfully obscured his own, never mentioning the fourteen-year-old daughter of the plantation's caretaker or her missed periods—she was *not* pregnant, his own doctor confirmed it— who was now the happy recipient of a Foxcroft education, all expenses paid. Or the caretaker, whose job was guaranteed by the next owner. In writing.

Ponce watched Jacqueline flee and let it go. She would ask her later. She headed to her table and found Red, facing her. She took her seat, between Gus and—oh, wasn't Jacqueline something?—Dr. Bain, rescuer of fallen soufflés. No sooner had she put the napkin in her lap than someone clinked a glass and M stood.

"I would like to welcome you all to my home," he said. "Soon to be our home." He smiled at Babette during a smattering of applause. "My young bride-to-be thinks I'm a sentimental old fool to throw a dinner like this, and I'm sure she's right. But I can't think of a better way to celebrate our lives together than by celebrating the way we met. I thank each and every one of you for coming tonight. It means so much to us both."

Ponce saw Neil staring at her from across the room and turned her face away.

"I would also like to thank y'all for giving me the opportunity to donate to your causes," M continued, laying on the accent. "There's no better way to learn where someone's heart is, no better way to learn how a community works and what it holds dear, than to embrace the giving patterns of the people who live there."

That earned some enthusiastic murmurs and a few table thumps.

"I must also applaud Jacqueline Posner on her superb taste in friends," M said. "I didn't get to meet most of you the last time we were gathered here, but I look forward to getting to know y'all so much better now. As a matter of fact, I ran into Red Evans earlier this week, and this evening, I would like to propose a toast to him." M raised his glass.

All heads turned. Some craned their necks. Red was a legendary newsman. Conservatives admired his writing even as they disagreed with him. They had read him all through Vietnam and Watergate, but he had never lived in New York. He was a Washington character. They wanted to see what he looked like. "I want to toast Red on his new job this evening," M said, and Shawsie whipped around in her seat to search out Ponce, who nodded reassuringly.

"As of next month," M said, "he will begin writing a national political column for *Time* magazine. To which many in this room will say, 'Amen!'"

Everyone applauded.

Red stood and raised his own glass. "I would like to thank M and Babette"—he bowed slightly in her direction—"for including me here tonight. I had been on Jacqueline's guest list for that famous dinner but couldn't make it, unfortunately. So it is especially meaningful to me to be here tonight, to say that, like M, I too am moving to New York City, for the very first time.

"I have long felt that the most important thing in life is friends, and I've decided it's foolhardy not to be with them. So on the first of next month, I will officially become a New Yorker."

"Where are you moving?" Shawsie couldn't restrain herself.

"A magnificent apartment, actually: 907 Fifth Avenue, 3C."

Shawsie jumped up. "Oh! Oh my God!" It was Ponce's address.

Red raised his glass. "To my irrepressible niece, whom I adore, to her delicious daughter, whom I look forward to watching grow up, to our generous hosts this evening, and last but never least, to my new and lovely roommate, I would like to say thank you. These last few years have been rough ones for me. I wasn't sure I would ever belong anyplace again."

He looked at Ponce, who held his gaze.

"Welcome home," she said.

ACKNOWLEDGMENTS

I am grateful to my editor, Peter Gethers, and my agent, Kathy Robbins, for their unflagging patience and encouragement during the last four years.

I would also like to thank Suzanne Goodson, Andrew Heyward, Nora Ephron, Nicholas Pileggi, Irwin Blye, Evangeline Morphos, Penelope Green, and Timothy J. Hill for helping to bridge fiction with fact, along with Benjamin Dreyer, Kathleen Fridella, Shilpa Nadhan, Carol Carson, and Coralie Hunter for their careful work on this book.

Closer to home, I am indebted to Cynthia LaBorde, Barbara Denner, Roberta Epstein, Caroline Harrison, and Evelyn Witchel for their invaluable help.

I am thankful, as always, for my mother, Barbara Witchel, and for her steadfast support of everything I do.

My stepsons, Nathaniel Rich and Simon Rich, are warmhearted, sharp-witted commiserators in the folly of book writing and I treasure their company and advice.

But most of all, I am indebted to my husband, Frank Rich: a brilliant writer, an incisive editor, and the most kindhearted, generous, funny person I know. He remains the true gift of my life.

A NOTE ON THE TYPE

The text of this book was set in Electra, a typeface designed by W. A. Dwiggins (1880–1956). This face cannot be classified as either modern or old style. It is not based on any historical model, nor does it echo any particular period or style. It avoids the extreme contrasts between thick and thin elements that mark most modern faces, and it attempts to give a feeling of fluidity, power, and speed.

Composed by
Stratford/Textech, Brattleboro, Vermont

Printed and bound by
R. R. Donnelley, Harrisonburg, Virginia

Designed by Virginia Tan